The Count

Volume 1

Mécénat

Hako Catchatoor

First edition published December 2025

ISBN 978 1 9193946 0 2

For my Mum and Dad – true adventurers both, for my Dad's brother Hrand, who died with him while serving God and others, and for Geoffrey who, nearly thirteen years later, joined the family for new adventures at home and abroad

FOREWARD

It would seem that, by accident, I may have written a book that appeals to both men and women. Of course, people are who they are and they like what they like, but broadly speaking the men who have read advance copies of the book seem to have appreciated the action, humour and clarity, while the women seem to have enjoyed the warm characters, interactions and romance.

Everyone has enjoyed the plot twists.

So, wherever you would put yourself on the action/logic – emotion/romance scale, I hope you enjoy it too.

It's a 'clean read' and I make no apologies for that. Hard core fans of dark, brutal thrillers may find it a little 'light', but I'd still say, give it a chance – you might be surprised.

ACKNOWLEDGMENTS

To everyone that has helped me, encouraged me and supported me through the writing and publishing process – thank you. Special thanks to Stu, Jen, Debby, Marianne, Sheila, Michael and Barbara who read the various drafts and provided invaluable encouragement and feedback. Finally, to my beautiful wife, Deborah, who has done all the above and so much more: thank you and God bless you.

CHAPTER 1

ANNA PARKER

To say that Anna Parker was beautiful would be like saying that on a clear, sunny day the sky is blue – true, but totally inadequate. Looking at her was like gazing at a deep blue sky filled with golden sunshine; the sort of vision that takes your breath away and touches your soul. It was more than simply physical beauty – although it was that, in spades – there was something about her that drew you to her, like you had – or desperately wanted – a soul connection. It didn't matter whether Anna felt anything in return, like the sky has no feelings for the onlooker, the feeling she engendered was real. With long dark hair, warm, soft brown eyes and the sort of features and complexion that could pass for British or continental, she would be as natural in Manchester as in the Mediterranean. She was well above average height for a woman, at around five feet nine inches, with a slim athletic figure that swelled at the chest and hips, and long legs, shapely and toned.

As far as the official records were concerned, the decision to place the returning operative in a safe house had been taken for her protection. As far as Anna Parker was concerned, it was for her confinement. The rationale given was that the successful mission would have upset some very powerful and ruthless people, and there was a risk that those parties may be trying to track her down. Unofficially, Anna Parker was under house arrest and constant surveillance to ensure that she couldn't run and couldn't contact anyone with whom she may have colluded in regards to the missing item.

Any attempt to escape would make everyone think she was guilty, she knew that. Not to mention the difficulty in getting past the "protection detail" that had been assigned, with agents front and rear of the house and two inside it. For normal protectees, one or two agents in total would suffice, but given Anna's situation and training, no chances had been taken.

On the other hand, she wondered, how was this going to play out? She'd been here at least three days already, she reckoned, post- the initial debrief in France, and whilst the disorientation tactics made keeping track of time difficult, she figured it must be Friday morning by now. The interview routine had been pretty much identical, with the same questions being asked over and over again, but in slightly different ways, trying to catch her out, trying to make her give something away. How could she make them believe that she was honest, loyal? It was as though the only thing that could break the cycle was giving them something that they wanted to hear, and she couldn't do that.

At least they're still playing by the rules, she thought to herself. That was another potential direction they could go in. A vehicle pulls up quietly in the middle of the night and whisks her off to a less salubrious venue where there were no neighbours within half a mile to hear her scream. *Is that what's coming next?* she thought. If so, then maybe running wasn't so bad an option after all.

She toyed with the idea of using her looks and charm to help her escape, but these guys were on their guard, and whether she tried to leave by the front or the back entrance, she would have to get past three of them and the chances of fooling or charming multiple alert agents in one go were negligible in this setting. She resolved to be patient, at least for a little while longer, and readied herself for the next visit from Sir Peter, and the next round of questions.

Sir Peter, she thought, the man who had sent her on the mission. The man who had steered her, even attempted to *control* her activities while she was out in the field trying to make a success of the job. At times it had been more like interference than guidance. It had annoyed her greatly and had put the mission at risk. And not just the mission.

There was movement in the hall. One of the agents had let someone in. *Here we go*, Anna thought, steeling herself for another round of sparring with Sir Peter. But when the door opened and a man entered the room, it wasn't Sir Peter; it was a tall bearded man with spectacles and slightly wild hair that looked like it had a mind of its own … a mind that it had yet to make up.

CHAPTER 2

THE OLD MAN AND THE ROBBERY

The officer viewed the CCTV footage from the robbery with a broadening smile. It was as much as his hardened professionalism could do to stop him laughing out loud. Armed robbery was serious, of course, but this footage was like something from a comedy film. He played it again.

There were just three characters: the terrified cashier behind the counter, the masked robber pointing his gun, and the old man seemingly oblivious to what was going on right behind him.

As the robber threatened the cashier, the old man was bending down to get a newspaper from the bottom shelf. Leaning heavily on his thick metal walking stick he couldn't quite get down far enough. Steadying himself with his other hand on the next shelf from the bottom, he moved his walking stick back so it was out of the way. The end of the stick went up between the robber's legs. As the old man turned to see what had happened, the stick got caught and pressed into the back of the robber's left knee, causing the leg to buckle. The two started to topple over and the old man tried to steady himself by throwing his arms around the robber, but ended up pushing him with even greater force to the floor. Unable to put his arms out to break his fall, the robber's head hit the hard surface with a smack, knocking him out cold.

Inspector Steve Gent, whose surname was pronounced with a hard "G" as in "Gap", couldn't resist watching it a third time, chuckling quietly to himself. It was hilarious. He let the footage play on. With some considerable assistance from the cashier, the old man was able to stand up. Gent allowed himself another chuckle – an armed robbery foiled and culprit knocked unconscious by the inadvertent slap-stick actions of a frail old man. Hollywood couldn't have written it better!

The video continued. The cashier quickly rang the police who, because of the serious nature of the crime and the fact that the thief was there to be grabbed, would be at the scene in minutes. Meanwhile the cashier tended to old Mr Tomms, whom he regarded not so closely as a friend, as Mr Tomms was away quite a lot, either visiting relatives in France or friends in … wherever it was his friends lived, but he considered him an acquaintance. Anyway, suffice it to say that when he was in Tooting, Mr Tomms was a valued customer – and a very pleasant and friendly one, if somewhat hard of hearing. The cashier was used to repeating everything to Mr Tomms, even though he'd already said it in a loud voice the first time. It was fine; that was just Mr Tomms.

Inspector Gent smiled. He could see the headlines now: PENSIONER FOILS ARMED ROBBERY! Of course, the aged hero wouldn't want his picture in the paper. It wasn't so much that he was far too modest, although he certainly was that; the real reason old Mr Tomms didn't want to attract much attention was, as Steve Gent knew very well, that he wasn't old, and his name wasn't Mr Tomms.

* * *

The man known as "The Count" had awoken that Wednesday morning with a fairly simple plan for the day, which was: firstly, to have a hearty, but leisurely breakfast; secondly, to maintain and reinforce the persona of Mr Tomms in that particular part of the city, and, thirdly, to meet a figure of some significance who wanted to discuss a matter of business with him.

For the Count, "business" could mean any number of different things, from dealing in art, finance or property, to performing services of a more secret nature for governments, corporations, or private individuals. His meeting that evening, he was fairly sure, would fall into one of the latter categories.

The house in which he stayed – when he was in that area – had two storeys, each of which purported to hold an apartment, and a basement, which belonged to the ground floor flat. Access from the street was via a single front door at ground level into a communal hallway and stairs up to the first floor flat. The Count – or old Mr Tomms as he was known in that area – lived on the ground floor in No. 37A, while another man had No. 37B.

Being quite a large property in terms of rooms and floor space, the ground floor flat plus basement was bigger than an elderly gentleman would normally need, but not so much so that it would draw attention. In reality, the whole house belonged to the Count and had been internally transformed into a most satisfying combination of comfortable living space and a place from which to conduct local operations. The Count had bought the property from the previous landlord to use as a base for a number of prior assignments, during which he had created the character of a kind, pleasant and rather deaf and doddery old gentleman, in order to preserve his anonymity and move around the area freely, asking questions, making contacts and so on, and – not least in importance in his line of work – to lie low from time to time.

In the three years since he had bought it he had made a few general acquaintances in the area, but as in all large cities, people generally kept themselves to themselves and that made his underground activity so much easier.

His leisurely breakfast was prepared for him by the man who "lived" in No.37B – the Count's personal chef, aide and, on the odd occasion when the Count felt he might be outnumbered more than three to one, bodyguard. Butler –

not his real name, but one that had amused the Count to assign him when taking him on – had other skills and duties, but the Count had to admit, he was a wonderful chef.

For many people, the idea of dressing up and applying cinema-quality make-up each morning in order to present one's self as someone else might seem a dreadful repetitive bore, but the Count quite enjoyed it. He had many characters and many places, and he loved acting as much as the greatest and most passionate thespian. On reflection, the Count mused, a great many people go through the daily ritual of dressing up and making up in order to present a different face and persona to the world. He wondered if they enjoyed it as much as he did, or whether they were just afraid to be themselves.

In the persona of Mr Tomms he had gone to the local newsagents / mini-supermarket to keep up the appearance of the elderly gentleman's normal life and to see what was happening in the locality. He greeted the cashier with a cheery smile and exchanged pleasantries, saying "Eh, what?" each time the cashier spoke to him and making the poor man repeat everything at least once. Yes, he was fine, thank you; although a little back pain was to be expected by an eighty-three year-old man. He'd shuffled round one of the aisles with his thick metal walking stick and was half-way up the other aisle, nearing the till, when a man wearing a ski mask burst into the shop.

Pretending not to notice, the Count faced the shelves opposite the cashier and sidled slowly up to the newspaper section. By now the man in the ski mask had pulled a gun and was demanding all the money from the till. Bending down slowly towards the newspapers on the bottom shelf, and leaning heavily on his metal walking stick, the Count sized up the position and stance of the intruder. With a deft movement he bent further forward and with a flick of the wrist drove his walking sticking back and up between the robber's legs. Pretending to react to the contact, the

Count turned, twisting the stick and taking the man's legs from under him. The robber's hands had instinctively moved down to the injured area and the Count grabbed him in a bear hug, pinning the man's arms to his sides so he couldn't break his fall. As the two went down the Count pressed down and forward, driving the robber's head into the floor.

The Count had allowed the cashier to help him up and make a somewhat ropey, but well-intended attempt at first aid, all the time replying, "Eh, what?" to everything his helper said.

The police had arrived pretty quickly and the Count had been pleased to see Inspector Steve Gent on the scene – not the only police officer who knew of the Count's shadowy activities, but one of a very, very small number.

Steve Gent was not a bent copper. On the contrary, he was completely trustworthy. In fact, the Count would not have chosen him if he had been anything less.

Was he on the Count's payroll? Far from it. He certainly benefited from the Count's activities in terms of securing an arrest or solving a crime, as he had done today, and occasionally the Count might choose to show his appreciation, but he was an honest man and fiercely loyal to his duty.

Actually, thought Gent, when he had reflected on it, the Count was a bit like an informant, a bit like a consultant, a bit like a specialist contractor. In fact, looked at it that way, he would have no trouble justifying it to his colleagues or superiors – not that he would ever dream of telling anyone else about it. That would be a betrayal of the Count's trust, and Gent would never betray trust. On the other hand, the Count could also be a bit like a second boss. He had to admit, at times the Count seemed to direct his efforts and make certain demands on his time, but it was often in line with Gent's policing objectives – and always for a good purpose. He also knew that he was covered from way up the command chain. He just hoped that the Chief Officer who had originally informed him of his "special duties", unknown to anyone else in the Force, had passed the information on to his successor ... just in case he was ever caught in an awkward situation.

But his special duties had gone well so far. He had done what the Count had asked of him and the Count had always come through. Considering how little he really knew about the Count, Gent trusted him absolutely.

For the Count's part, that feeling was fairly mutual, although the Count was extremely cautious when it came to people and there were only a handful people in the world in whom he trusted absolutely. One was his sister, another was Butler. However, Inspector Steve Gent ranked pretty highly among those in whom the Count had placed his trust. The very fact that he had revealed as much as he had to Gent was testimony to that. And Gent had proved loyal, discreet and good at what he did. Qualities that the Count valued highly. Whether he would include Gent in whatever business arose from his meeting that evening remained to be seen.

The Count did not know it yet, but as things would turn out, he would be depending on Inspector Gent very heavily over the next few days.

CHAPTER 3

THE MEETING

Leaving the house promptly at 7pm in the guise of old Mr Tomms, the Count headed up into the city, carrying a small and somewhat shabby case. He took a bus, a train and a short walk to reach his destination, which was the Riverside Club, a down-market version of the more aristocratic gentleman's clubs in the well-to-do areas of town. Not that the Count couldn't afford membership in one of those – indeed, he was a member of several, but this meeting had been arranged by someone else. The Riverside Club wasn't as stiff and starchy – or as aloof and discriminatory – as some of the posh city clubs, but it was a far cry from the seedy meeting places of the criminal underworld. And the "conference room", as it was affectionately known, was secure and private. The Count was content with the choice of venue.

The management and staff of the Riverside Club were very discreet. No questions were asked, no identification was required – in fact, the management would not have been surprised to learn that most of the conference room bookings were under false names. There were no security cameras in the conference room, no hidden microphones, no one-way mirrors. Conversations were, and had to be, completely confidential; that was the whole point of the conference room, and the reputation of the Riverside Club depended on it.

This evening the conference room had been booked by

someone under the name of Mr Charleston Clarke who, rather like Mr Tomms at the newsagent/grocery store, was not exactly a regular, but was certainly a valued client, and who, like the Count, was also using a false identity.

However, unlike the Count, Charleston Clarke did not have to make any effort to make himself look elderly. He was in his sixties to start with, but a rare genetic disorder had caused his skin to age prematurely, giving him the appearance of a much older person. And so it was, a meeting of two old gentlemen took place in the Riverside Club; amusing, but not remarkable to anyone who might have bothered to notice who had been discreetly ushered past the burly bouncer, through to the conference room.

"A pleasure to meet you." Clarke stood and offered his hand as the Count entered the room. The Count shook it and they both sat down.

"Although," continued Clarke, "I had expected you to be a little …", he hesitated.

"Younger?" The Count intervened to ease the awkwardness. "I am more sprightly than I look." The Count smiled and Clarke could see a twinkle in his invitee's eyes.

"Indeed." Clarke gathered himself. "We have never met, but I have read a couple of reports in which your assistance is mentioned."

"Actually, we have met." Surprise registered on Clarke's face. "But," the Count continued, "I looked rather different on that occasion."

There was a pause as the man calling himself Charleston Clarke searched his mind.

"I don't recall." he fumbled.

"It matters not." said the Count. "However, I suspect that what you are about to tell me matters a great deal."

"It does." replied Clarke. "A great deal – to me personally, and to the country's international relations." He leaned forward as if he was about to share a secret in a public place. The Count noted the movement and recognised a second reason that the man had not risen beyond the lower echelons of senior intelligence officers in the British Secret Service – an inherent insecurity and lack of awareness of his surroundings. The first reason the Count had observed was predictability. It had not taken the Count long to identify the man who had contacted him, giving the name Charleston Clarke. The man had used that name regularly as an alias and so had been fairly easy to track down for someone with the Count's abilities and contacts.

Clarke rubbed his hands together slowly, as if trying to wash them clean of some offence.

"I would like to hire you to retrieve something. Something that was … lost – or perhaps stolen. I'm not yet quite sure which."

"I see." said the Count. "Could you give me a little more detail?"

"Yes, yes, of course." Clarke was clearly uncomfortable. "The item was obtained during a …" he hesitated, trying to find the right word, "… a job on the continent, but whilst the job was successful and the person undertaking it returned safely, the item did not return with her."

"Ah. That is awkward. I have no doubt that you interrogated the operative thoroughly?" Clarke almost jumped at the word *operative.*

"Of course."

"And she claimed that in no way had she been negligent, nor indeed that she herself had disposed of the item for her own personal profit?"

"Correct."

"I see."

"She *seemed* genuinely distraught to have been unable to resolve this one area of the otherwise highly successful … job."

"And nothing untoward showed on the lie detectors?" The colour was draining from Clarke's already grey face and he simply nodded vaguely.

"Which, of course, she was trained to fool in any case."

Clarke resigned. "Yes." There was a moment's silence. "So, you see my dilemma."

The Count leaned back in his chair, relaxed, but deep in concentration.

"I do." He paused. "And I think I may be able to help you with it."

The tension visibly eased from Clarke's wrinkled face.

"I'm relieved to hear it."

"But first," the Count continued as if Clarke's words had been an interruption, "I must ask you something."

"Of course." Clarke responded, although the worry was now returning to his face. "What do you want to know?"

"As you may have gathered," the Count now leaned forward assertively, "I know who you are; that is, I know your real name and for whom you work."

The man using the name Charleston Clarke sat back, but not in relaxed concentration. On the contrary, he was shrinking away from someone who clearly had the upper hand. It was a feeling he was familiar with. He was solid in his job, reasonably intelligent and experienced, but he knew that there were those who outshone him in every way. He had done well with the talents God had given him, but there were times when he felt very much at the limits of his abilities. It was not so much that he disliked being out of his comfort zone, although that was as true of him as it is of anyone else, it was rather that his comfort zone was somewhat smaller than he would have liked. The Count went on.

"Given that you work for the intelligence services and that the *job*," the Count emphasised the word, "was in fact a covert mission ..." He did not wait for Clarke to confirm. "... you have a number of highly-trained operatives on whom you could call. Granted, some may be otherwise occupied, but nevertheless you have in-house resources at your disposal. So I ask myself why you have called on me instead?"

Clarke seemed unwilling to answer.

"Unless," the Count ventured, "you have not yet informed your superiors of the event?"

Clarke's defences collapsed and the whole story came gushing forth. It was like therapy and he felt so much better for sharing it.

He had been in charge of the British side of a joint Anglo-French operation against a secret criminal organisation called the Mécénat. He pronounced the word with a reasonable attempt at a French accent: "May-say-nat'", although he sounded the "t" at the end of the word, which most French people wouldn't do; they would cut it short, "May-say-na'". The society had originated in the less salubrious areas of the French capital and had grown quickly until it had established its presence throughout the whole of the greater Paris area, at which point it had settled and continued its illegal activities at too low a level to involve the security services. In recent times, however, it had become much more aggressive and now operated not only throughout France, but across Europe and into Asia.

Mécénat. Translated into English it meant "patronage" or "sponsorship", implying some kind of benevolent care, but the only people it looked after were its own members and the only things they sponsored were serious criminal operations, with trafficking – drugs, weapons and people – being a speciality. Little or nothing was known about the head of the society, known simply as "the Boss", or *Le Patron* in French. It was hard to infiltrate and its members were fiercely loyal to the group and, by liaison up the ranks, to the Boss. The few that had been caught never talked, and had all died in suspicious circumstances shortly after capture, whether by their own hand or by another. Being in custody seemed to make no difference; the reach of the Mécénat extended to wherever it was needed. The French Secret Service was trying desperately to get to the heart of the organisation, but it was always one step ahead of them.

The agent that Clarke had sent into the field was on her first real mission. She had been assigned to work with the interior branch of the French Secret Services – the DGSI – and under the supervision of one of its agents a raid had been carried out on a Mécénat site in the Paris area. The operation had been a success in its original objective, but it was suspicious that the rookie British agent had survived while the experienced DGSI agent had not – and at the same time, a high-value item had gone missing.

When he had finished, Charleston Clarke looked searchingly at the Count, hoping for deliverance.

"I accept …" said the Count. Clarke's wrinkled face eased. "… but I have certain conditions."

"Name them." replied Clarke.

The Count did so and Clarke agreed without hesitation to all but one.

"I'm happy for you to refer to me by name on my secure communications, why are you insisting that I must never refer to you by any name whatsoever!"

"It is a matter of security."

"Security is my business!"

"You sit on the sidelines. I am in the field. My identity is more than my business. And I will not have any clue to it leaked, overheard or compromised in any way." His voice was calm, but the authority was clear. "You must use no names. If you cannot follow this simple rule, then I cannot help you."

Clarke knew he was beaten. He needed the Count and though it hurt his ego to be on unequal terms in this regard, he would have to swallow his pride. He would be in control, though, he would just have to establish that after securing the Count's services.

"Very well." he conceded. "Agreed."

* * *

The Count was pleased with how things had gone with Charleston Clarke – or Sir Peter Shackleton, as he was really called. The case was intriguing and challenging, two factors that really motivated the Count. The fee – half up front and half on completion – was very agreeable, being as it was, quite sizable, but whilst the Count would find a good use for it, he did not need it as such, and it did not rank too highly among his criteria. No, the third significant motivating factor was that it was for *good*, that is, it involved putting right something that was wrong, and bringing an end to an illegal operation that thrived on the misery and oppression of others.

At the Riverside Club, the Count had suggested to Sir Peter that he should start by meeting with the suspect operative on Friday, to form an initial impression and that the precise course of action would depend on how the meeting went. That was certainly true, but was only part of the story. In reality, the Count had already begun forming a plan and had a good idea of how things were going to develop. If he had held the same level of confidence in Sir Peter Shackleton that he had in Inspector Steve Gent, he would have shared at least some of his intentions with him. But that wasn't the case. Sir Peter had wanted too much direct involvement with the operative's mission, the Count had been able to discern that much from the meeting at the Riverside Club, and he didn't want him interfering with what he had planned. Sir Peter had been keen for the Count to meet the operative the very next day, but the Count had suggested that she be left to stew for another twenty-four hours. The meeting would take place at the safe house on Friday, which was the day after tomorrow, and the Count would start with a psychological examination.

And so it was that a space had been created for the Count to do some background research and for old Mr Tomms to take a trip to the area in which the safe house was located.

* * *

One advantage of walking very slowly, the Count

reflected, was that it gave plenty of time to observe. Another benefit of his character's age and condition was that it made apparent confusion quite believable. So when old Mr Tomms walked up and down the street, carrying a tattered old case, pausing outside various houses and looking at a scrap of paper, as if trying to find somewhere but not really being sure where he was or where he was going, the agent in the van across from the safe house wasn't suspicious of him, but actually pitied him. He was tempted to get out of the van and help the poor old fellow, but he couldn't risk being seen, so he did his best to ignore him.

After a few minutes of wandering, the old man stopped outside the house next-door to the safe house, then walked up the path and knocked on the door. A few moments later, the door opened and the lady of the house appeared. A few words were exchanged – the agent only had cameras, no sound – and then both lady and elderly gentleman disappeared into the house. Five minutes later, the old man left the house, went down the street to another house. The lady had clearly been able to help him find the place he was looking for. The old man knocked on the door and waited. There was no answer. He knocked again, and again, then, patently heart-broken, shuffled off down the street and round the corner.

Poor old duffer, thought the agent, *I wonder how far he'd come and how long he'd been searching? And who had he been searching for? Maybe a long-lost relative, a son or daughter with whom he'd fallen out years ago, and who he wanted to make up with before he died?*

Things had gone well for the Count. The lady who lived in the semi-detached house next to the safe house had been a little surprised to see an elderly gentleman at the door, but she couldn't help but take pity on him, slightly confused as he seemed and, moreover, asking to use the bathroom. The nearest public toilets were nearly a mile away in the park and the thought of such a dear man having an unfortunate incident on the street was more than she could bear. That short visit was all the Count had needed to have a quick look round the house and as he was thanking the lady and commenting on how nice her house was, referring to this or that feature, he was able to glean useful information about the layout and features of the house next door. He also learned that, although Mrs Martin's husband had passed away several years ago, she was managing quite well and had some good friends, like Marjorie Vickers, who lived on Templeton Avenue and took her out for afternoon tea at a certain time every Tuesday and Friday.

"Oh, yes," she rounded off, "I know most of the houses on this road, and I used to go next door quite a lot when the Bryce's lived there – before the new neighbours bought it. Funny lot, they are." she said, with a scowl. "Hardly ever see them, hardly ever hear them, but at least they're no trouble. Not like the ones at 22. My friend Sarah – at 24 – she's had a nightmare with them! I'd much rather have the ones here. He must be in the building trade, there's always some van or other parked across the road. I don't have a car – Marjorie takes me out – so I don't mind an extra vehicle on the street."

It was amazing how much someone could say in just two minutes, but it was gold dust to the Count and from it he formed the rest of his plan. A plan that he would put into operation tomorrow when, in the guise of a psychologist, he would visit the safe house to interview the suspect agent who was being held there.

* * *

Inspector Steve Gent received the urgent request from the Count with excitement, even though it was a routine research job on a lady who lived on Templeton Avenue, a certain Marjorie Vickers. It was fairly basic; the Count wanted to know about the woman's age, how she looked and dressed, her routine, what car she drove, etc. That was all relatively straightforward; the challenge was how quickly the Count wanted it. Gent took it as a compliment. The Count wasn't one of those arrogant bullies who made ridiculous demands in an attempt to make people work harder and faster. The "I want it yesterday!" brigade. Gent could think of a few senior officers in the force who fitted that bill very well. No, the Count only gave a tough deadline when he really needed it and when he had confidence that the person to whom he was entrusting the work could do it. From the Count, it was a mark of respect, and it made Steve Gent feel highly valued to know that the Count had the confidence that he would come through. And he did.

Gent would have loved to know what it was all about, but he was satisfied with one thing: whatever was going on, he was part of it.

As far as the Count was concerned, there was a lot more work to be done, but that would be for himself and Butler, and when Friday morning came he was ready.

* * *

The agent from the protection detail ushered the Count into the middle room on the ground floor. The room had no windows, although from the outside it looked for all the world like it did. There was a window in the outside wall and there were curtains that opened and closed. Behind them were net curtains, preventing anyone from seeing in when the curtains were open, and there was a source of light which came on when the curtains were drawn shut, but it was all a trick; the recess was only inches deep and a brick wall separated it from the inside of the house.

The Count took in the room at a glance and noted that particular deviation from what would have been a mirror image of the house next door. He would need to check what, if any, other alterations had been made, as he started the real game. The décor and furniture were plain, functional and uninspiring; however, the room held one stunning feature – Anna Parker.

CHAPTER 4

THE GAME BEGINS

The agent who had shown the Count in closed the door behind him, leaving the Count alone with Anna. The two of them stood in silence for a few seconds, each taking the other in. There was something there, the Count felt it immediately and for a moment he gazed intensely into her eyes, but whilst he felt a strong desire for a response, there was none. He wondered whether it would have been different if he was meeting her as himself rather than in the disguise of a tussle-haired, bearded and bespectacled psychologist. The padding that he was wearing around his waist was also, no doubt, something of a passion-killer for someone like Anna Parker. Perhaps the question would be answered eventually, but it was for another time. That said, he was already enjoying the game and this just raised the level of interest even further.

For Anna's part, she had noted the confidence of the man's eyes, targeting and locking hers, which stirred something in her, but not enough to compensate for his mild-mannered professor look and unkempt hair and beard. She would have said that he was reasonably well-built, had it not been for the slightly bulging waistline.

"Miss Parker." The Count said calmly. "A pleasure to meet you." He held out his hand, not as a man does to another man, palm to the side, but palm up, as a gentleman does to a lady. The move took Anna Parker by surprise and she found herself reaching out, palm down, in response. The Count took it with a gentle, but strong touch, and for a brief moment as his eyes met hers again, he felt an impulse to kiss her hand, as he would have done in higher society, but he dismissed the urge and softly released it.

Anna had expected the man to continue by introducing himself, but he didn't. In such awkward social situations even a couple of seconds seems like an age. She was suddenly unsure of herself, not knowing what to do or say. "Who are you?" seemed abrupt – rude, even, but she felt that compelling urge that many of us do in a similar position; the urge to say *something*.

The Count smiled, relieving the tension.

"You must be wondering who I am. But, please, sit down."

"Where do you want me to sit?"

"Where do you usually sit?"

"You mean when Sir Peter questions me?" She pointed to a rather straight-backed chair with minimal padding. "Here."

"Well, let's go with that." replied the Count, easing himself into the larger and much more comfortable chair opposite. Anna noted that not only had he taken the bigger, better chair, but he had also avoided telling her anything about who he was.

OK, thought Anna, beginning to recover her composure, *you're trying to establish a position of dominance.* That was the angle she needed to regroup her defences and ready herself for the game, for that was what she was sure was coming. A game of cat and mouse, in which she was the mouse.

The Count was a very good judge of people. He watched Anna's expression, and her eyes in particular, reading at least in part what was going through her mind, how she was feeling, and how she was likely to react. He saw the shift and knew he had to re-establish the connection.

However, he also knew that whilst Sir Peter had reluctantly agreed to stay away, as his presence might put Anna even more on her guard, he would nevertheless want to feel in control and would be desperate to know what was going on. That is to say, he would be listening in and watching via the camera and microphone hidden in the room. By establishing the normal seating arrangements used during Sir Peter's questioning sessions, the Count was fairly sure that the camera would be pointing at Anna Parker. He would still have to be careful, but he had planned accordingly.

"Miss Parker …" The Count hesitated. "May I call you Anna?" There was a warm tone in his voice, but Anna was suspicious. She had now set the mental context that they were on opposite sides and she wasn't going to be fooled by a smooth-talking charmer.

"I suppose so." she replied, somewhat stiffly, but then … what do I call you?"

"Thank you – and fair point." said the Count. "Please call me Edward."

"Not your real first name, I imagine."

The Count smiled. He liked this woman; she had spirit. He shook his head.

"No. And I'm glad you know that." He held her eyes again with his.

"You're glad that I know you're lying to me?" Anna retorted.

Anna noticed there was a twinkle in his eyes. Was he trying to tell her something?

"Knowing when someone is pretending and when they are genuine is extremely important, don't you think?" Was he talking about her, or about himself? Anna couldn't decide.

His expression changed and he reached into his briefcase. Taking out three folders, he began to speak more formally.

"Miss Parker …"

"Anna." she interrupted, "remember?" But there was no humorous response, no flicker of a twinkle in his eyes now. He continued.

"Anna. Sir Peter has asked me to speak to you regarding your last mission. I am not going to make you go through it all again; I've read the transcripts of your de-brief and subsequent ... conversations." He tossed one folder onto the coffee table. "I want to know a little more about you."

"You mean my background, upbringing – all that kind of stuff?"

"No. I've also read your file." He tossed a second folder onto the coffee table. "I want to know about you."

Oh, great, Anna sighed to herself, *He's a shrink!*

The Count opened the third folder.

"I'm going to show you some pictures."

Oh, please, moaned Anna inwardly, *Not this rubbish.* The Count saw the change of expression.

"I see that you don't think much of this technique."

"It's your show." said Anna. "And it doesn't look like I can do much else right now."

"Thank you for cooperating. Now, I want you to be calm, relaxed and dispassionate. When I show you a card, I want you to remain completely passive and simply say what you think the picture represents and avoid any expression of emotion, doubt or confusion. Be decisive and tell me immediately your first impression of what the picture represents." He looked directly into her eyes. "I repeat. Remain passive."

"Okay. Passive it is."

"Good." said the Count and held up the first card. It took all Anna's training and will power to stop the shock registering on her face.

* * *

Sir Peter monitored the interview from the comfort of his luxuriously upholstered leather chair. Being only in the lower tier of the senior officers, despite the knighthood which he had received for reasons unrelated to his role in British intelligence, his office was small, but it was very nicely presented. Oak panelling, vintage light fittings and plush carpet complemented the polished wooden shelves and beautiful mahogany desk with shiny brass handles.

By contrast, the high-tech equipment that sat on the desk and around the room seemed strangely at odds with the antique ambience. For Sir Peter, it was a suitable blend of familiar, classical comfort and old-world prestige, with the power, potential and somewhat more flashy status symbols of the modern era.

The Count certainly looked very different from the elderly gentleman he had met at the Riverside Club. His face had only appeared briefly on the screen as he turned to nod his thanks to the agent who had led him into the room, but he looked thirty years younger at least. The hair was brown, rather than grey, and there was a lot more of it. It was slightly untidy, as was the beard, as one would expect from someone more focussed on the inner person than the exterior appearance. The glasses, however, indicated a good degree of success in his profession, being of the sort of style and quality that the average person is instantly drawn to when the optician asks them to choose the frame that they would like for their new spectacles, but whose price instantly propels them to the other end of the display cabinet. However, once the interviewer and interviewee had taken their seats, Sir Peter could only see the Count from behind, as the camera had been set up to monitor the person being interviewed.

He watched with interest at the initial sparring between the two protagonists. He admired the Count's smooth approach and unruffled nature. His own interviews with Anna had not gone quite so smoothly. There had been open antagonism and it had grated on Sir Peter. He felt he had not been in control, as he liked to be. The Count had managed to keep things contained – cool, perhaps, but at least not aggressive.

That said, he wondered what the Count could possibly learn from Anna Parker's responses to various pictures, but perhaps he was just warming up and playing the part. Perhaps the sucker punch would come when Anna was least expecting it.

* * *

The shock flooded Anna's body with electricity and adrenaline. She immediately understood why the psychologist had told her to remain passive and avoid any expression of emotion, doubt or confusion as she was currently flooded with all of them. The card read:

SAY "DUCK"
REMEMBER THE FOLLOWING ...

Stunned, Anna controlled herself and said in a flat tone, "Duck".

The Count put the card face down onto the coffee table and held up the next one.

1PM GREEN
2PM RED
SAY "CAMEL"

"Camel." said Anna, sounding almost bored, although her heart was racing. She repeated the message in her head, not understanding it at all, but knowing it was vital. The Count showed the next card.

3PM LANDING
ALONE
SAY "HEART"

"Heart." she responded. *What on earth ... Never mind, just remember it!* she told herself, *1pm Green, 2pm Red, 3pm Landing – alone.*

The cards went on, but now they were just abstract shapes and Anna knew that she had been told everything she needed to know. She wasn't sure how she knew it; after all, she didn't understand it, but there was something in the manner of the man in front of her that exuded not only confidence, but capability. It had been there from the initial introduction, there in the twinkle in his eyes, as if he was enjoying playing a game. It was there in the message about it being important to know when someone was pretending and when they were genuine, and now the audacity of the messages on the cards. This man was a professional – and probably not as a psychologist. What's more, he was playing against Sir Peter. She wasn't sure what that meant, but she knew that Sir Peter was most definitely not on her side, so, whoever and whatever this man was, right now, he was her way out of this incarceration.

Anna played along and said whatever came into her head as each picture was presented. Pretending to have had enough, she broke the rhythm of the picture – response cycle.

"Are you remembering all this?" she said sarcastically. "I see you're not taking any notes." The Count smiled.

"I'm sure you're aware that this interview is being monitored and recorded. I'll receive a transcript within an hour."

"I figured as much." She made it sound aggressive and even slightly disdainful.

"Although I must say," the Count went on, "I believe I've learned a lot about you already." He smiled and Anna fought the urge to smile back, but the Count's tone continued to be formal so as to give nothing away to the watching Sir Peter, for whom the primary indication point of any untoward behaviour or intent on the part of the Count would be his voice.

"And if Sir Peter is still unhappy after whatever it is you've got to tell him?"

"Sir Peter is his own man and will make his own decisions," replied the Count, "but I wouldn't be surprised if you were taken to a specialist in more … shall we say, practical methods." Anna winced inwardly, but showed no sign of it.

The Count gathered his papers and stood up. Anna noticed that he had put the folders back into his case, but the cards into his jacket pocket.

"Is that it?" asked Anna.

"For now." replied the Count. Anna stood. The Count had not turned away. She repeated the message in her mind to keep it there: *1pm Green, 2pm Red, 3pm Landing – alone. But what does it mean?*

The Count held out his hand. She took it, and instantly knew she had the answer.

As Anna reached out and took the hand of the psychologist she felt him pass her a tiny plastic tray, no more than one centimetre by two centimetres, like someone had cut out a couple of tablets from a packet. A tingle ran through her body. He held her gaze momentarily, then stood tall and took two or three seconds to fasten his case fully, blocking the camera just long enough for her glance at the tray and to hide it down the front of her jeans.

"Thank you for your cooperation." he said. "I may need to see you again."

"Will there be more pictures?"

"I'm afraid not. Did you find them interesting?"

"Some more than others."

"Indeed. And now I must head off to review the transcript and draft my report, which I must do by 5pm this afternoon. Let's see … " He looked at his watch. "It's 12:55 now, so I should have time." And with that he turned and left.

* * *

Sir Peter pressed a button and spoke to the agent in the hallway of the safe house. As the Count moved towards the front door the agent blocked his path.

"May I have the cards, sir?" It was more of an order than a request.

"Sorry?"

"The picture cards. They're in your left jacket pocket. Sir Peter would like me to copy them to him right away."

"I'm not sure they'll mean much to Sir Peter. He's not really …"

"I'm afraid I must insist." the agent interrupted, and the Count had no option.

* * *

While the transcript was being prepared Sir Peter studied the picture cards. The first was an abstract splodge that vaguely resembled a duck, although Sir Peter thought it made him think of a cannon. The other cards were similarly innocuous abstracts of the sort used in personality tests. He had no idea what the Count would learn from Anna's responses, but there was nothing untoward in the cards. *Just as well to have checked, though,* he told himself, *one cannot be too hands-on.*

* * *

The Count chuckled to himself as the taxi drove away from the safe house. He had judged Sir Peter rightly, and so he had taken the precaution to wear one of his jackets with hidden pockets – which, in fairness, was most of them. Each side had two compartments; one that was almost impossible to spot and went quite deep, the other deliberately made highly visible to draw the eye with coloured stitching or a contrasting material. Anticipating some kind of search or a demand to show the cards that Sir Peter had been unable to see, he had brought two sets: one that he would use to communicate with Anna, and one that he would produce if needed for Sir Peter. He had slipped Anna's set into the hidden pocket and produced Sir Peter's set from the other. *Elegant and effective,* he thought to himself, *quite beautiful.* Then he realised that, in addition to the trick he had just pulled off, he was also thinking about Anna Parker.

CHAPTER 5

AFTERNOON TEA WITH FALSE PLATES

The agent in the van had just finished his lunch when the blue Toyota Corolla pulled up across the street. Was it still lunch at 2:30pm? Meal times were often a bit hit and miss on surveillance jobs. He mused on the incongruity between the high tech gear that was crammed into the back of the van versus the portable toilet that he had to pull out and use as necessary – all while keeping a close eye on the screens. Good job the bad guys didn't know when he needed to go.

He clocked the car and checked the registration number on the system. Okay, the registration matched the model and the car belonged to Marjorie Vickers, a friend of Mrs Martin who lived next door to the safe house. Another note on the file advised him of their afternoon tea routine. He relaxed and thought about using the toilet. He watched as Marjorie went up the path, rang the bell and went in. *Yep, now's a good time to go,* he thought.

It was a full half hour later that the two ladies emerged from the house and drove off for afternoon tea, but it was only ten minutes after that when he got an urgent call from one of the agents in the house.

"We can't find Anna Parker! Have you seen anything?"

* * *

Anna had followed the psychologist as far as the doorway and had heard the confrontation in the hall, heart pounding as the agent forced him to hand over the cards. Would he look – would he see? But there was no alarm, no fight, no arrest. What did that mean?

She stood there, momentarily stunned, heart racing, brain overloading. Who was this man? Was this all a trick – a test devised by Sir Peter? She didn't think so. Sir Peter wasn't that creative. And it was just like Sir Peter to check on his own representative, interfering old beggar that he was. No, the psychologist wasn't following Sir Peter's plan, but whose plan was he following and how did she fit into it?

One thing she did know, she now had just three minutes to decide whether she was in or out. But she already knew, head and heart, that she was in.

She repeated the message to herself: *1pm Green, 2pm Red, 3pm Landing – alone.* Now she understood, at least the first two parts. The plastic tray that had been slipped into her hand contained two small pills: one green, one red. It was obvious that she was to take the green pill at 1pm and the red pill at 2pm. It seemed reasonable to assume that "Landing" referred to the area at the top of the stairs rather than, for example, the time a plane was going to land, as the word had been followed by an instruction to be alone. So, that was it, the whole picture. Take the green pill at 1pm, the red pill at 2pm, and be alone on the landing at 3pm. What the pills would do to her and was going to happen at 3pm she had no idea, but if she was going to trust someone and follow their plan, it wasn't going to be Sir Peter. And if they were going to move on to more direct means of getting information out of her … that was not a great option.

She had located the cameras in every part of the safe house within the first twenty-four hours of being put there. There weren't many blind spots, and those that there were weren't very large, but she knew them all. She left the room and saw that the agent from the hallway had gone into the back room to send copies of the cards to Sir Peter.

She moved to a spot in which most of her body was out of sight and, without looking down, retrieved the tray from her jeans and quickly prised out the green pill. Pretending to cough she leaned forward slightly, just enough to identify the green pill, which she then popped into her mouth as she coughed. That was long enough. An agent would be coming any second to make sure she was safe and secure.

She sat down, this time taking the padded chair – as much a statement of defiance as for her comfort. Almost immediately the door opened and the other member of the in-house security detail entered and sat down opposite her. They sat in silence and for the next five minutes nothing happened. Then it started. She rushed upstairs to the bathroom and threw up.

The agent followed her. Hearing the commotion the other agent spoke via their earpiece comms.

"What's going on?"

"Anna's being sick."

"Is it genuine?" asked the agent downstairs, wary of being caught off guard by a fake show of illness.

"Oh, yes!" came the reply, "big time."

Anna felt terrible. The initial wave had passed, but she felt like there was more to come. She flushed the toilet, groaned and curled up on the bathroom floor.

"Okay," said the agent, wrinkling his nose at the smell, "I'll leave you to it."

For the next twenty minutes, Anna lay there, and then it hit again. *What have you done to me, you psycho psychologist?!* But there was no time to dwell on it, the impulse got her up on her knees, head over the toilet, just in time. She groaned loudly.

The agent was already on his way back up the stairs.

"Phew, that's a stinker!" he remarked, seeming to enjoy the spectacle.

"Thanks for your concern." Anna spat back sarcastically, wiping her mouth with several pieces of toilet paper. She flushed again and lay down. "That's twice in what … fifteen minutes?"

The agent checked his watch.

"More like twenty. You're first one was at five past one, or just after, and it's 13:26 now."

"Great." Anna moaned. "I hope this isn't going to be every twenty minutes. Right now I'd settle for a 30-minute respite."

"I'll time you," said the agent, smirking. "We can make a game of it. I'll come back at in half an hour."

Anna hated the way he was enjoying her discomfort, but she was delighted at the way she'd managed to manipulate a time check. As soon as she'd been locked up they'd taken away all means of her keeping time: her watch had been confiscated (*Unfortunate but predictable,* Anna had thought, as it contained a few "extras" that field agents might require in a tight spot), along with her phones. She had no access to TV, radio or internet, and most of the inner areas of the house had no natural light, but had lighting controlled centrally, not following the normal day-night cycle. This was fairly standard disorientation procedure.

Anna had hoped the effects of the green pill would wear off after a while, but they didn't. At least she made it through the half hour. The agent returned, a broad smile on his face on seeing her leaning over the toilet again.

"Hey, you got your half-hour" he said cheerily. Anna threw up again. "Whoa! There she blows!" His smile faded. It had struck him that this could potentially be something more significant. His tone was a little more serious.

"Are you feeling any other symptoms?"

"Other than wanting to die – no." She had an idea. "But if this is still going an hour from now, I want a doctor."

The agent paused. He didn't want to be seen as having panicked, but then Anna Parker was a top priority and he couldn't risk anything happening to her.

"Okay, well, I'll check on you in an hour – but yell if anything new comes up … Whoops! Sorry, I mean, if there are any new symptoms."

Great, thought Anna, it must be about 13:58 now, and the agent's return would tell her when it was just before 3pm. She knew that she was in view of a camera – there was no privacy for a suspected traitor – but through the nausea she'd been working out her plan. For a couple of minutes she rolled over every now and then holding her stomach, until she figured it was 2pm. She rolled and writhed again, but this time as she appeared to hold her stomach in pain, she retrieved the red pill from down the front of her jeans. Sitting up and turning towards the toilet, she pretending to wretch, putting her hand over her mouth and popping the pill in. What would this one do? Put her in a coma, so she could escape in a fake ambulance? She hoped desperately that it wouldn't be any worse than the green pill.

* * *

Butler was having a busy couple of days. Yesterday the Count had asked him to source a vehicle and had been very specific about the make, model and year – and the registration number that should be on the set of detachable plates that he was to put on it. He had also been instructed to purchase two particular sets of clothing with a matching tote bag for each, one of which was to be packed with a certain set of tools, some trainers, a polypropylene boiler suit, two pairs of latex gloves and a pair of tickets for afternoon tea at the Ritz Hotel up in central London. These items were to be put in the boot of the car ready for the Count and the car was to be left at a precise location by 2pm this afternoon, which he had just managed to do, with a few minutes to spare.

Butler thrived on clarity, variety and challenge – and

this had certainly been all of those things. Life with the Count was never boring, that was for sure. His final instruction was to move on to the Manor and prepare rooms and dinner for the Count plus one. He took a taxi back to where his own vehicle awaited him and drove out of town and into the English countryside.

* * *

As with the green pill, there was no marked change in Anna's condition for the first few minutes after swallowing the red pill, but she gradually became aware that she was starting to feel a little better. Her first thought was that this was good news, but then it struck her that the only reason the agents were leaving her alone was that they believed her to be pretty much incapacitated. Now she understood. She needed to be fit and well for whatever was going to happen at 3pm, but it had been necessary to establish a genuine illness in order to put the agents at their ease and give her a good chance of being alone on the landing when the time came. It had been horrible, but she had to admit, it was working well. It was now down to her to keep the plan on track by keeping up the appearances of being ill.

* * *

The Count, made up and dressed as Marjorie Vickers, drove the blue Toyota through the suburbs and parked outside Mrs Martin's home, next door to the safe house. When Mrs Martin answered the door she was slightly confused, firstly by Marjorie's early arrival and secondly by her appearance. Having anticipated this, the Count bustled in with gusto and confidence, and closed the door behind him. He quickly apologised to Mrs Martin for the interruption and inconvenience, then promptly administered a sedative that would leave Mrs Martin unharmed, but without recollection of what had happened, when she woke up about 40 minutes later.

Carrying her gently through to the lounge, the Count set her comfortably in her armchair, sleeping peacefully. He put on a pair of latex gloves and picked up Mrs Martin's phone. Dialling the number he had memorised, he practised Mrs Martin's voice one more time. He felt he'd got it about right after his visit as Mr Tomms, but it never hurt to get into character.

"Hello, Marjorie?" said the Count, "I won't be coming to afternoon tea, I'm not feeling very well." Marjorie expressed concern from the other end of the line, but the Count needed to keep it short. "Oh, it's nothing, dear, I just need a rest, that's all; you go without me. See you on Tuesday. Bye."

He hung up, then hurried softly up the stairs and into the bedroom. He closed the curtains and took from his tote bag a set of clothes in Mrs Martin's style, but in a slightly taller woman's size, laying them neatly on the bed, along with a grey wig. He hitched up the dress he was wearing and pulled the plastic overalls up over it and switched from his Marjorie Vickers heels into the trainers.

Moving swiftly on to the landing, he picked up the loft pole, opened the hatch and pulled down the loft ladders. Climbing quickly and gracefully, he was up in the loft within seconds.

He extracted the necessary items from the tote bag and set to work. His first task was to remove some bricks from the partition wall that joined on to the safe house attic. He had to be quick, but careful not to make a noise. Using a combination of chemicals and tools, he managed to remove the necessary 12 bricks in a little over 15 minutes. Moving through the hole like a snake, he found the safe house loft boarded – that made moving around easier and, on top of the insulation, would help to deaden the sound.

He conducted a rapid inspection of the area and located the wiring for the security camera that covered the landing area. Tapping into it, he connected a device that enabled him to see the picture from the camera and also control the feed from it. Seeing that the landing was clear, he took a snapshot and readied the device to send that picture as the signal as soon as he pressed the button.

The loft ladders were still attached to the loft hatch that he'd spotted from the hallway on his visit earlier in the day. That was fine, although he'd brought a length of climbing rope as a back-up. He checked his watch – 14:49. He secured the hatch to a beam using high strength parachute cord and made sure it was tight, then set to work on releasing the hatch. Cutting a rectangle in the plastic cover, he exposed the locking mechanism and drew back the twin bolts that held the hatch up. The parachute cord took the strain and the hatch stayed put. The Count checked his watch again – 14:54. He sprayed the hatch and ladder joints with lubricant to make sure they worked and didn't squeak. Now he just had to wait and hope that Anna did her part.

* * *

Knowing she was constantly on camera, Anna kept up the pretence of being ill, although she felt better and stronger with each minute that passed. The vomiting nausea was subsiding, and now she could feel the butterflies in her stomach that signalled the nervous tension as she prepared for whatever was going to happen at 3pm. She heard the agent coming up the stairs.

"How's the patient?" the agent enquired. Anna groaned and rolled over slightly for effect.

"No worse. Maybe even a little better, but …" she suddenly shot up, pretended to throw up into the toilet, then flushed quickly.

"Whoa! Okay. Anyway, at least we don't need to make a fuss. Just stay here and try not to make a mess. I hate mopping up sick." Anna waved him away without turning round.

"Just leave me alone. You're not exactly helping."

Relieved that the condition wasn't serious, the agent reverted to his former joviality.

"That's one reason I didn't become a doctor – terrible bedside manner!" And with that, he left her to it. Anna lay down and rolled over – towards the landing. The bathroom wasn't large and she was now by the open door, just a step away.

* * *

As the seconds ticked towards 3pm the Count pressed the button to start the camera feed, then took the strain and released the highwayman's knot that was holding the loft hatch in place. There was a tiny beep from the Count's watch and he swiftly and silently lowered the ladders. Anna caught a glimpse of the movement and was up on her feet in a flash. The ladders had barely touched the carpet when Anna was already on her way up. She moved like a cat, strong and supple, but as she stepped into the loft she stopped like a clumsy child when she saw the middle-aged woman in plastic overalls poised by the hatch.

The Count grinned, "Keep moving." he hissed, pointing to the hole in the brickwork. "Through there!"

She responded instantly and the Count took less than a minute to pull up the ladders, hoist the hatch and secure the bolts. Moving efficiently and with speed, he removed the security camera device, restoring the normal camera feed, gathered all the rest of his equipment into the tote bag, and snaked through the hole. Anna was waiting for him on the side.

"Who *are* you?" she panted, breathless from the sprint up the ladders while still recovering from the pills.

"I'll tell you later." said the Count, smiling. "But right now, put on these gloves, go down to the bedroom and get changed – your clothes and wig are on the bed." Anna stared at him. "Quickly!" ordered the Count in a voice that radiated authority, but bore no malice, and Anna found herself responding to it.

The Count gathered the rest of his gear, descended and closed the hatch. Anna was still dressing when the Count joined her. Despite the urgency of the situation, he couldn't help noticing – and admiring – her figure. Anna clocked it and couldn't resist flirting.

"Oh, Grandma, what a deep voice you have!" she said, in a mock Little Red Riding Hood voice. The Count laughed. He definitely liked her.

"All the better to direct you with, my dear." he parried. "Now, get a move on." And this time it was her turn to laugh, and though she had no idea who this man was or what he really looked like, she thought she might like him too.

Two minutes later they were heading through the hall.

"One moment." said the Count and he stepped through into the lounge. Anna followed him. The Count quickly checked that Mrs Martin was OK. Anna thought she heard him whisper, "Sorry, Mrs Martin – and thank you."

Just before he opened the front door, the Count reached into his tote bag, pulled out an envelope addressed to Mrs Martin, and dropped it on the floor, as if it had been posted through.

"What's that?"

"A little gift from me, to make up for the inconvenience." the Count replied, "Two tickets for afternoon tea at the Ritz Hotel."

What sort of man checks on a woman that he's drugged, apologises and leaves her tickets for the Ritz?! she wondered, half amazed and half enchanted.

Composing themselves, they left the house confidently, apparently deep in conversation about something or someone further down the street, so that her heads were turned away from prying eyes and cameras, got into the car and drove away.

* * *

Sir Peter had no idea what had happened, but he was furious. He watched the security camera footage again. He could see Anna Parker roll over towards the landing, stand up and step out of the bathroom camera's picture, but she never appeared on the landing camera. It was as though the bathroom doorway was a portal to another dimension. Sir Peter didn't believe in science fiction, and no country or agency on earth had got anywhere near teleportation. He was at a loss. The panic started to rise again within him, as did the acid indigestion that came with it. Not only had his agent lost the item, but he had now lost the agent. He wasn't going to be able to keep it under wraps for much longer. He made sure that the agents on duty – and those on the replacement shift – told no one without his express instruction. He ordered the obvious things: a full search of the house and an inspection of the cameras, then focussed on the footage front and back, and grilling the agent in the van.

He studied the transcript of the Count's interview with Anna a second time, but could see nothing untoward in it. No clue that anything like this was going to happen.

* * *

The Count hadn't had time to study the transcript in detail when it came through, within the hour as predicted. He had skimmed it, editing out names, location and anything else that might give away who, where or what this was about, then emailed it securely to the top London psychologist from whom he had obtained the personality test cards and whom he had paid to be on standby ready to analyse the responses, write a report and send it to the Count by 4pm.

It was now ten past three as the Count drove Anna through the suburbs. A few streets away from the safe house they passed another blue Toyota Corolla going the other way, driven by a middle-aged lady. Anna caught the number plate – the same as the car they were driving. She immediately put two and two together.

"Is that …?" she remarked casually, but couldn't help the note of admiration at her rescuer's planning and execution.

"Identical to this car? Yes. That's Mrs Martin's friend, Marjorie. They go for afternoon tea together on Tuesdays and Fridays."

"But when she gets to the house they'll know what

happened."

"Don't worry," said the Count, "She's going straight to the church hall."

"How do you know?"

"Marjorie got a call earlier to say that Mrs Martin wasn't feeling very well and wouldn't be going for afternoon tea today."

"A call from you, I suppose?" The Count said nothing, but his face showed he was loving it.

"Wouldn't it have been easier to just "borrow" the car?" Anna suggested, "That way there'd be no chance of both cars being there at the same time and giving the game away."

The Count's expression and tone hardened slightly.

"I don't like to cause unnecessary distress – especially not to little old ladies."

Anna had never met a spy like this before – if, indeed, that was what he was. Anna had a hundred questions, but that last remark felt like a rebuke and she fell silent.

The Count pulled over into a quiet spot, got out of the car and removed the false number plates. He then got back in and drove on. No automatic number plate recognition cameras would be tracking them now.

The Count drove a few miles further and stopped on a back street outside a row of lock-up garages. He pulled out a remote control and used it to open one of the doors, then parked the car inside. He got out and Anna followed.

"If you wouldn't mind getting changed once more." he said politely, pointing to yet another set of clothes and a wig stacked neatly on one of the shelves.

"Sure."

They both changed in silence. The Count faced away from Anna, but as she dressed, she stole a few glances over at the man who was calling the shots at the moment. He was a little above average height, probably a whisker under 6 feet tall. He was muscular without being pumped up like a gym junkie; more like a gymnast, she thought. When he removed his wig and make up she could see that he was handsome, with a classically stylish haircut and probably in his early- to mid-thirties. And he was putting on a casual, but very smart outfit. Her clothes were in a similar vein, casual – very comfortable and probably very expensive, judging by the labels and the cut, and they fitted perfectly. She thought about asking him how he knew her sizes, but she already knew the answer. He had read her files and obviously had an excellent eye for detail.

"Ready?" asked the Count.

"Ready." replied Anna and smiled. The Count returned the smile. *At last,* thought Anna, *I thought I'd made him angry with my challenge.* Of course he'd have considered taking the lady's car and drugging her as well, but he was much bigger and better than that.

For his part the Count was pleased and impressed with Anna's response. She could have replied, "Ready for what?", but she didn't, she just said, "Ready." And the Count liked that.

"Then let's go." he said, heading for a break in the shelves, where a door led through to the adjacent garage in which a silver Mercedes gleamed under the motion-triggered lighting.

CHAPTER 6

THE MANOR

The Count drove a little faster, keeping to the speed limits, but not slowing down much if at all on bends. She noticed that whenever he wanted to straighten a bend, to enable it to be taken more quickly, he would only cross the centre lines as far – and would drive only as fast – as his view of the road ahead would allow. His driving was exhilaratingly quick at times, but also curiously safe. Anna wasn't sure whether he was driving like his true self now, or whether it was all part of the new persona, driving less like a middle-aged lady and more like a suave and confident businessman. She ventured a question.

"So … who are you?" she asked.

"That's an interesting question, but unfortunately one that has many answers and none of them simple." Even out of the corner of his eye he could see that she wasn't satisfied by his reply. "In certain circles, including the one in which we are currently involved, I am known as 'The Count'."

Well, that's something, thought Anna, *but not much.*

"And does the Count have a name?" Anna pressed.

"Many." smiled the Count, "Almost as many as the characters I have to play."

"You make it sound like you're an actor."

"Indeed I am," said the Count, "but this …", he waved his hand, indicating the world at large, "… is my stage."

"I think Shakespeare said something similar was true of

all of us." countered Anna.

"Yes, but he was referring to the single character that most people play."

"Themselves."

"Correct. However, in my covert occupation I am called on to take on different parts and different characters depending on the play that I happen to be in at any given time."

"And whose play are we in just now?" asked Anna. The Count nodded, pleased and impressed with her insight.

"That, my dear, is a far more important question."

"And will I get an answer?"

"Oh yes," said the Count, "over dinner."

* * *

The Count indicated then turned the Mercedes off the country lane and through a gate that opened automatically as the car approached and closed behind it when it had passed through. The drive arced to the left through a small area of woodland and then right, leaving the woods behind and leading into grounds that fitted the old manor house very well. The whole estate consisted of only one and a half acres, but it was pleasantly spacious. The high walls that marked the boundaries were 19th century brick, some ivy-clad, others decked with trellis-work and climbing plants such as clematis and roses, the very earliest-flowering of which were starting to come into bloom. The manor house itself had a particularly beautiful climbing rose around the front door portico and either side to the large leaded windows. The Count pulled up in front of the sturdy oak double doors, one of which opened immediately, revealing a tall, tough-looking man with a jovial expression. They got out of the car.

"All went well, sir?"

"Very well, thank you – due in no small part to you and our drably-dressed friend. Well done, Butler. Much appreciated."

Butler beamed at the Count's genuine expression of

recognition and gratitude.

"Anna, meet my trusted associate and friend, Butler."

"I bet that's not *your* real name either." said Anna, half-wondering why she felt so much at ease in the company of these men about whom she knew next to nothing. The Count and Butler both laughed.

"Now," said the Count in a business-like tone, "if you would be so good as to follow Butler, he'll show you to your room. I have a little matter to attend to. I'll see you for dinner at six." And with that, he left Anna in Butler's care.

The drive from the lock-up garage had taken around 45 minutes. The Count checked his watch – 16:15. *Good,* he thought to himself, *still on track.* He headed directly to the study and checked his emails. He went straight to the one from the psychologist in London and scanned the report, paying special attention to the summary and conclusion. Next, he edited it slightly to remove references to the originator of the report and make it his own, then he quickly readied a secure email with the report as an attachment and picked up the phone.

* * *

Sir Peter looked at the antique clock on the wall in his office. Time was ticking on and he still had nothing useful from any of his agents. He had done well so far to hide the loss of the item from his superiors, but he wasn't going to be able to hide things much longer. He ran through the possibilities:

1. *One of his agents had betrayed him* – but he had multiple agents on site and the likelihood of them all being in on it was remote, plus he had camera footage that showed the exits and the agents' movements. He discounted this scenario for now.

2. *Whoever had the item had now come for Anna*, either to retrieve her as a valued operative, or to silence her. He didn't know how they'd extracted her, but it was a real possibility.

His mind drifted to the Count. Could he be involved? His reputation was spotless, but then, he was the only new factor in the equation …

His thoughts were interrupted by the ringing of his telephone. He pulled himself together and answered in his customary sharp tone.

"Shackleton."

"Sir Peter," the Count's voice was smooth and reassuring, "I wanted to let you know that I've just put the final touches to my report from this morning's interview and am sending it to you now. Could you please check that it has arrived safely?"

Sir Peter looked again at the clock. It was 16:25; a full thirty-five minutes ahead of schedule. He checked his emails.

"Just a moment, checking now …", he refreshed the list and saw the Count's email at the top. "Yes, I can see it there, with the attachment."

"Good," said the Count, "I think you'll find it interesting – at least as a starting point. Perhaps we could discuss it after dinner – say, 9pm? I will, of course, need to spend more time with Miss Parker at some point to delve a little deeper."

Sir Peter groaned inwardly. He frantically opened the attachment and scrolled down the document. It was certainly thorough and even on a quick glance through, randomly checking here and there, he could see that it was a genuine analysis of Anna's actual responses. It must have taken the Count a couple of hours to write it. There was, therefore, no way that he could have been involved in Anna's disappearance. It was time to go all in.

"Yes, about that," said Sir Peter slowly, "I'm going to need to extend the requirement for your services a little." The Count let a moment or two go by, for effect.

"In what way?"

"Well," said Sir Peter hesitantly, "in addition to ascertaining the level of Anna Parker's loyalty and locating the item …" he paused.

"Yes?" prompted the Count.

"I also need you to locate Anna Parker."

"What do you mean?"

"I mean," Sir Peter was struggling to even say it out loud, "that Anna Parker is missing."

"Missing?" gasped the Count, "but how? She was in one of your safe houses."

"I don't know how." groaned Sir Peter, "but she's gone. I'll double your fee if you can find her and bring her back."

The Count smiled to himself. He had plenty of money and it wasn't his primary motive, but sometimes it just fell into one's lap. In any case, he could put it to good use in any number of ways, perhaps through one of his charities, or via gifts to folks he came across who were in need.

"Very well," the Count accepted, "I'll need to view the scene, the footage and to speak to the agents. I'll also need you to be a little more forthcoming about who you suspect may be behind the loss of the item. They might have strong motives for wanting to get hold of Anna."

"Of course." replied Sir Peter. "And I had the same thought."

"Good," said the Count, "then we're on the same wavelength." *At least on what you're aware of,* added the Count in his head.

"I assume you've secured the scene?"

"Naturally."

"We can't wait until tomorrow. I will be there by eight-thirty. Will you be able to meet me there?"

"I will be there from eight." said Sir Peter.

Of course you will, thought the Count, *You'll want to be a step ahead of me, in control.* He chuckled silently, *Not much chance of either of those happening, though.*

"Until tonight." he said soberly.

"Until tonight." replied Sir Peter.

CHAPTER 7

DINNER AND DETECTIVE WORK

Anna's bedroom was like an up-market period boutique hotel room – but without the style-over-substance pretention. Everything was quality, beautifully furnished, decorated and finished. She'd half-expected another set of clothes or perhaps an elegant evening dress to wear over dinner, but instead there was simply a dressing gown and a pair of men's pyjamas on the bed, although the dressing gown was the sort of soft and luxurious kind that you could snuggle up in beside a log fire. It was quite quaint, really. It was homely and gave her an odd feeling of being treated more like family than a guest – and nothing at all like a prisoner.

She looked out of the window. There were no guards, no one patrolling the perimeter. From her window on the west side she could see the sun setting over the picturesque stone-built parish church half a mile away across the neighbouring fields.

There were some mints in a bowl on the bedside cabinet and Anna suddenly realised that her breath must have smelt awful the whole time she was with the Count. She hurriedly popped one in her mouth and meandered around the room, examining the books and various objects on the shelves and tables. There were no family photographs, she noticed, just a couple of tasteful paintings and a cross-stitch text in a wooden frame that read:

with a small sub-text, "John 8 vs 32".

The truth, thought Anna, was more likely to get her locked up than set free.

She decided to take a shower. The en-suite bathroom was immaculate, beautifully tiled in a classic, yet modern style. The water was hot and it felt good to wash away the feel of the safe house. The towels were as thick and soft as the dressing gown. A hairdryer had thoughtfully been placed on the dressing table, along with a men's hairbrush. It struck Anna that there was clearly no lady of the house and that any ladies who visited had come here under different circumstances and brought their own accessories. *But it's the thought that counts,* she said to herself, and then laughed, because that sounded quite like: "It's the Count that thought!" *Yes, he is thoughtful,* she mused, remembering the Count's kindness to Mrs Martin and consideration for Marjorie Vickers.

Anna sat on the bed for a while, still wondering why, given that she was at the centre of an international affair and was now effectively on the run from the British Secret Service, she felt so calm and free. But was she free? Or was she being held here? She tried the bedroom doorknob; it turned and the door opened. She wandered along the corridor and down the stairs into the hall. It really was charming. Everything was neat and tidy, yet homely. Antique, but not crusty. A perfect blend of good taste and order.

She moved towards the front door.

"Can I help you, Miss Parker?" She turned to see Butler standing not far behind her. He was holding a large and very sharp kitchen knife.

"I was just looking round."

"Might I suggest a stroll around the sunken garden and on to the ornamental pond and fountain? It's very pretty."

"Er, okay, thanks." said Anna, amazed that she wasn't

being prevented from leaving the house. And that, she thought to herself, was precisely why she felt at ease in the place.

"I'll be in the kitchen if you need me, miss." He held up the knife. "The veg won't chop itself!"

She followed Butler's advice and wandered round the gardens. He had not misled her, even in early spring they were very pretty indeed with camellias, hellebores and primroses among the ones she could recognise and name. Further round she saw a small paddock, but there were no horses in the stables, although it seemed likely that there had been relatively recently. The stables were clean and tidy, but there was hay and feed, and the odd hoof print in what little dirt there was on the floor. She surmised from this that, assuming this was the Count's property, he must enjoy riding, but he was only here from time to time, and he would keep the horses elsewhere and have them brought over when he wanted to ride.

All this added to the picture she was building in her mind of the man who had helped her escape from the safe house, despite being in some way associated with the Service. After all, he'd been there on Sir Peter's instructions, but then again he'd been double-crossing Sir Peter the whole time.

Whose play are we in just now? she thought, reprising the key question. *Not Sir Peter's.* She reflected that, had Sir Peter had the imagination to think of the world as a stage and the things that were going on as a play, he would have thought of himself as both the playwright and the director – prescribing exactly what people would do and say, and constantly telling them exactly how to do and say it. But now the actors were ad-libbing, or worse still, they were following someone else's script. But whose? The Count's? Or was he simply another actor in the play, with someone else directing from behind the scenes? Did the Mercedes and the manor house even belong to the Count, or were they just props, like the copy of Marjorie Vickers' car? The Count had promised to answer her question over dinner, but would he – and if he did, would it be the truth or just another line in the play? And how would she know the difference?

She suddenly felt cold. She'd been lost in thought for a good while and late afternoon was turning to early evening, bringing with it the coolness that falls at the end of a spring day. But there was another reason why Anna Parker felt a chill. *What if the Count knew her secret? What if he knew that she really had taken the item?*

She turned back towards the house. The Count was standing at the corner, watching her.

* * *

Sir Peter couldn't wait. He ordered a taxi, then rushed out and peered into the distance, anxious to see his ride as soon at it appeared on the street. He never saw a man step up behind him, or realise that the man had slipped something into his coat pocket. He just felt someone brush past him and continue walking down the street.

He phoned ahead so that the agents would be ready and standing to attention on his arrival. As soon as the taxi pulled up outside the safe house Sir Peter swept into the building to take charge of the investigation personally, but instead of lining up in the hall, like 19th century domestic servants when their master arrived home after a weekend away on a shooting trip, two were at the top of the stairs and two were nowhere to be seen. One of the agents called down to Sir Peter.

"She escaped through the loft, sir."

Sir Peter was conflicted. On the one hand this was good news, but on the other hand he had wanted to be the one to solve the riddle. He started up the stairs.

Sir Peter was briefed as he surveyed the whole scene, from the bathroom, still faintly reeking of vomit, to the loft, which he managed to climb up to with some difficulty, and the gap through to next door's attic. An agent had gone through the hole and lit up the scene.

"The hatch is secure, sir, but she must have gone down through here; there's no other way out."

"Who lives next door?" demanded Sir Peter, shouting with unnecessary volume through the hole.

"A Mrs Martin." replied the agent stood behind him, the one who had been in the van, "Widow, 63 years old, totally clean."

"Blast!" muttered Sir Peter, "Dirty move, that, involving civilians. Has anyone interviewed her yet?"

"I don't think she's back yet, sir."

"What do you mean, not back yet?"

"She went out for afternoon tea with her friend. They go every Tuesday and Friday afternoon."

"I'll wager they didn't go today." rasped Sir Peter, "I believe we'll find Mrs Martin bound and gagged in her own home. Monsters!" He made his way down the loft ladders, puffing and wheezing as he went. Taking one of the agents with him, Sir Peter stormed round to Mrs Martin's front door, broke it down and burst in.

Mrs Martin dropped her cup of tea onto her slippers and screamed.

* * *

The man who had been lurking outside Sir Peter's office walked at a nondescript pace so as not to attract any attention. The bug that he had placed in Sir Peter's pocket was tiny and unlikely to be noticed for some time. *Marvellous, really,* he thought, *a super-sensitive listening device and a tracker in such a small piece of kit.*

Now the Mécénat would be able to find where the British Secret Service was hiding Anna Parker. The Boss would be pleased.

* * *

As it turned out, the Boss's pleasure was short-lived. Having heard, via the listening device, the address Sir Peter had given to the taxi driver, the Boss immediately called a nasty-looking man with a hooked nose and thick dark eyebrows, gave him the address and a terse instruction.

"Go and get her." The man wrote down the address.

"I'll take a team." he said, "she's going to be guarded."

"Try not to make too much mess." said the Boss, "You're not on our turf now. We need to be ... what do the English say? ... discreet." The hook-nosed man grimaced.

"I'll do my best."

He was looking forward to it. Arturo loved a good shoot-out. He'd be careful, though, this time – discreet. He'd spend, oh, at least ten minutes casing the place before he would take out the inevitable agent holed up in a van nearby, disable comms and video feeds and then blow the front door – discreetly, of course, and take out any agents inside. He'd be careful with Anna Parker, the Boss wanted her in one piece – and from the photos the Boss has sent through she was a good-looking woman, why waste that? Sure, she could fight, but this had been her first proper field mission, and you can only learn so much in a training environment. There are things you learn out in the real world, where people are really trying to kill you, that no camp on earth can teach you. That takes time and experience. And Arturo had had a lot of both.

His phone rang. It was the Boss.

"Stand down. She's not there."

"Wrong place?"

"Right place. Wrong time. She escaped this afternoon."

* * *

Both the Count and Sir Peter had read the summary and conclusion of the psychologist's report on receipt of it, but since then the Count had studied it in more detail. The summary showed that Anna was complex, showing traits that at times seemed to be contradictory. She was sometimes logical, sometimes imaginative. Passionate, but showing the potential to be detached. Humorous, even playful, but with a dark side. Strong, but with indications of repressed fear. In short, the report was inconclusive, but recommended that she be treated with caution. Sir Peter was satisfied so far; from his point of view it looked like events had proven that the report had assessed her correctly. The Count had read the commentary on each of the un-prompted responses and they had certainly set alarm bells ringing. He locked the report in a desk drawer and locked the study behind him.

He checked in with Butler, who told him that Anna was taking a walk round the grounds. The Count stepped out briskly, spotted Anna and followed her silently. She seemed to be enjoying a stroll round the small estate, but it was hard to tell what she admiring and what she was assessing in terms of escape, potential weapons, etc. Even a gardening fork could be deadly, but the tool shed had still been safely locked up when he'd passed it.

He thought she seemed at ease, which pleased him more than he'd expected. It was good for the Count's plan that she was relaxed, but somehow he was glad that a connection had been made, something personal, something … and then he had seen it. The sudden change of demeanour, her arms almost hugging herself, the look on her face when she saw him watching. It was guilt – and fear.

Anna recovered quickly.

"It's turned chilly." she said with a smile.

"Yes," the Count responded, "shall we go inside?"

As they walked back together Anna made polite conversation.

"You have a lovely garden."

"I'm glad you like it." He checked his watch. "Just time for an aperitif before dinner."

As they entered the house, the Count's phone rang with the ominous *da-da-da-daah* from Beethoven's fifth symphony. The Count answered and despite the inner tension that Anna was just about managing to hide, she couldn't help laughing out loud when she realised to whom the Count had assigned this ringtone.

"Hello, Sir Peter."

* * *

"Stand down." barked Sir Peter.

"I'm sorry?" queried the Count casually.

"No need to come to the safe house; we know how she got away."

The Count covered the phone and motioned for Anna to go on without him.

"Excellent. And how did she do it?"

"Well, she had help, of course. Wouldn't have been able to get past my team without it."

"I agree – and, of course, if you have any ideas who might have helped her, it could aid my search tremendously, but out of interest, how *did* they do it?"

"Quite clever really. She got out through the loft."

"The loft?" said the Count, sounding surprised.

"Yes, the accomplice came in through next-door's loft, tampered with the camera feed and opened the hatch from above. They escaped through the other house, bold as brass, disguised as Mrs Martin and her afternoon tea crony."

"Mrs Martin?"

"The old lady who lives next door. Poor thing was terrified."

I'll bet she was, when you got to her! thought the Count, but what he said was, "Oh dear!"

"We're dealing with professionals and it looks like Anna Parker's in league with them."

"So who do you think these professionals might be?" the Count asked.

"There are two primary possibilities," answered Sir Peter, "both powerful and when cornered, lethal: one is the criminal organisation I told you about at our meeting ..." He hesitated.

"And the other?" the Count pressed.

"The other is the French Secret Service themselves."

* * *

Anna had moved on when the Count had signalled to her, but only to a point where she could listen without being seen. She gained little from the first part of the conversation, other than the fact that Sir Peter – *or, more likely, his team*, she thought – had worked out how she had managed to escape. The latter, and no doubt more interesting, part of the conversation had been conducted in the Count's study and Anna was frustrated not to have heard it. She would have to see if she could prise it out of the Count over dinner. Not that the Count struck her as being someone who could be easily prised, but she had charms, and she knew how to use them.

Once she realised there was nothing more to be gained by hanging around, and quite a bit to be lost if she was caught lurking, she wandered through the drawing room to the modest library. With windows in the side and rear walls there was a light and airy feel to the room, moderating the effect of the dark wooden shelves lined with books of many genres. There was seating for four people in the form of a three-seater sofa under the large window and a large chair that resembled a well-padded throne. There were a few books of obvious sentimental value placed in strategic positions, one of which was a heavily-worn black leather-backed Bible. Anna picked it up. Inside the front cover was a hand-written inscription:

TO MY PET,
MAY THIS BOOK BE A LAMP TO YOUR FEET AND
A LIGHT TO YOUR PATH.
ALL MY LOVE.
MUM

There was a date underneath. Given its condition, Anna had expected the book to be much older than it turned out to be. To her great surprise it was only about twenty-five years old. *Wow, this book must have seen some action,* she thought, wondering why anyone would take so little care of a book that clearly seemed to mean a lot to the Count's family – or had it just been read, a lot? And was the Count his mother's little "pet"? He'd be about the right age, she supposed. That would be so cute. *I must remember to keep that one up my sleeve for later.* Replacing the Bible carefully as she found it, Anna went back through the drawing room and across the hall into the dining room.

Butler came in from the kitchen.

"A little something to drink before dinner, miss?"

"Would a Campari be possible?"

"Of course. Negroni or Spritz, miss?""

Anna was taken by surprise. She had not expected anything but the basics.

"Spritz, please."

"Certainly, miss."

Butler returned momentarily with a large ice-filled glass containing her drink garnished with a slice of orange.

"I felt a slightly larger one might be in order, given the excitement of the day." he said with a smile.

Anna couldn't help smiling in return. If Butler was supposed to be guarding her, he was the most lovable prison warder she could imagine. She sipped the cocktail as she awaited the Count.

"This is excellent – thank you."

Butler smiled again and returned to the kitchen to prepare to serve. There was a comfortable-looking chair that looked out through the patio doors onto the small breakfast terrace on the east side of the house. She sat down and admired the gardens as day began to turn to dusk.

The Count, having finished with Sir Peter and having made a couple of short phone calls, entered just as the hall clock struck six.

"Sorry about that. It seems Sir Peter has another little

problem that requires my assistance."

"And what's that?"

"It appears that someone has gone missing." said the Count with a dry smile.

"I wonder who that could be?" said Anna coyly.

"I wonder."

Butler popped his head in from the kitchen.

"Ready for me to serve, sir?"

"Yes, please." The Count indicated to Anna to sit and held the chair for her. Anna was in two minds about whether to be offended or flattered. *I'm perfectly capable of pulling my own chair in,* she thought to herself, *but then, it's nice for someone to go out of their way to treat me as someone special.*

The Count walked round the table and suddenly stopped.

"I'm terribly sorry," he said, "with all that's been going on I forgot to make sure the red pill had worked fully. Are you feeling well enough to eat?"

Anna appreciated the genuine show of concern, but noted the oversight. *So he isn't infallible, that's worth remembering.*

"I'm fine, thank you for asking. In fact, I could eat a horse!"

Butler appeared with the soup.

"I'm afraid the horses aren't here at the moment, miss," he said with dry humour, "and I'm not sure the Count would let you eat either of them anyway." Anna laughed. Wow, it was hard to think of these guys as potential enemies, but she had to keep the walls up until she was sure it was safe to do otherwise.

The table looked like it could be extended to hold up to ten or twelve guests, but tonight it had been drawn in to its most intimate setting. The Count sat facing her, and the two tall candles, thoughtfully placed to either side so as not to interfere with their view of each other, added a warm tone to the already agreeable ambience.

"So what did Sir Peter tell you?" Anna asked nonchalantly.

"Oh, he was very complimentary about our escape – he called us professionals." chuckled the Count. "He wants me to track you down, of course."

"And if you find me, what then?" probed Anna, "Will you turn me in?"

"That depends." said the Count calmly.

"On what?"

The Count looked directly into her eyes.

"On you." he replied.

Anna felt as if he was peering into her very soul. She'd been trained for this and met his gaze with one of her own. It was like a battle of wills, with him wanting her to open up and her not wanting to let him in. But somehow neither one wanted to force the other; it was strong and steady, but strangely gentle and not antagonistic on either side.

"I was rather hoping to *bring* you in, not *turn* you in, and only when the time was right and certain matters had been resolved." They looked at each other again. Could she trust him?

Butler was an excellent chef and the food was amazing, but Anna couldn't appreciate it just now. The butterflies in her stomach were taking the edge off her appetite. The next few minutes might determine whether or not she would have an ally or an enemy.

"You said you were going to answer my question over dinner. So … here we are, having dinner. Whose play are we in just now?" She repeated the question verbatim, as if restating the terms of a contract to someone who might try to renege on it. She needn't have bothered, the Count was a man of his word.

"Right now we are involved in at least three plays: Sir Peter's, mine and that of the Mécénat." At the mention of the latter, Anna looked up from her meal. *The Mécénat.* The group that had been the focus of her mission. The group that had killed Michel.

The Count continued.

"Do you remember Pyramus and Thisbe?" he asked.

"A Midsummer Night's Dream – the play within a play."

"Precisely. Sir Peter's is a play within a play. As I recall, Shakespeare describes that inner play as "the most lamentable comedy" and, from what I have seen to date, that is an apt description of Sir Peter's production. First, the loss of the item, and now the loss of the leading actor."

"The mission was a success in other respects." countered Anna, defending her own involvement rather than Sir Peter's. The Count nodded in agreement.

"Your own performance was, if I may say so, quite brilliant. Quite brilliant." He looked at her again. "But not perfect." Anna looked away, but the Count carried on.

"The question I have is: What was the flaw in your brilliant performance?"

Anna looked at him again, confusion on her face.

"I don't know what you mean?"

"I mean, said the Count firmly, "Was the flaw that you lost the item, or was it that you failed to convince Sir Peter that you were not involved?"

There was a momentary silence and Anna wondered whether he was being rhetorical.

"Are you seriously asking me that?"

"Yes. It was a direct question and I want you to be honest with me."

"Like you've been honest with me?" Anna retorted. The Count was unruffled.

"But I have been honest." he insisted. "Don't you remember what I said when I interviewed you at the safe house, about it being important to know when someone is telling the truth and when they are pretending?" Anna nodded.

"I wanted you to be clear on which was which – and you were."

"But you were pretending to be someone else at the

time – isn't that lying?!"

"All lying is pretending, but not all pretending is lying. When you go to the theatre to see a play, are the actors lying or pretending?"

"Pretending, of course – but that's okay because you know they're pretending!"

The Count let the words hang in the air.

"Exactly." he said simply. Anna couldn't fault his logic, but another angle came to mind.

"Okay, you were straight with me – sort of, but, what about Sir Peter? You double-crossed him!"

"No," said the Count, "I needed to avoid his interference and I simply haven't given him the revised script yet."

"Well, what about the old lady next door to the safe house? You drugged her and put her in danger!"

The Count looked remorseful, as if it pained him to think of taking advantage of a vulnerable person, but he remained resolute.

"It's true that I drugged her, but she suffered no injury or stress from me, and she is in no danger from others. I hardly think that Sir Peter or anyone else would expect her to have anything useful to say about your escape. In fact, I expect that she is rather looking forward to afternoon tea at the Ritz on Tuesday."

"And what about the hole you made in the her loft wall – who'll pay for that?" Anna was determined to find something to pin on the Count. He laughed.

"Don't worry about that; the British Secret Service will have it repaired in no time, and no one will be able to tell the bricks had ever been removed."

Sensing a pause in the conversation, Butler entered and, seeing that both of them had finished the soup, removed the bowls and side plates.

"Would you like a brief pause between courses, sir?"

"No, thank you, Butler, we'll press on with the main course, please."

"Certainly, sir."

The light was starting to fade and through the glass doors Anna saw the garden suddenly be illuminated by a string of festoon bulbs around the breakfast patio, lights within the ornamental fountain, and other lights, both at ground-level and at well-planned elevated points. It gave the place a fairy tale atmosphere that was in stark contrast to what was going on in inside the house.

Butler returned with their main course. Anna hoped she had dodged the question, but the Count had not been diverted.

"My question still stands, Anna," he said, "and it will be very helpful if you would please answer it honestly." Anna composed herself, smiled and put on a teasing voice.

"Helpful for whom – me or you?"

"Both." the Count replied, unmoved by her game. Anna leaned forward seductively.

"And what will you do to me if I won't answer?" she said, using the naughty schoolgirl voice that had worked with so many men. The Count leaned towards her in turn, his face stern and his voice sharp and filled with distaste.

"I am not a toy, Miss Parker. Do not treat me with so little respect again." Anna's face drained. It felt like being slapped across the face and publicly humiliated all at once. The Count glared at her without retreating and she realised she had made a serous mistake.

"As to what I will do to you if you won't answer – nothing, except to expel you from this house and thereafter you will be on the run from the British Secret Service, the Mécénat and, probably, the French Secret Service. While you are with me, you are under my protection. If you now reject my *bienveillance* you will be alone against them all."

He leaned back in his chair.

Anna was in shock. It had felt like a game while she had gone along with his plan – his play, but now that she had stepped out of her role she realised how serious things were. Danger was looming for her on many fronts, and she was at risk of losing her only ally. But there were other matters that she needed to finish, other people whose lives were hanging in the balance, and she mustn't fail them. The Count had a script, but it didn't take into account the things that only she knew about. Sir Peter had thrown it all into chaos at the critical moment in the mission, and she couldn't risk the Count doing the same now. Besides, she still didn't know what his agenda was or how his play would end. And in the few seconds that it had taken for those thoughts to run through her head, she had decided.

She was going, and she was going alone.

CHAPTER 8

NIGHT MOVES

Inspector Steve Gent hung up. The Count's request was strange, but fairly straightforward. He was on duty until ten, but the job only had to be done by 8am the next morning, so he carried on as normal until his shift was over, then put on his coat and gloves, and headed out.

He found the blue Toyota in the garage where the Count had said it would be. The automatic door had been set to manual mode by the Count before he had left, so Gent could pull it up by hand. He got into the car, found the keys under the seat and drove the vehicle out of the garage. He reset the door to automatic mode, pressed the button to close it and ducked quickly under it as it came down. As instructed, he drove the car via a route that avoided any traffic cameras and parked it neatly where he had been told to.

He walked back to his car and went home. There was no need to tell the Count that the job was done. The Count would expect nothing less.

* * *

Butler was disappointed, the main course had not been finished by either one of the diners and Anna had left the table before dessert.

The Count was disappointed. He had hoped that even in those few hours he would have developed a relationship of trust with Anna, and it had seemed to be going well, but then she had made a crude attempt to manipulate him and he had reacted badly to it.

Anna was disappointed. She had been both clumsy and unwise. Everything she had learned about the Count since noon that day showed him to be clever, kind and principled. She wasn't used to dealing with men like that. All the significant men in her life had been very different – her father and brother, her lovers … had any of them really cared for her? She wasn't like some women, who seemed to hate men in general, despite looking like they were doing their very best to *be* one, she just found it hard to trust them and believe that they could be givers and not just takers. The Count he seemed to be a giver, but he hadn't told her what he was really after. He might be trying to manipulate her, just like them.

The Boss, however, was not disappointed. Listening in to Sir Peter's telephone conversation had been very helpful. It had been no surprise that Sir Peter had mentioned the Mécénat, nor the French Secret Service, and the information on Anna Parker's means of escape had already been received via the listening device, but it had nevertheless been most enlightening. The Boss now knew there was another player involved. One who seemed to be operating in the shadows.

* * *

There had been a short period of silence as they continued to eat, then Anna pushed back her chair. "I think I'll go to my room." She stood & the Count did likewise. For a moment Anna thought he was going to stop her, but then she realised he was standing up out of habitual good manners.

"Very well," said the Count, "Can we talk again in the morning?"

Talk all you want, thought Anna, *I'll be long gone by then.* But what she said was, "Okay."

She had searched her room for anything that might prove useful and stuffed it into the tote bag that still held the clothes & wig she had used to escape the safe house in the guise of Mrs Martin. She was surprised at what previous occupants had left behind, but their loss was her gain. She didn't bother getting changed into the pyjamas; she had no intention of sleeping that night.

The Count had eaten most of the excellent main course that Butler had prepared and, having called Butler in to join him after Anna's departure, he waited for Butler to eat his soup & main, then they could have dessert together. It was a mark of their friendship and though he appreciated it hugely, Butler never let it stray into disrespect or any doubt about who was in charge. As Butler ate, the Count gave him instructions. Butler appreciated the Count's orders, they were always clear and concise. He nodded, still chewing on the tender veal cutlet, to indicate that they had been received and understood.

* * *

At around 1am Anna slid open the bedroom window that overlooked the narrow strip of flower bed and the path that ran along the side of the house, separating it from the paddock and neighbouring fields. It was a full fifteen foot drop to the ground, but she had been trained for this and the ground on which she would land was soft. Lowering the tote bag as far as she could reach, she let it fall to the ground. There was a small thump, but she had used the pillow case and clothes to wrap and muffle any solid items that might have banged together and made a noise. She climbed out of the window and sat on the ledge, then pushed off and away from the wall, landed well and rolled to absorb the impact. Grabbing the bag, she sprinted silently round to the front of the house where the silver Mercedes was parked, the keys still in the ignition. *Tut, tut, Count. Careless.*

Sliding into the driver's seat, Anna closed the door as quietly as possible and found that, despite being almost three inches shorter than the Count, she only needed minor adjustments to the seat & mirrors due to her long legs. She strapped in and turned the key, hoping that it wouldn't make too much noise. She needn't have worried, it made no noise at all. The car wouldn't start.

There was a tap on the window.

* * *

The alarm had gone off in both Butler's room and on the Count's phone as soon as the sash window had been opened by more than six inches. Butler had been on first watch and headed to the front of the house, as per the Count's instructions, but the Count himself was up almost as quickly and moved swiftly to the rear. As Butler opened the front door he heard the car door close. He stopped and watched from the doorway. The interior of the vehicle was illuminated by courtesy light, and he saw Anna making her adjustments then reach down to turn the key in the ignition. That was his cue. He strode casually forward and tapped on the window.

The Count came round the side of the house, passing by the paddock overlooked by Anna's bedroom window and round to the front, where Butler was standing by the silver Mercedes. Anna opened the car door as the Count stepped in next to his employee.

"Perhaps now might be a good time to have that talk." He turned to Butler. "Would you be so kind as to make three hot chocolates? A good dash of brandy in each."

Butler nodded and smiled at Anna.

"You'll be glad you stayed, miss. Trust me." He winked at her and went back into the house. Somehow it took all the sting out of the situation. The Count, however, was more serious.

"I'm sorry we fell out and I apologise for being an ungracious host." He said. The sincerity in his voice was unmistakeable and Anna was surprised to find that between them the two men had got under her skin.

"No, you were right. It was crude manipulation. I'm sorry too." The Count held out his hand, and although she didn't need his help, she chose to take it. Their eyes locked and neither broke away until Anna was out of the car and they turned to go back into the house.

It was a moment they would both remember. And there would come a time when each of them would hold on to it for dear life - literally.

Anna was ashamed to admit it, but she had only just in that moment realised how much the Count had actually opened up to her. For example, she knew what he really looked like (strikingly handsome, she thought) and she knew where he lived, at least some of the time, and she knew the whereabouts of one of his secret lock-ups. She doubted that the Count had revealed any of these things to Sir Peter. He had not blindfolded her, drugged her, or in any other way tried to prevent her from gathering this information. He had been perfectly charming, not in an attempt to seduce her or manipulate her (at this thought she shuddered with shame), but simply because that's who he really was.

The Count led her into the drawing room where two chesterfield chairs sat either side of the fireplace, turned slightly towards the matching sofa that faced the fireplace directly. The fire wasn't lit, but it was a cosy, relaxed space nonetheless, illuminated as it was by the two wall lights in the recesses either side of the chimney breast and the warm glow of the small chandelier on a dimmed setting.

The Count indicated for Anna to take the sofa then, when she was seated, he took the chair to the left of the fireplace. They sat in silence for a couple of minutes as Anna took in the ambience and admired the craftsmanship of the antique fire surround, the ornate mirror frame and the two pictures, one in each recess, occasionally glancing over at the Count. He appeared to be resting, or deep in thought, with his head back and eyed closed. In reality, through his long dark eyelashes, he was looking at Anna. She really was beautiful.

Butler appeared carrying a tray with three hot chocolates, fully loaded. He placed the drinks on the side tables next to Anna and the Count, then placed his own next to the empty chesterfield chair and sat down.

"Thank you." said the Count, seeming to wake from his reverie.

"Yes, thank you." said Anna, keen to show her appreciation too.

The Count noted the shift in her behaviour and Butler smiled at her and then at the Count, who nodded.

Anna was keen to get things moving, but knew it was better to wait for the Count to drive the conversation.

The Count took a deep breath, exhaled slowly, then took a quicker breath and was about to speak ... when his phone rang with the tones of Beethoven's fifth.

* * *

Sir Peter had been restless and sleep had evaded him. He had set up a makeshift bed on the couch in his office, as if it was the command centre of the operation and he was in charge. This protocol wasn't unusual in Service missions that ran intensively over a period of days and nights, and in differing time zones, but this wasn't a standard Service mission and, whatever Sir Peter would like to think, he wasn't in charge. The first few hours of any manhunt were critical and there had been no news. It was still a good few hours to dawn and he wondered what the Count was doing about his problem. He picked up the telephone and rang the Count.

* * *

The Count was furious, not only for the interference, which he took as a personal insult, but even more so for the interruption at such a crucial moment. He took a moment, then answered the call calmly.

"Sir Peter," he stated rhetorically, "what has prompted you to call me in the middle of the night?"

"I need an update on progress." he demanded.

"Why?" challenged the Count firmly.

"What?" spluttered Sir Peter.

"Why do you need an update?"

"What do you mean, why?"

"What if I have nothing to tell you yet – and if I did, what would you do?" said the Count coldly in a tone that made Sir Peter feel both stupid and impotent at the same time.

"Well ..." he bumbled. The Count sought to end the conversation.

"I have someone on it, and I expect significant news to report by morning. I will contact you then." However, like an addict or the fool who will not stay down, Sir Peter could not see when he was beaten.

"Now look here, C...."

"NO NAMES!" thundered the Count in a voice that made Anna jump.

"Yes, yes, indeed." spluttered Sir Peter, realising his schoolboy error.

"You will abide by my rules or this association is terminated – and your career with it." The Count's manner was chilling and Sir Peter felt the full force of the threat.

"Of course, of course." he muttered humbly.

The Count's expression softened slightly, not that Sir Peter could see it, and Anna noticed a devious smile forming on his face, as if an equally devious plan was forming in his mind in that instant.

"Until morning, then." said the Count firmly, closing the conversation.

"Until morning." echoed Sir Peter, smarting.

Butler spoke first.

"You have a plan, sir?" The Count took a sip of his chocolate.

"I do." He smiled again. "Excellent chocolate, Butler."

"Thank you, sir."

* * *

The Boss was pleased again. The little listening device was paying dividends. Significant news in just a few hours. The opposition was divided. And, most importantly, the shadowy adversary had a name, and it began with the letter C, or possibly K. Progress indeed.

CHAPTER 9

THE MISSION

Anna looked over at the Count, relaxed, leaning back in his armchair, sipping his hot chocolate and brandy. How could he be so cool after being so furious only moments before? She knew that feeling of fury, though. Sir Peter was an infernal meddler. She broke the silence.

"How do you do it?" she asked.

"Do what?" asked the Count in return.

"Shift from fury to harmony in just a few seconds. I mean, Sir Peter …" She could feel the volume rising as she felt her own anger at Sir Peter, "… he rang you in the middle of the night when he should have waited 'til morning, he breached the rules about your identity …!" She cut herself off.

"It's true, I was extremely annoyed. Sir Peter is a liability and that, Anna, is why I cannot take him into my trust." He paused a moment and looked directly into her eyes. "You, on the other hand …"

Anna waited. What would his judgement be? What did he think of her after the events of the night so far?

"… I believe I can trust. The question for you now is: do you believe you can trust me?"

Anna looked deep into his eyes, her mind a swirl of images and data, but through it all there was a path, some kind of link that joined them, and at the end of that path there was light. There was light inside his soul and that light was reaching out to her now through all the melee of her thoughts and emotions. Something solidified deep within her and she spoke unfamiliar words with a strange new confidence.

"Yes," she said simply, "I believe I can trust you."

"In that case," said the Count, "please tell me what really happened."

Anna nodded silently, closed her eyes for a moment, then told her story.

* * *

The previous Monday ...

She had been quite enjoying working in France for the last few days with the Direction Générale de la Sécurité Intérieure, or DGSI for short – the special intelligence service run by the Ministre de l'Intérieure, the French Interior Ministry. With its roots stretching back though the DST (Direction de la Surveillance du Territoire), founded in 1944 and further to the RG (Renseignements Généraux) created in 1907 by Georges Clemenceau, who received the nickname Le Tigre – the Tiger – due to his brave and ferocious manner, it was well-organised, well-equipped and well-informed. Strong links with EUROPOL and NATO had been established and international operations with other security and intelligence services helped with the fight against international terrorism and organised crime. She had been particularly looking forward to the evening's operation on a suspected Mécénat storehouse site in one of the seedier areas of outer Paris. The lead had come in only that morning and it looked like the person who had been observed had been aware of their blunder. That meant there was every chance the site would be cleared by morning, so a team had been put together and assigned surveillance and, if the lead proved good and the level of opposition and firepower looked manageable, to intercept and apprehend the Mécénat personnel , along with as much evidence and whatever was being stored there as possible.

Anna hoped it was drugs, not weapons. Not just because this was her first field mission and she was understandably as anxious as she was excited, but who in their right mind would want to take on a group of criminals that had a huge range of high-powered weapons to hand?

The revised orders had come through at around 5pm, just as the team was in final preparation mode. Something about a prominent politician's daughter having been kidnapped by people-traffickers – not the Mécénat, but a rival gang. Resources were being diverted to the hunt for the child and the gang. There would now be only two of them on the operation tonight instead of the original six that had comprised four DGSI and two British agents. The French had reassigned three of their agents and, in an attempt to curry favour with the French and to take some credit if the new operation went well, Sir Peter had offered up one of his agents. That just left Anna on the British side and Michel from the DGSI, so it was going to be surveillance only unless the Mécénat numbers were very low.

They installed themselves just as the twilight brought the dim grey light and shade together in a blurring effect. The team had researched the area and identified a disused warehouse building just 50 metres down the street, on the opposite side. Anna hoped that they wouldn't find kids hanging out there; she didn't want to tip anyone off by having startled teenagers making a ruckus, and she didn't fancy holding a group of kids at gunpoint, tying them up and gagging them until the operation was over. *Still, needs must,* she thought, *whatever it takes. This is real field work.* Michel seemed more relaxed. He was more experienced and had been given the lead, for which Anna was grateful just now, although she was keen to progress and lead her own operations before too long.

They entered the building from the rear, so that neither they nor their vehicle, which would be unfamiliar and therefore suspect, could be seen from the Mécénat hideout.

Entry to the building was easy with their tools and training, and they worked their way quickly to a room on the front side of the first floor. The original plan had been to have two pairs on the ground floor, a spotter/sniper on each of the first and second floors and at opposite ends so as to cause confusion and make return fire targeting more difficult, plus two in the van to block or pursue any vehicle that tried to make it away from the scene. All that had gone down the pan and now that it was just the two of them, Michel had decided that they should stay together and watch from the first floor.

Their target was a run-down detached building in its own compound, purporting to be a scrap metal business. The yard that ran round the front and right-hand side of the building contained plenty of scrap and was protected by a six-foot high metal fence whose sturdy posts, topped with sharp metal spikes, were just a hand-breadth apart. The gate, which was wide enough for a medium-sized lorry to pass through, was made of similar stuff, although turning round in the yard would have been difficult, due to the piles of scrap littering the place. There were no windows on the ground floor, and all but one window on the first floor had been bricked up. A quick pass round at a safe distance by a drone with a high-zoom, high-resolution camera a couple of hours earlier had shown the up-to-date state of the building and surrounding area. The rest of the building was the typical ugly commercial/industrial brick and metal construction with no other windows. There were two doors: a conventional door at the front and a large metal roll-up door big enough to reverse the back of a lorry into for loading out of the side of the building. There was a brand-new black BMW parked in the shadows. *The scrap metal business must be doing well,* Anna thought to herself sarcastically.

For a while nothing happened. That was not unusual on stakeouts like this, things often happened in the middle of the night, but shortly after 9pm a light went on behind the blinds of the first floor window and a faint glow appeared under and around the edges of the roll-up door. Things were moving.

A few minutes later a large truck pulled up outside the site. Two armed men came out of the main door and opened the gates, allowing the truck to reverse into the yard. They closed the gates, then went back inside the building. The truck driver backed up to the roll-up shutter and waited until the men had opened the roll-up door from the inside, then reversed the rear end of the truck into the gap, leaving the front two-thirds of the truck sticking out into the yard. He climbed out of the truck and went in through the main door. The fit of the truck to the loading bay was pretty good, no doubt deliberately matched to almost eliminate the possibility of someone viewing in from outside, but from their vantage point Anna and Michel could just see a sliver of the activity. Anna had the slightly better view, being on the left side of the window, but they could both make an informed guess about what was being loaded. The truck was being loaded with large, heavy crates, each one taking two men to lift it into the back of the truck. The crates were too big and heavy to be drugs.

Oh no, thought Anna, *it's weapons.* On the plus side, the crates were sealed ready for shipment, so it would take a good few seconds for them to be accessed, and a few more seconds for clips to be loaded, so once the initial rounds had been fired, they might have a brief period to take control. Assuming that all the crew were working on shifting the goods, Anna reckoned there were just four of them: two lifting onto the truck and two stacking the crates in the back of the truck.

"We could take them." she whispered, not that anyone would have heard if she'd used her normal speaking voice.

"Maybe," said Michel, "but there could be a lieutenant overseeing the job. That would make five of them, one of whom probably already has a weapon at the ready. That's a very different scenario to the two of us against four men with crates in their hands."

They took pictures of what little they could see and logged a good description of the truck. It would be tricky to tail it in one vehicle without being spotted, but Michel was keen to try. If they could track it to its next port of call, that in itself would be valuable information about the Mécénat operation. Maybe they could call in additional resources to help out before too long.

Michel had been right. Part-way through loading a fifth figure had come into view. Armed with an assault rifle, he had been gesticulating and directing the stackers to move some crates over to the left side of the truck. Anna was relieved that she hadn't jumped the gun and led them into a fight that they would have most likely lost. And this wasn't a video game; in this business, losing might mean coming away with a life-changing injury – or coming away in a body bag. Game over.

Within just a few more minutes loading was complete. Anna marvelled at the speed and efficiency with which the criminals worked. Was it fear or reward that motivated them? Or was it some twisted pride in making a good job of something bad? She thought of the phrase, *Honour among thieves.* As though they could pretend that they were anything but despicable low-lifes by inventing and adhering to some "code" that really just amounted to "Don't tell on me and I won't tell on you." Rather than being a mark of honour and bravery, it was really just a way of covering up their fear of being caught. *Professional criminal.* They wore it like a badge of honour, like it was something to be admired, and not what it really was: a person too lazy, scared or selfish to compete on equal terms in the real world. Anna despised them.

Suddenly, something caught her eye. It happened so quickly that she almost missed it. The lieutenant had disappeared from view for a few seconds, then returned dragging something – was that a child?

"Michel! Was that ...?"

But before Michel could answer, there was a gunshot and the lieutenant fell to the ground, executed by one of the others, probably for compromising the site, Anna thought.

"Move!" ordered Michel grabbing his rifle. They ran full tilt down to the front door. which they had readied on arrival, just in case they needed a swift exit that way. Opening it a crack, they saw one of the men carry out the dead lieutenant's body and dump it in the boot of the BMW, while the truck driver climbed into the cab and eased the truck forward. A third man started the shutter mechanism and went to start opening one of the gates.

"The fourth man must be in the back of the truck with the child." Anna whispered, this time with good reason. Michel nodded.

The BMW headed out of the gates almost as soon as the car would fit through the gap. *He's keen to get rid of his cargo,* thought Anna. The truck followed, but pulled up on the street so the driver could help close the gates. The BMW was crawling down the street so as not to get too far ahead, but was now just passing Michel and Anna. Michel saw the opportunity and took charge.

"You take the man on the gate, I'll take the driver." In an instant they were both running towards their respective targets, pulling out their weapons of choice as they went. For Anna it was an extendable baton and she wielded it with ruthless efficiency. Due to the noise of the truck's engine running, her target only heard her footsteps in time to turn and get a hand to his gun, but the baton struck his head with such force and accuracy that one blow rendered him unconscious immediately. She turned and ran round the side of the van to where the driver, who had jumped back into the cab to make a getaway, was being held at gunpoint by her colleague.

"Quietly now," said Michel softly to the driver, "Get out of the truck." Anna drew her pistol and covered the driver as Michel guided him back towards the yard and cuffed him to the fence. Michel rapped twice on the back of the truck. Muffling his voice he called out, “The gate’s stuck. Give us a hand.” He unlocked the rear door and stepped away as he opened it, so that the man inside couldn’t see him. There was a shuffling sound as the man moved towards the rear, but he was suspicious.

“What’s the problem?” he called. Michel stepped quickly into view, gun in hand, but it was dark in the back of the truck and that gave the man inside the half second advantage. There was a burst of gunfire and both men fell backwards. Anna leapt into the truck, torch in one hand, gun in the other. She was on top of the Mécénat man before he could take his last breath, but then his head slumped to the side. She felt his neck to be sure, then jumped out to check on Michel. The vest had saved him from the first bullet, but the second had caught him in the neck. He needed urgent attention. She dragged him to the fence and sat him up, talking to him all the time, trying to keep him conscious.

There was a screech of tyres and a bright light; Anna turned to see the BMW bearing down with the sole intention of crashing into them. There was nothing Anna could do to save Michel, she threw herself to one side as the car crashed into the fence, killing Michel outright.

No! Anna screamed in her head. *If only Sir Peter had stuck to the original plan there would have been three of us and Michel would still be alive!*

The car’s airbag had gone off, giving Anna valuable seconds to regroup, and the system had automatically unlocked the doors. Like lightning she opened the passenger door and fired three rounds towards the driver’s side, then dived to the floor in case of return fire, but none came. Her heart had never beaten so fast and she had never been so scared in her life. She waited a good thirty seconds. Nothing.

“He’s dead, you idiot.” called the truck driver

mockingly from the fence where he was chained up. "Haven't you killed anyone before, little girl?"

Anna got up, walked over to the driver, looked him in the eye and knocked him out with the butt of her pistol.

"Who are you calling 'little girl'? And who's the idiot now?", she muttered.

Running quickly to the driver's side of the BMW, she confirmed that the threat had been neutralised. The adrenalin was rushing through her body and she felt nauseous, but she stopped short of being sick. She went to the gate and cuffed the first man she'd knocked out to the fence. It was only then that she heard the crying above the noise of the truck's engine. *The girl!* It had all happened so fast and she'd been so intent on staying alive that she'd momentarily forgotten about her. Anna walked softly back to the open rear door of the truck and called gently.

"Are you okay?" There was no reply, just a gentle sobbing. "It's safe now. They're all ..." - Anna tried to think of another word than "dead" or "unconscious", and doing that in French made it even harder – "... asleep." *Some for longer than others,* thought Anna, but she kept that to herself. She gently pulled herself up into the back of the truck and edged round the crates, shining her torch more downwards than forwards, so as not to dazzle the child, although all she had to do was follow the sound that was coming from under the khaki blanket in the corner.

"My name's Anna – what's yours?" The sobbing stilled to an occasional sniffle. "I'm here to help you."

The blanket shifted slightly and two bright eyes peered cautiously over the hem. Anna positioned the torch on top of one of the crates, so its light was more evenly cast on them both and their surroundings. She smiled reassuringly.

"Hello," she said calmly, "I'm Anna. Shall we get out of this horrible place?" The girl nodded. She let Anna help her stand up, though she kept the blanket wrapped round her, as much for comfort and security as for warmth.

Anna reckoned the girl was about 6 years old.

"Don't look, now. It's better if you close your eyes for a minute." The child nodded and pulled the blanket back over her head. Anna jumped down, found the keys to their car in Michel's pocket, then lifted the child out of the back of the truck and carried her round to the front, holding her close. Reaching into the truck she turned off the ignition and put the keys in her pocket. Child in arms, she crossed the road and made her way through the stakeout building to the vehicle. Once inside Anna turned to her new ward.

"You can look now." A little face appeared, tear-stained and frightened. Anna kept it light. " I'm afraid we don't have any child seats – are you okay sitting in the front with me like a big girl?" The child nodded.

"Okay, let's get you strapped in." said Anna in a matter-of-fact voice, reaching over and securing the seat belt. "Good. Now I'm just going to have to make a call to let the authorities know what's happened."

The girl's reaction took Anna by surprise. She seemed scared again and was clutching onto the blanket for dear life.

"It's okay," Anna soothed, but the girl only huddled up tighter. Anna called opened communications on her radio, identified herself and gave a brief summary.

"Mécénat site confirmed. Need urgent assistance. Weapons shipment secured in a truck outside the yard, along with four Mécénat personnel – two dead, two chained to the fence. DGSI agent down, killed by Mécénat. Also, …" The child suddenly grabbed Anna's wrist and shook her head violently, her eyes pleading. Anna stared at her. What on earth was the matter? Why was the child so scared? Something was wrong.

"Go ahead." came the voice over the radio.

"Also, …" Anna picked up again, looking at the terrified child, "I need to check myself out. I took a few knocks. I'll leave it to you guys to clear up the scene. I'll report in later. Out."

She put the radio down and the girl burst into tears. Anna leaned over and put her arm around the child.

"Let's get you somewhere safe."

* * *

Anna paused. It had not been easy to re-live the event, but the Count had asked for the truth and she had given it. Out of the blue the cross-stitch she had seen in the bedroom came to mind. *The truth will set you free.* Strangely enough, she *did* feel freer for having shared it.

"So Sir Peter guessed correctly," mused the Count, "the *item* is the girl." Anna nodded, thinking back to those initial interviews, where Sir Peter had thrown all sorts of ideas and accusations at her, while she sat there stony-faced and silent. She had been trained for that, but she had never envisaged she would need to use that training with her own people.

"I never confirmed it, but he kept pursuing it."

"And you know who the girl is, of course?" asked the Count, semi-rhetorically. Anna nodded again, but hesitated, reluctant to divulge the secret of the terrified child that she had held so close and protected so far.

"It's okay," the Count said reassuringly, "Is Camille still safe?" Anna sat up straight on hearing the name.

"How do you …?" The Count waved the question away as if dispelling a childish impression that a magic trick had just been performed.

"I keep up with the news … and I have the odd contact here and there. I had put two and two together before Sir Peter had even given me his theory."

"Which was?"

"Which was that you had abducted the daughter of a prominent French politician."

"So, now you know it's true." said Anna.

"On the contrary," said the Count brightly, "now I know that it is absolutely *not* true!"

Anna frowned, confused.

"But I *did* take her." she insisted, "Don't you believe

me?"

"Of course," replied the Count, "but you did not *abduct* her – far from it. You took her into protective custody."

"Yes." Anna's relief was evident in her voice.

"And your silence was simply to protect the child." Anna nodded in response. "If you had given Sir Peter the details he would have gone after the child and delivered her to the DGSI, with no concern for the child's wellbeing, but simply to further his own career within the Service and ingratiate himself with the French hierarchy."

"Exactly!" said Anna, amazed at the Count's insight.

"However," said the Count, now taking his turn to frown, "we have a dilemma."

Anna's heart momentarily froze. Was he now going to reveal that this had all been a trick to get her to divulge information? She looked in panic at Butler.

CHAPTER 10

THE COUNT SETS A TRAP

Butler caught Anna's look of panic and gave her a reassuring look, then glanced over at the Count, who had not been oblivious to Anna's reaction.

"I'm sorry, Anna. I didn't mean to alarm you. The dilemma is simply this: On the one hand we have a mother separated from her daughter – and who are we to divide a family? On the other hand, we have a young girl who is clearly terrified to return to the environment which she now sees as unstable and terrifying."

"There's always the French social services." offered Butler. Anna shook her head.

"They would just return her and if there's someone on the inside who will still be there if she goes back, then ..."

"Then she will never feel – or be – safe there, irrespective of mother or guards." said the Count darkly.

"Did she give you any idea of who that might be?" asked Butler.

"No." said Anna. "She was pretty traumatised. She barely spoke in the short time we had together, before I put her into hiding."

"And where was that?" asked the Count, knowing that this would be a genuine struggle for Anna, if she had any traces of mistrust left within her.

"At the Monastère des Clarisses in Senlis, about an hour's drive north of Paris. I have a contact there. The nuns trust my contact and ask no questions. Their concern is only for the welfare of the child."

The Count leaned forward and put his hand on hers.

"Thank you, Anna. Your trust means a lot to me."

Butler beamed at Anna. She was family now. He turned to the Count.

"And what of your plan for Sir Peter, sir?"

"Ah, yes." smiled the Count, rubbing his hands together, "Given Sir Peter's serious lack of judgement, we need to determine whether or not his calls are secure, and then …", he turned to Anna, "… I think a little spiritual retreat would do us good."

"At the Monastère." ventured Anna.

"At the Monastère." confirmed the Count. "But before all that, let's get some sleep." He checked his watch. "Hmm, not too long, though. I need to call Sir Peter just before eight. Shall we meet here at 07:50 to set the hares running?"

"Shall I re-enable the Mercedes, sir?"

"What would I do without you, Butler?" smiled the Count. "Yes, please."

* * *

Anna made a point of being a minute early. Butler was busy preparing breakfast in the kitchen, but the Count was nowhere to be seen. On the dot of ten to eight, he appeared from his study and strode into the drawing room, phone in hand. Butler joined them.

"Shall we?" said the Count, indicating the chairs and sofa. They sat down. The Count called Sir Peter, putting the call on speaker so the others could hear, but indicating to them to be silent.

"Shackleton."

"Good morning, Sir Peter."

"That will depend on what news you have for me."

"Good news. The car that took Anna from the safe house has been located and we have a good lead."

"How good?" retorted Sir Peter stiffly.

"Well, it's not one hundred per cent, as the vehicle was

found a few streets away from the nearest CCTV and ANPR cameras, but from what we can see, the gang switched vehicles …"

"Gang?" exclaimed Sir Peter.

"I'll use that word as it looks like more than one person was involved and they were certainly highly organised." He winked across at Anna and Butler. "Anyway, the first vehicle disappears off the streets covered by the cameras, then a couple of minutes later another vehicle appears."

"Could be a coincidence." snapped Sir Peter, "Could be completely unrelated."

"Possibly." acknowledged the Count, "But I personally am not a great believer in simple coincidence. Besides, we know where the other vehicle went to."

"You have a location?"

"Leave it to us, Sir Peter." The Count was enjoying dangling the carrot tantalisingly under Sir Peter's nose.

"I demand to know! What if something goes wrong and you need back-up?"

"There will be less chance of anything going wrong if the place is not buzzing with your agents. However, if you agree not to come within three miles of the property …"

"Yes, yes, agreed." gushed Sir Peter, uncontrollably keen to get the location.

"Very well, " said the Count, "there is a manor house a few miles off the M25 …"

Sir Peter scribbled the address down frantically. Anna looked in shock at the Count while Butler, his hand over his mouth, stifled his laughter.

"Remember," warned the Count severely, "not within three miles."

Before Sir Peter could reply, the Count hung up. He looked at Butler, who was still grinning.

"Nice one, sir." he said.

"Are you seriously using the manor as a honey pot to attract potential enemies?!" asked Anna, incredulous.

"Yes, of course," said the Count breezily, "but not *this*

manor."

"You mean …"

"There's a ruined manor house ten miles from here. It's quite exposed from most sides, so we'll be able to see if anyone comes and we should get a good look at them if they do." The Count stood up. "I reckon it will take twenty minutes or so for whoever's coming to make a plan and at least forty minutes for them to get there, so that gives us twenty minutes for breakfast, five minutes to change, fifteen minutes to get there and we should be there well before anyone else."

"And will we be fishing or hunting, sir?" asked Butler.

"Fishing today, Butler – *fly* fishing to be exact." said the Count with a knowing smile. Butler chuckled.

"Very good, sir."

Although she had not known these two men for long, Anna had learned by now that, despite sometimes communicating even life and death matters in a manner that seemed to border at times on schoolboy banter, they were formidable characters who understood each other perfectly and took their business very seriously. The light-hearted demeanour was simply an indication of their confidence, trust and unfailing competence.

Butler half-turned to go, then checked back. "Your car or mine, sir?"

"Oh, we'll be going a little off-road, so we'll take yours, if that's okay."

"Of course, sir." Butler nodded. That was so like the Count, to ask his permission even though the Count had bought the vehicle for him. He left the room and began to get things ready.

"You know that Sir Peter will have agents in the area, right?" said Anna.

"Naturally, but then, we can easily predict where they will be positioned."

"And where's that?"

"On the only road that goes anywhere near the old

manor, precisely three miles either side of it."

* * *

The Count was not wrong.

Sir Peter pored over the map and, much to his relief, found that there was only one road that went within three miles of the manor house, namely the road that went past it. With his limited number of agents he could only have placed a maximum of six road blocks, allowing two agents for each of them, even if he called in all three shifts at once. This way he could have two cars at each point, each car with two agents, and still have one shift resting. He picked up the phone and began giving orders.

* * *

The Boss was busy handling multiple activities and despite being alerted to activity on the tracker/listening device, had not been able to drop things immediately to listen in. However, the set-up made it easy to replay what had gone on. Sir Peter's shadowy friend had done the hard work and now it was Arturo's turn to earn his money. It would not be straightforward, though. There would be the "shadow's" people to deal with, and then Sir Peter's agents as well, but thanks to the listening device, the Boss now knew where Sir Peter's agents would be. Arturo would handle it. He would know when, where and how to strike.

The Boss made the call.

Armed with the information provided by the Boss, Arturo studied his own map and formed his plan accordingly. Given that Sir Peter's agents were already on the move, there was no way they could get there and get in and out without running into them if they went by road. Parking up, say three and a half miles away and going in on foot across fields, fences, dry stone walls, etc. would take far too long. Not having access to air transport, which would have been noisy and a potential give-away to whoever was holding Anna Parker, there was only one option left – the river. He traced its course with his finger until he found a marina six miles from the manor. He could hire a motor boat, and if there wasn't one to hire, he could just take one. Either way, he didn't care.

* * *

The three fishermen steered their inflatable rib downstream a few hundred yards and across to the opposite bank, and tied it to an old mooring post. One of them set up a small pop-up fisherman's tent on the bank and disappeared inside, while the other two readied their gear, cast out, set their rods on the stands and sat down on padded folding chairs. It was a fresh morning and the hoods of their camouflage-style fishing coats were pulled up over their heads.

Anna's clothing was actually not a bad fit, considering it was a man's outfit. She stared across the river and downstream towards the old manor just a quarter of a mile away over the fields. From her vantage point she could see the manor clearly, and further downstream, to her right, the area of woodland between the river and the house itself. Looking further to her right she had a clear view of the waterway for half a mile before it meandered round a curve and out of sight.

"I thought you said we were fly-fishing?" she said, confused. "I don't know much about fishing, but I'm pretty sure it's different to this." The Count grinned slyly.

"Actually, Butler will be doing the flying; we'll just be fishing."

Anna wasn't sure she was any the wiser, but at least it seemed she'd been right about the different types of angling.

"So, what happens now?" she said, rubbing her hands to keep them warm. The Count handed her a pair of expensive roof prism fishing binoculars.

"You watch the house, the river to your right and, every now and again, your float."

"And what am I looking for?"

"Any movement near the house – although I suspect

there will be none initially. On the river, any boat coming this way – especially if it pulls up by those woods – alert me immediately."

"And the float?"

"Well," said the Count in a matter of fact tone, "if the float disappears, you yank the end of the rod upwards."

*   *   *

Arturo had no trouble getting hold of a boat. It was low season and there were plenty for hire. The proprietor had asked to take a copy of his passport, but Arturo played the struggling foreigner.

"Passaporte … 'otel …, sorry, sorry …". He flashed cash in front of the owner who decided it was easier just to let it go.

It wasn't a large boat, nor was it fast, but it was big enough for him and his four-person team and could maintain a steady 12 knots on still water, equivalent to around 8 knots against the current on this stretch of the river. It would take about forty minutes to get to their target.

*   *   *

Anna was getting bored of watching the float and the river. Sir Peter was also restless and frustrated. He desperately wanted to be there when the action broke, to take control and be able to claim a major part in the recapture of his errant spy. He had had a hard time deciding which of the two road blocks he was going to join and it frustrated him greatly that he couldn't be in two places at once, however childish and unrealistic he knew that notion to be. The minutes ticked by quietly and so far the only traffic had been an overweight middle-aged man in a skin-tight cycling outfit on a bike so thin that it seemed barely capable of supporting his considerable bulk, and a grumpy farmer, irritated at being stopped, questioned and searched.

What was the Count doing? Patience had never been Sir Peter's strong suit, and right now the waiting was driving him mad.

* * *

Nothing was moving at the house or on the river – including Anna's float. *How do people do this for a whole day?* she thought to herself, amazed. *How much longer before something comes along?* Then, just like buses after a long wait, two things came at once.

First a boat appeared round the bend and headed towards the trees on the far bank. Anna alerted the Count, who turned to the tent.

"Butler, you're up." There was a sound of tapping and clicking from inside the tent and Butler said, "Ready." And then …

Anna's float disappeared.

"Strike!" said the Count to Anna.

"What?"

"Yank the rod!"

Anna grabbed the rod and yanked. She felt a tug at the other end and the rod being pulled away from her.

"What do I do now?" she yelled, utterly confused by both the fishing process and why it mattered just at the point when the bad guys had turned up.

"Let it run!" said the Count, coming to her assistance.

"What do you mean, 'Let it run'?" gasped Anna , "it hasn't got legs!"

The Count almost snorted with laughter. *How can he be so relaxed? Doesn't he know these people are killers?!* thought Anna.

"Okay," said the Count, "let it *swim*!" Steadying Anna's rod with one hand, he gently but firmly moved her hand off the reel handle, allowing the reel to spin and the line to go out.

"Let it run." repeated the Count softly. "It will tire itself out and make it easier to bring in." She felt him close to her, his hand still on hers, the combination of voice, touch and powerful self-assurance mixing in with the danger of the mission and the excitement of the catch and making chemicals swirl in her head and body. From the outside one would have thought that the Count was unaffected by it all, but on the inside he most certainly was. People talk about "chemistry" between a couple, and most, if not all of us, have experienced those chemical feelings within ourselves, but in moments like these the chemistry somehow crosses over; something is released that the other can feel. Something more than body language, like something released into the air, breathed in by the other, recognised and added to the mix. It's said that certain animals can smell fear. Who knows, maybe humans can smell attraction?

The moment was broken by a humming noise from the other side of the fishing tent. Butler's head popped out through the opening.

"Say when."

Swaying the rod downstream slightly, the Count sneaked a casual glance downstream.

"Go."

The humming grew louder and a drone emerged from the other side of the tent, three feet off the ground, then up and over the Count and Anna, and out over the river. Flying slowly and carefully, just a foot over the water, the drone headed downstream towards where the boat had been tied up.

The Count released Anna.

"Now we reel in a little."

"Are you talking about the fish or the hit squad?"

"Both." said the Count with a smile.

* * *

Arturo and his team had rounded the bend and caught sight of the manor.

"Pull over to the bank by those trees." he ordered.

One of the team jumped onto the bank and moored the boat to one of the sturdy old trees growing right by the river's edge, while the rest of the team grabbed their gear. Arturo scanned the area with his binoculars. It was all clear, except … a quarter of a mile away a couple of fishermen were on the opposite bank, but they were in the middle of trying to land a fish that seemed intent on trying to get away. The one with the rod was clearly a beginner and the other one was trying to help, as well as flailing around for the net that they would shortly need to use. Arturo relaxed and got on with his job.

Working their way through the cover of the trees, the team approached the house. Arturo scanned it with his binoculars. It was a bit more run-down than he'd expected for a safe house, but maybe it was just somewhere to hold up briefly. He moved slowly and silently to the edge of the tree line. It was still thirty yards to the house, but there was no sign of anyone on this side of the building. It was all quiet. He signalled to the team: two to go to the right-hand corner of the house, two to the left. They moved with barely a sound on the soft grass. It was still quiet … or was it? What was that faint humming sound?

He looked around, but could see nothing. The house was still. The team members were now in position and looking at him for further instructions. The sound increased gently, but the trees made it hard to pinpoint. Suddenly it ramped up a notch and in the two seconds that followed, Arturo got a clear view of the drone and the drone got a clear view of Arturo.

Arturo raised his gun and fired at the drone, but it hopped up six feet in a flash. He fired again, but the drone skipped teasingly to the side, then swooped up and away.

"It's a set-up!" yelled Arturo, "Abort!"

The team set off back through the woods. It was a race now and it was looking like they were going to lose it. Two of Sir Peter's vehicles were three miles down the road towards the marina and were bound to get there first, but even so, that would be only four against Arturo's five. Not bad odds, thought Arturo as he sprinted over the bracken and fallen branches, especially if they jumped ship before the marina and let the boat coast in on its own. Arturo leapt into the boat, quickly followed by the rest of the team. He pointed his binoculars upstream to check on the two fishermen. They were now busy landing their catch. If they had heard the gunshots, they clearly weren't bothered. Probably thought it was a farmer shooting rabbits or something. They were far too occupied with their fish.

"Full speed!" shouted Arturo. The craft had a maximum speed of fourteen knots; plus the 4 knot current in their favour this time, that made eighteen knots. It would be tight.

* * *

"Shots fired, sir." shouted the agent with the long distance parabolic microphone. Sir Peter leapt into action. Ignoring the Count's instructions he barked orders to the agents at both road blocks.

"All agents to the manor – now!"

There was half a minute's frenzy as the road blocks were moved and the agents piled into their high-speed pursuit vehicles and sped off, tyres squealing, towards the old manor house.

* * *

Butler took the drone over the manor, away from the river and out towards the road so that Arturo would have no idea where it was going, then he banked it round in a wide semi-circle back to the tent, so as not to give away their base of operations. Meanwhile, the Count and Anna played the fish, letting it run and reeling it in, until it grew tired. They heard the shots and Anna looked round, but the Count pulled her back.

"It's okay to look once, but now ignore it. They'll be back at their boat soon and we need to appear to be completely absorbed in our fishing, with no interest in what's going on around us."

Anna nodded. The Count took hold of the rod.

"You grab the net and get into the water, but keep your

back to their boat. We can't risk you being recognised." Anna picked up the net and stepped down from the bank. After taking just two steps into the river the water was almost up to the top of her wellington boots.

"This okay?" she asked hopefully. The Count nodded, concentrating on the catch. Gently reeling in the flagging fish, he drew it over to where Anna was waiting with the net. She could see it now, wriggling and splashing as the Count raised the rod to bring the fish to the surface so Anna could slip the net underneath.

"Wow, it's a big one!" she exclaimed, lifting the net clear of the water.

"Not bad at all – and excellent for your first catch!" agreed the Count.

"Well, you did most of the work." Anna admitted.

"Nonsense!" said the Count, "We did it together."

"So, what do we do with it?" asked Anna.

"Well, first we take a picture of you holding it, and then we put it back."

"Put it back?! After all that waiting and effort?"

"Of course," said the Count, "we either release it, or we eat it – and we don't have time to dine at the manor. We have bigger fish to catch." He glanced downstream. The boat was disappearing round the bend at a fair rate of knots. "Speaking of which ..." He took out his phone. "While our fish is running, I need to have the net ready."

He rang Sir Peter's mobile. After a few seconds the call disconnected.

"Strange," said the Count, "there's plenty of signal here." He tried again and got the same result. His face darkened.

"The idiot! He's gone in!"

* * *

It took nearly four minutes for Sir Peter and his agents to reach the manor house down the winding country lane. All four vehicles arrived at the same time, doing well to avoid a head-on pile-up as they screeched to a stop, two from each opposite direction. Sir Peter was first out, shouting instructions even though he'd barely assessed the scene. The heavy metal gates were closed and a heavy padlocked chain held them firm.

"Bolt cutters!" barked Sir Peter. One of the agents ran to the rear of his vehicle, fumbled around for a while, then reappeared bolt cutters in hand.

"Quickly, man, quickly!" shrieked Sir Peter, now at fever pitch. "Every second counts!"

The gates proved to be heavier than expected, being old wrought iron rather than any modern alloy, and they had also dropped slightly over the years, so that they dragged and stuck in the ground as the agents tried to force them far enough apart to get the vehicles through.

"Never mind!" yelled Sir Peter, "Get in there on foot!"

The eight agents, all armed to the teeth, ran down the long meandering drive. The old manor was a much larger estate than the Count's modest property ten miles away, and it took the agents almost a minute to reach the house itself. They arrived panting, then spread out in twos. Sir Peter was still a hundred yards away, half jogging, half walking, and gesticulating furiously, as if the agents would be looking back at him, rather than trying to avoid being shot by unknown enemies in the house. One pair went left, one pair went right; the other two pairs went forward, either side of the grand front door.

All was silent. Each pair signalled 'all clear' so far and there was a moment's respite. It was difficult to say whether it was Sir Peter's footsteps or his rasping breathlessness that drew their attention first, but in any case, the agents turned to see their leader arrive. One of the senior agents spoke up.

"No sign of activity here, sir. House looks abandoned, no vehicle tracks – and that gate hasn't been opened in years."

Sir Peter swore under his breath.

"Check round the back – and be careful. *Someone* fired

those shots."

As the agents started to creep round the sides of the building to the rear, Sir Peter's phone rang again and he knew it was the Count. As he so often did, Sir Peter masked his shame with bravado and aggression.

"What's the meaning of this wild goose chase?" he demanded angrily. It was well for Sir Peter that he was on the phone and the Count was not physically present, otherwise he might have found himself flat on the floor with a sore chin. However, the Count's anger was obvious.

"You meddling idiot!" he snapped, "Why did you not answer my calls?"

"What? I was in pursuit …"

"In pursuit of *whom*, you blockhead?" bellowed the Count, "I was ringing you to tell you where you could pick the villains up!"

"But there were shots fired here …"

"And I told you not to come within three miles of the place. If you'd obeyed my instructions you'd almost be at the marina by now, in time to intercept them."

"Marina? What are you talking about?" spluttered Sir Peter.

"I'd planned all this out carefully, " said the Count, "and as usual you've blown it."

"But , but …"

"I warned you before, Sir Peter. I gave you another chance and you've failed again. And when I bring Anna Parker in – as I most certainly will – rest assured that the Service will know of her innocence and your incompetence."

"But …"

"And by the way, your calls have been bugged."

"What?!"

"Consider our relationship terminated."

And with that, the Count hung up. Anna looked at him, concerned.

"Was that wise? Don't we already have enough enemies?"

The Count took a deep breath.

"You may be right. But having that moron on our side was like having an enemy in our camp anyway. He's already hanging by a thread and if he tries to mount further operations, he'll just expose himself even more. The higher ranks of the Service won't be fooled for long. He'd be an idiot to try to go after us."

"But that's the point – he *is* an idiot."

* * *

Arturo gave the orders for the boat to slow down as it came in sight of the marina. No point drawing unnecessary attention. He scanned the area for any sign of Sir Peter's men. It looked quiet, but could be a trap. A message pinged on his phone. It was from the Boss, who had heard the whole phone call.

"All clear at the marina if you are quick. Sir Peter has bungled again."

Arturo relaxed a little, but stayed alert. They had no trouble at the marina. The Boss, however, was troubled. The shadowy opponent had outwitted them and alerted Sir Peter to the tracker bug. It wouldn't be long before it was found and destroyed. The Boss was even more displeased to hear Arturo's report later on and learn that it was likely that the drone had captured Arturo on camera. That was a serious compromise. If it had been one of the lower ranks the solution would be obvious, but it would be hard to replace Arturo. *Let things take their course for now,* thought the Boss, *and if the British have proven fruitless, perhaps the French might be more useful.*

* * *

Sir Peter's head was reeling. He was in a very bad position, but perhaps something could be salvaged. He cleared his head, gathered his agents and drove to the marina. They were too late, naturally, but at least they could ask around. And, as it happened – not that Sir Peter would recognise it – that was the third smart thing he had done in relation to Anna Parker. The first had been to assign her to the mission, the second had been to hire the Count to determine her innocence or guilt.

A little bit of old-fashioned detective work had provided a rough description of a man who had hired a boat earlier that morning and returned it just a few minutes ago. Tall, dark, but not handsome. And a hooked nose. The descriptions of the others with him were sketchier, as the boat owner hadn't interacted with them directly, but there had been about five of them in total, he thought, one of whom was female, but the description was nothing like Anna Parker. This woman was quite short. Whilst it is relatively easy for a person to change their hair or general appearance, it is almost impossible for them to knock five inches off their height. He was still no closer to finding his renegade agent.

* * *

Back at his office Sir Peter worked frantically on his options, which were, frankly, limited. He also conducted a search for the listening device and found it in his coat pocket. He placed it gently on a handkerchief that he'd put on his desk to eliminate the sound of contact with the polished oak, which might have given away that it had been discovered.

After a while, he had worked through the possibilities and decided on his strategy.

It had boiled down to two options: tell the truth and face the consequences, or lie blatantly and try to save his career and pension. He had chosen the latter. After all, thought Sir Peter, spying and lying went hand in hand. In his view of the covert world there was no truth and falsehood, only perception. The plan was simple: he would report that Anna had been recruited by the traffickers, was involved in the abduction of Camille Dupuy, and was now on the run and being aided by unknown persons. He paused. Dare he mention that he had hired the Count? His superiors probably had more faith in the Count than in Sir Peter himself. No, better to say nothing about the Count, but if the Count was caught in any crossfire, well, that was his own fault.

Now, he thought, what tone to strike? It would seem more believable if he admitted some minor error on his own part rather than trying to blame other people for the entirety of the mess. Yes, that would work. He crafted his wording carefully, then picked up the phone and made his report, knowing that whoever had planted the listening device would now also have the information.

Afterwards, he let a couple of hours pass normally, then pretended to remember the listening device.

"Blast!" he feigned annoyance, "The bug! Where are you, you little beggar?"

Making a noisy show of searching the office, talking to himself to give a running commentary for whoever might be listening, he eventually got round to his coat. Rummaging in the now empty pocket, he exclaimed, "There you are!"

He picked up a heavy paperweight and smashed the device. He didn't like being spied on, but it had served its purpose; he had been able to sell Anna and the Count out to two groups at once. *You are a cunning fellow!* he thought to himself. All memories of past failures erased in his own mind, Sir Peter felt the part – a real spymaster – no, a *great* spymaster.

* * *

The Boss was much encouraged. Granted, the listening device had been discovered and destroyed, but not before Sir Peter had passed on information that not only corroborated, but added slightly to, the information the captured men had passed on before, well, passing on. The Mécénat had a contact in the detention facility who was unable to get the men out, but could at least manage a quick conversation and supply the suicide pills.

Apparently, one of them had been unwilling to take his, but the other had resolved the issue and eliminated the risk of compromise. The loyal man's family would be well-provided for. In its twisted way, the Mécénat lived up to its name, providing patronage, sponsorship and support for its members while they were alive and for their families if the worst should happen. The fact that this support came from the proceeds of criminal activity, the impact of which was horrific on those who suffered as a result of the drugs, weapons, human trafficking and abuse, was swept under the carpet. In their minds it was loyalty, care, belonging. And so the devil appears as an angel of light, as he does in so many less blatant ways for the rest of us in our daily lives. As for the other family … well, disloyalty would have to be discouraged. As calmly as if ordering a pizza, the Boss picked up the phone and ordered a punishment hit on the disloyal man's family.

"Fernand Gobet has betrayed us. You will burn his house down at midnight tonight."

"Very good, *Patron*. But … at midnight his wife and children will be asleep upstairs."

"And?"

There was a short pause.

"Nothing, *Patron*."

The Boss hung up. That should send a signal to anyone else who might consider breaking the code.

As for Anna Parker, it seemed she had not taken the girl to England, which meant the girl could still be in France, but who was this rogue agent working with? Sir Peter had said she had defected to traffickers, but the Boss knew for a fact that it wasn't the Mécénat, so who was it? Being in the organised crime business, the Boss had a good knowledge of the rival gangs and syndicates, so there were three lines of attack. One was simply to put the feelers out generally on the street and in the underworld. The second would be to put Mécénat surveillance on the rival gangs – and maybe lean heavily on the more likely candidates to extract information. The third was to keep Arturo's team on finding Anna Parker. There was every possibility that she might flee from England to France to meet up with whoever she was now working for.

CHAPTER 11

MADELEINE DUPUY

It had been a very difficult week for Madeleine Dupuy. On Monday her daughter had been taken by traffickers – the very organised crime gangs she had been publicly campaigning against. Although still a *Secrétaire d'État*, similar to a junior minister in the UK, she was a rising star, having ascended through the ranks rapidly, and she looked set to go higher still. A single mother, she had campaigned on many issues of concern to families: education and equality, the rights of working women, and increasingly since the death of her husband four years ago at the hands of organised criminals, had waged a political war on the trafficking of drugs and people, especially children. Her career had taken its toll on her family life, and things had not become any easier when she finally made it over the line into a ministerial position; if anything, the workload had increased. Furthermore, her proactive stance against organised crime had made her the target of death threats on more than one occasion.

Late on Tuesday afternoon Madeleine had called her secretary, Emmanuelle Carnot, into her office in the Ministre de l'Intérieure.

"Any news, Emma?" asked Madeleine, using the short version of her secretary's name.

"Nothing yet, Madame."

Emmanuelle waited, but there was no response. "But as you know, the DGSI have some leads." she added encouragingly.

"They have the letters that threatened this would happen. But what good are they now? I get so many, I didn't take them seriously until it was too late."

"At least you kept them and passed them on straight away. There could be vital clues in there. For example, the small grammatical errors indicating they were written by a foreigner. They're on the track of the Albanian trafficking gang even now."

"But it's been almost twenty-four hours." replied Madeleine, with a desperate edge to her voice.

Emmanuelle knew she was fighting a losing battle, but to her credit, she persisted, clutching at straws.

"And they stopped the Mécénat weapons shipment and have two of the gang."

"They won't talk." Madeleine snapped, "And anyway, success as it was, it was a weapons smuggling operation, nothing to do with the kidnap."

Emmanuelle resigned herself to defeat, but tried to end on a positive note.

"I'm sure they'll find her."

"They might." replied Madeleine, the stress unmistakeable in her voice, "They might."

The rest of that day had passed with no progress, but the following day Madeleine received a call from Eric Mazet, the DGSI agent leading the search for the missing girl.

"Sorry for the interruption, Madame, but I thought you would want to know that there has been an incident at the facility where the two Mécénat weapons smugglers were being held."

"What do you mean, were being held? Have they been moved?"

"Yes, Madame."

"Where to?" There was a short pause at the other end.

"To the morgue, Madame."

"They're both dead?" Madeleine's voice went up a

couple of notches. "But they were in custody!"

"Yes, Madame."

"How did this happen? No one should be able to get to them there."

"Absolutely, Madame. But it seems that one killed the other and then committed suicide. They would rather die than be disloyal."

"Perhaps, although in this case it looks like only one of them felt that way."

"It would appear so."

"Did they talk at all? Did we get anything from them?"

"Nothing, Madame. I'm sorry." Madeleine leaned back in her chair and took a deep breath.

"There will be a full investigation." It was more of a statement than a question.

"Yes, Madame."

"Okay. Thank you for letting me know."

* * *

Two more days had passed and despite the stress of her missing daughter, which would have floored many people, Madeleine was at her desk in the Ministre de l'Intérieure. It was not unusual for her to be working at the office on a Saturday. Of course it had meant significantly less time with her daughter and she was aware that young Camille resented it hugely; however, on this particular Saturday Camille was not waiting for her at home with the nanny, nor was she at her ballet class, she had been taken and Madeleine was determined that she be found.

The DGSI had made little progress in the intervening days, but were reasonably convinced now that it was not the Albanians who had abducted Camille. Madeleine tried to concentrate on some Interior Ministry matters, but just before lunchtime her phone rang. It was Eric Mazet again.

"Madame, there have been some developments in the search for your daughter."

Madeleine sat upright. "And?"

"Well, there is good news and bad news."

"Just give me all of it!" snapped Madeleine, then softened her tone. "Sorry, Eric. As you can imagine, this is a very stressful time for me."

"Of course, Madame. The good news is that the British have informed us that one of their agents has defected to the traffickers and they strongly suspect that agent is involved in the abduction of Camille."

"And do we have details of the agent – name, pictures, whereabouts?"

"Name and pictures – yes. In fact, it's the agent who was on the Mécénat weapons operation a few nights ago." She looked down at her notes. "Anna Parker."

"And her whereabouts?"

"Last seen in England yesterday, at a safe house operated by the British Secret Service."

"That is progress. Thank you – but what is the bad news?"

"She escaped from the safe house yesterday afternoon."

Madeleine's face darkened.

"*Idiots incompétents!*" she thundered. "How is this possible?"

"The British say she had help from outside."

"Do they know who helped her?"

"They're not sure, Madame, but they say Camille was being held with the weapons shipment and that this Anna Parker took her from there."

"The Mécénat?"

"I'm sorry, Madame. This must be very painful for you." Worry was etched on Madeleine's face.

"It is, Eric, it is." Recovering her composure a little, Madeleine managed a measure of appreciation. "Thank you."

CHAPTER 12

ACROSS AND A CROSS

The Count had calmed down by the time they reached his manor house. Butler had picked a few good shots of the team that had arrived on the boat, and particularly of the man who appeared to be their leader. They were well-equipped, but with a minimalist efficiency, allowing maximum speed both in movement over the ground and in the logistics of loading and unloading gear from one mode of transport to another. The Count congratulated Butler on a job well done.

"And you too, Anna – you were excellent as a fisherman!"

Anna shrugged.

"I suppose I can see why people do it. It was boring as anything for ages, but then it was so exciting to actually get a catch!"

"Well," said the Count ruefully, "Butler got his catch and you got yours, but it seems I was the only one to come away empty-handed."

"That wasn't your fault, sir." said Butler, "It was that wretched Sir Peter."

"I know, I know. But now we must move on. Anna and I will go to the monastery at Senlis. You can follow on later – I'll send instructions – but I need you to work with our drably-dressed friend to identify this team – who they are, especially the leader, and who they work for."

"Very good, sir. I'll keep you posted." He looked at

the Count with a serious look for once. "But call me if you need me."

The Count nodded. "I will."

Anna wondered who the drably-dressed friend might be, but knew that Butler would understand the Count's coded allusion well enough.

"Right." said the Count, snapping into action mode, "*On y va!* By the way, Anna, are you claustrophobic? There was nothing in your file, but I thought I'd better check."

"Well, no …" said Anna hesitantly, "but what exactly have you got in mind?"

* * *

It didn't take the Count long to prepare for the journey. Butler had made the booking on Le Shuttle, the train that would take them through the Channel Tunnel over to France. Complete with false moustache and slightly padded cheeks to match the passport photo, he was travelling as Jonathan Martin, successful businessman, and Anna was travelling as … well, luggage. It had taken some persuasion to get Anna to agree, but she knew he was right, the British would certainly have put out an alert for her at all ports and airports, and it was possible that the French had done the same. The Mécénat would be on the lookout, and even though they didn't have direct access to the facial recognition systems at these key points they would most likely have their own people in place. They may even have gone as far as putting out a bounty on her to all the underworld "freelancers". France was a big place and it would be much more efficient to focus efforts on the points through which cross-border travel was funnelled.

They had stopped en route at an alpine sports shop at which the Count bought lots of skiing equipment and clothing. Anna had stayed in the car, wearing the wig she'd used when escaping from the safe house, and some distracting make-up that, to the human eye, would change the shape of her features. It wouldn't fool facial recognition, but it would just provide that bit of extra help over and above the considerable care that they were taking to keep her out of sight. The windows of the Mercedes were tinted and would prevent anyone seeing in, so the risk was minimal as long as she stayed in the vehicle. There were additional measures she could employ later, if necessary, such as sunglasses and a wide-brimmed floppy hat that a previous guest had left at the manor.

The Count folded down the back seats before setting off and loaded the equipment and clothing into the sizeable space created by doing so. They had driven to a secluded spot a few miles from the Eurotunnel Terminal at Folkestone, at which point Anna had to ditch the hat and wig in favour of a helmet and a pair of ski boots. With Anna lying full length in the extra-large ski bag, the Count packed clothes around her and on top of her, topping it all off with skis and poles. He zipped up the bag, leaving a small gap to ensure Anna could breathe easily, then shut the boot and returned to his luxurious leather seat.

"Sorry, Anna." he said sincerely, "Let's hope you get a more comfortable crossing on the return leg." There was a muffled reply, but the Count wasn't sure it was one of appreciation.

* * *

The terminal was fairly crowded and the Count had to manoeuvre the Mercedes through the mass of vehicles edging to get on the next train, irrespective of their scheduled time. The officials did their best to wave people this way and that, and the drivers did their best not to bump into each other. Things were busier than usual as the French had added temporary security checks to their usual passport inspections. The Count had no difficulty at the UK border control; however, a rather surly and suspicious official conducting the French border checks was not so easy to please. The Count made the effort to speak to him in French, but the guard was not impressed. He had noticed that the booking was for two people – which to

Anna's utter amazement the Count had insisted upon, as it was "only fair in the circumstances".

"Mon collègue a été, er, délayé *[My colleague has been diluted]* - er, non, pardon, il a été ..." The guard interrupted with palpable disdain.

"I speak English, you know." *Yes, with a heavy French accent!* thought the Count, but he decided it was best not to vocalise it.

"Ah, good – thanks." bumbled the Count.

"So your colleague, 'e was delayed?"

"Yes, something cropped up this morning, so he will be coming over tomorrow, God willing."

The official walked round to the back of the car and tapped on the rear window. The Count could see him motioning for the Count to release the boot.

"Lie still, Anna. You're about to be inspected." he whispered, just loudly enough for her to hear. Knowing that the guard couldn't see through the tinted windows, he reached behind him and subtly slid the two zip fasteners as far down the bag as he could manage, then released the boot.

The guard could hardly wait for the lid to rise of its own accord and was scanning the contents of the boot as soon as he could get his head inside.

"You are going skiing?" he asked in a somewhat suspicious and confrontational tone.

"If the opportunity arises. It's partly a business trip, but I'm hoping for some pleasure while I'm there."

For some reason as he said the last few words he thought of Anna and he wondered whether she had read his mind. The guard rummaged around a little, then turned his attention to the ski bag.

"Do you mind if I look inside?"

Anna's heart began to race even faster than it had been. She tried to apply her training, slowing her breathing and calming her thoughts. The Count remained cool, but ready.

"Not at all."

The guard took hold of the zip fastener nearest to him and pulled it towards him, revealing the skis, poles and the toe ends of the boots that Anna was wearing, as it was the best way to hide her feet at the end most likely to be searched. The guard tugged the sides of the bag wider apart, but could see that it had been stuffed with ski clothes, gloves, goggles, etc. He paused.

"You ski wizout 'elmet?"

"Goodness, no. I packed it at this end." replied the Count cheerfully, rapping firmly on the bag where the helmet was, with Anna's head inside it. She felt the hard knocks and made a note to give the Count a rap on his own head when she got out of the ski bag. The guard zipped the bag back up, then tried a parting shot.

"You expect snow at zis time of year?"

"Of course!" the Count replied enthusiastically. "Still another two weeks left in the season – and there's always the glacier resorts if the snow's melting elsewhere."

"Okay, you can go."

"Thank you – er, *merci*." said the Count appreciatively, "*Au revoir*."

The guard shook his head as if dealing with a lesser being.

* * *

Inspector Steve Gent was not surprised to be called on again, but this time the Count had asked him to work directly with Butler. An easy-going man with a dry sense of humour, Gent would probably have been amused to find out that the Count had referred to him as "our drably-dressed friend", a coded reference to his being a plain-clothes detective. The task was simple: Butler would supply him with pictures of certain persons engaged in nefarious activity and he was to identify them using whatever systems and contacts he had, locally and internationally. He had until 14:00 the following day to respond. The fact that today was a Saturday didn't pose too much of a problem as law enforcement – international, just as territorial – was a 24/7 activity. He was confident that he would find people to assist.

Several drop-off points had been established over the last few years; for this job it was a locker at his gym. Butler had given him the locker number and combination. That part was easy enough. The difficult bit was knowing that Dave, the hyper-enthusiastic personal trainer, would be asking him yet again why he only came once or twice a month.

"There's only one way to get fit!" he would chirp, "If you can't run 10K in less than an hour you've only got yourself to blame!" and Gent's personal least favourite, "There's no gain without pain!"

He recalled the first time he'd been accosted by Dave on arriving at the gym for a session. He'd shown his membership card and Dave had picked up on it straightaway.

"Steve, is it?" he said, eyeing the card closely, "Steve Gent." He pronounced the "G" as a "J", but before Gent could correct him, Dave burbled on. "Must be great having your own special toilets everywhere you go. Get it – *GENTS*?!"

"I get it.", groaned the Inspector, wishing he had a pound for every time he'd heard that one on the school playground. "Actually, it's 'Gent' – as in 'go' and 'get lost!'." The references went over Dave's head.

"Where's that from, then?"

"Well, way back it's from Belgium."

"You should have a proper English name like mine – Griffiths!" Dave had said proudly.

"I thought that was Welsh?"

"Yeah, well … same thing."

Back in the present, Gent's fears were realised.

"Here again? … Finally!" smirked Dave.

"It's been a week or two." said Gent wearily.

"Three, at least." countered Dave.

"I haven't had the time."

"You've got to *make* time!" enthused Dave. "You've got to make sacrifices …" Gent closed his eyes. *Here it comes* … "There's no gain without pain!"

You're the biggest pain around here! Gent thought to himself as he side-stepped the trainer, who was practically blocking his path.

He skirted the room full of cross-trainers, exercise bikes and running machines and stepped into the men's changing area. The appointed locker was only three further along from his own, but at ground level. The combination worked first time. Inside the locker were: a large envelope containing photographs, a USB stick that he assumed contained the photos in digital form, plus anything else that the Count had asked Butler to give him and, enclosed in a transparent plastic case, an extremely rare vinyl record in its original cover, in mint condition. The Count knew him well. A note was stuck to the plastic case; it read simply, *Thanks. Appreciated.* Gent whistled softly. *That must have cost a pretty penny!* But what a record! He carefully placed the envelope into the gym bag that he'd brought with him. Closing that locker, he moved along to his own and took out a sweaty gym hoody.

He headed back towards the entrance, hoping that the cheery trainer had moved on the pester someone else, but he hadn't.

"Leaving before you've started?" he piped up, "You'll never get fit that way!"

Gent held up the sweaty hoody.

"Just needed to get this – it hasn't been washed for weeks." He thrust it under the fitness-meister's nose. "Here, have a whiff at that!"

Dave reeled back.

"Oi! Leave it out!" he yelled.

Waving the hoody victoriously, Gent marched out of the gym, a smile on his face and a spring in his step. *Did me a world of good, that did. I should go to the gym more often!* he thought to himself as he walked the fifteen yards to his car and drove the half-mile back to his home.

* * *

The crossing only took half an hour and soon the Count and Anna were driving through the French countryside. Sticking to the *Routes Nationales* and *Départementals*, that is the main roads and country lanes, the Count drove at what might be called a swift, but leisurely pace; that is, as fast as one could go without drawing attention. Still enclosed in the bag, but able to breathe a little more easily as the Count had taken the earliest opportunity to move the zip fasteners back to their original positions, Anna rolled gently from side to side as the car took one bend after another. After maybe twenty or thirty minutes (*It's hard to tell when you're inside a ski bag,* thought Anna), she could feel the car come to a complete stop and heard the engine switch off. First there was the sound of a door opening, then the boot, and finally, the zip being undone. Anna pushed aside the skis and poles and sat up. The Count peered in.

"How are … ?" Anna rapped him smartly on the head with her knuckles. "Ouch!" yelled the Count and they looked at each other and laughed.

"I suppose I deserved that – although I was just trying to make sure the border guard was convinced.

"Yeah, I'm sure."

"I was!" the Count protested, but they were both laughing like schoolchildren.

"How's the toothache?" enquired Anna with a sly grin.

"What? Oh, yes." He reached into his mouth and pulled out the padding from his cheeks.

"That's better." laughed Anna.

He undid the ski boots she was wearing, then gently slid them off. Taking each one in turn, he softly massaged her feet and calves.

"Mmm, that feels good. " she said, settling back and closing her eyes.

"We don't have long," said the Count, "but you deserve a treat after what you've just had to put up with."

"You know what?" Anna whispered, "You know how to make a girl feel special."

The Count smiled and gently laid her foot down.

"You *are* special."

He reached over and took Anna's hand. She responded willingly as he gently pulled her up towards him. She edged nearer to the back of the car, going side-on and drawing up her long shapely legs so she was almost huddled over her knees. He slid one hand under her legs and the other around her back. Instinctively she put her arms around his neck and allowed him to lift her out of the car. She felt his gentle strength and he felt her supple body. He held her close for a moment, then lowered her feet to the ground. As their arms withdrew, somehow their hands found each other and they stayed briefly trying to see what was in the other's eyes.

Anna had never met anyone like the Count. It was not so much that he was handsome – though he was, nor was it his muscular body – which looked and felt great. It wasn't just that he made her laugh, or even that she felt so relaxed around him. It was that, in addition to those things, she *admired* him, she *trusted* him – she *respected* him. She had never before found a man who was all of that.

The Count had seen his share of beautiful women, but Anna would stand out among any group of them. For all her strength and obvious abilities, she was caring, fun, and there was a sweet vulnerability under the tough exterior. And, within just a little over twenty-four hours, they had become friends that enjoyed being together.

The Count looked at his watch. "Time to get moving." he said. He grabbed the wig and floppy hat from where they had been stowed out of sight and shoved them onto Anna's head.

"There," he teased, "you look so much better!"

Anna gave a him a friendly shove and walked

seductively round to the passenger door. With a flick of her head like a film star, she opened the door and got in. The Count laughed and took his seat beside her.

"So, where are we exactly?" asked Anna.

"Just north of a small town called Marquise. About half-way to Boulogne-sur-Mer."

"Boulogne is on the coast - aren't we going to the monastery?"

"Yes, but it's a quieter, more scenic route. We'll stop briefly in Marquise to eat and get you some clothes."

"Okay," said Anna donning her sunglasses, "but it might be as well if I do the talking. Your French was … how shall I put it? Typically English!" The Count roared with laughter.

"I shall take that as a compliment!" he said proudly. And with that, he put the car into gear, did a neat three-point turn and exited the clearing. Taking a left onto the main road, they made their way into the town centre.

Parking on the Place de la Mairie, the Count and Anna walked the hundred yards to a Café Restaurant. The Count let Anna do the talking, nodding and saying the occasional *Oui* and shaking his head with the occasional *Non*, smiling benignly all the time. The meal was good, as was the coffee, and they were both glad of the *Toilettes*. From there it was a similar distance back up the road and round the corner to a women's boutique store, where they bought a few items to get Anna through the next couple of days. It was late afternoon now. They had minimised their visible presence, but it was time to move on.

The Count continued to drive south towards Boulogne, then to Anna's surprise, just before the town he turned off towards the coast.

"Where are you going? We should go straight on for Paris!"

"Yes, but we need to change to a rather less obviously English vehicle – that is to say, a left-hand drive one with French plates." The Count paused for effect and Anna just knew that some cryptic comment was coming. "And besides," the Count continued, "Jonathan Martin needs to spend a few days by the sea."

"Does that mean you'll be losing the moustache, then?" joked Anna, picking up on his meaning.

"Would you miss it?" asked the Count.

"Not in the slightest!" replied Anna with a broad grin.

"Then, yes, the moustache will be coming off!"

Following the coast road for a short stretch, past the beach, the Count wound his way through the streets of Boulogne to a quiet area with a few nice detached houses. He pulled onto the drive of one of them and parked next to a decidedly run-down Renault hatchback.

"Who owns this place?" asked Anna.

"Why, Jonathan Martin, of course!" the Count retorted, jumping out of the Mercedes and starting to unload the boot. Anna looked at him, staring in amazement as he merrily hauled the ski bag and a couple of other bits to the front door, rifled in one of the bags for the keys, and entered the house. A moment later he reappeared.

"Are you coming in?" he called.

Anna shook her head in disbelief, but got out of the car anyway and went inside. It was nice and had a good view too. Shame they didn't have time to stay and enjoy it. The Count went round the house, checking things and picking a few things up.

"Right," he said brightly, "Now we can head inland."

He loaded all the gear from the house and the Mercedes into the hatchback and opened the passenger door for Anna.

"I prefer the Mercedes." grumbled Anna.

"Well, this one's not quite as refined, of course, but it does the job. And it's French."

"Exactly." muttered Anna under her breath.

It took a little under two and a half hours to drive south and slightly east to Senlis on the north side of Paris. They talked easily for a while about all manner of things: the countryside, the history associated with it, their adventures so far, likes and dislikes, etc. then the conversation lulled The Count wondered if Anna had fallen asleep, she was certainly reclining in her seat and it had been a short night between two very busy days, but as it turned out, she was wide awake. She turned her head towards him and he felt her beautiful brown eyes looking at him.

"I still don't know anything about you." she said softly. The Count returned her gaze for a moment, then went back to watching the road.

"Does that bother you?" he asked, equally softly. Anna paused and thought for a while.

"In some ways, yes … and in other ways, strangely, no."

"In what ways does it bother you?"

"Well, you've read my file, you've done a psych profile on me, I've told you about my mission and what I did with Camille – no one else knows that … but I don't know who you are. I mean, people call you "The Count", but I know that there's no such thing in the English nobility. There are Countesses, but not Counts."

"That's true," admitted the Count, "and I don't think I would want you to call me 'Count' anyway."

"So, what? Am I supposed to call you 'Sir' like Butler does?" Anna had got the bit between her teeth now.

The Count sighed.

"Of course not."

"Then what? What do I call you? What's your *name*?"

"I told you on Friday that you could call me Edward."

"Aargh!" exclaimed Anna, frustrated to breaking point. "You're impossible!"

The Count took his eyes off the road and fixed her with them and she could see the same twinkle that she had seen on their first meeting.

"In public, call me by whatever name I'm travelling under. In private, call me Edward."

There was some coded message in there, Anna was sure

of it. She'd seen this time and again now, with her, with Butler, and somehow the Count had always been straight. She didn't know how, but deep down she knew that he was being straight with her now.

"Okay," she said grudgingly, "*Edward*."

The Count relaxed visibly and Anna felt some of her tension drift away too. They looked at each other again, emotions high with a heady mix of longing, frustration, anxiety and relief. It was incredible how much could be said without words.

Two hours later they turned off Rue du Moulin Saint-Etienne into the grounds of the Monastère des Clarisses. Anna looked up at the cross on top of the chapel and hoped it had provided protection for Camille over the five days since she had rescued her from the Mécénat …

CHAPTER 13

SANCTUARY

Five nights earlier ...

The young girl was still shaking with fear as Anna pulled the DGSI vehicle off the main road onto a side street.

"We need to change vehicles. This one could be tracked. Stay here, I'll just be a minute." The girl nodded and hugged her knees, feet up on the seat. Anna jumped out of the vehicle, rummaged around in the back and came alongside the passenger window, a slim jim in her hand. She smiled encouragingly, nodded at the child, and held up an index finger.

"One minute – okay?" she mouthed silently. The girl nodded. Anna moved along the street, selected a car and jimmied the lock. She opened the door and got in. A few seconds later she was ready. Holding the child close, Anna brought her down the street and settled her in their new transport. She finished hot-wiring the car, started the engine and drove off into the night. The whole thing had taken less than two minutes.

"Are you okay?" Anna asked as they drove along. The girl didn't speak. "You must be terrified, you poor thing. Did those men hurt you?" The girl shook her head. "Did they frighten you?" asked Anna. This time the girl nodded and burst into tears. Anna stopped the car.

"Oh my darling." she said and hugged the child. They

stayed there for a couple of minutes until the sobbing died down. "I know you're scared to go back." The girl nodded. "Is there someone there that you're afraid of?" She nodded again. "Can you tell me who it is?" The girl's eyes widened and she shook her head. Her whole body was shaking too. The girl was obviously terrified of an individual; she had probably been abducted by someone who was supposed to be protecting her – a nanny, a member of the security detail ... a double-agent in the DGSI, but she was so scared of them that she couldn't bring herself to identify them. Anna held her close.

"It's okay, it's okay." Anna reassured her, " I'm going to take you to stay with some ladies who will hide you and protect you. Just for a few days … until I can find out what's going on and make it safe for you – okay?" The girl nodded. Anna held her hand for a few seconds, then re-started the car.

For a while Anna talked gently to the frightened child, just trying to bring a sense of normality. She chatted about horses and pets, asking if she liked this or that. Occasionally the girl would nod or shake her head, but no words came. Anna tried playing "I spy" (which in the circumstances, she thought, was ironic, as that's exactly what she did), but got no response. In the end she just let the child rest, and occasionally pointed at something of interest along the way.

After forty-five minutes they arrived at the monastery. Anna held the girl's hand as they walked to the door and rang the bell. A light came on in the hallway and the door was opened by an elderly nun in a dressing gown.

"Can I help you?"

"We're looking for Sister Colette."

"All the sisters are in bed – except for me now, of course."

"I'm sorry to disturb you, sister, but it is most urgent." Anna looked down at the girl. The nun nodded and crouched down to the child's level.

"Are you in trouble, my dear?" she asked kindly. The girl nodded sadly. Sister Rosa stood up and addressed Anna quietly. "Is the child's home an unsafe environment?" Anna nodded. Sister Rosa opened the door wide. "She can stay here tonight, but we will need to inform the authorities tomorrow." Anna shook her head.

"This is why I need to speak to Sister Colette. It's a ... *special* case." Sister Rosa straightened and looked quizzical, then her face softened and she nodded.

"You had better come in. I will get Sister Colette."

They had not got long to wait before a young nun with intelligent eyes and an air of quiet authority appeared. She broke into a smile and practically ran towards them.

"Anna!" They hugged each other.

"Oh, Colette, it's so good to see you!"

"You too! But what are you doing here?" She looked down at the girl. "Is this ... ?"

"No, no," said Anna, "I haven't started a family yet – nowhere near, in fact, but ... look, the thing is ... I need your help, Colette. I *really* need your help."

Sister Colette looked puzzled. "What's going on, Anna? Why are you here and why are you wearing riot gear?" Anna pressed her lips together, grasping for some way to explain without compromising herself, the girl, or indeed Colette herself.

"I can't explain, but I need you to trust me – no questions asked. I work for the British Government and I'm over here working with the French. This girl is in grave danger and I need to keep her safe and hidden – just for a few days."

Colette was stunned, but if there was one thing she knew about Anna Parker it was that when she talked like this, she was serious.

"Okay ..." she said cautiously. "One week – tops. If we haven't heard from you, then we'll have to go to the authorities." Anna grasped her hands.

"Thank you, thank you, Colette!" She turned to the

girl. “Sister Colette will look after you until I come back.”

Sister Colette knelt down beside the girl.

“What is your name, my dear?”

“No questions, Colette – please.” Anna cut in.

“Very well,” said Sister Colette, smiling warmly and taking the child’s hand, “we shall call you … Sister Clarisse. Do you like that name?” The girl smiled and nodded, liking the idea of playing a game, then, in a way that only precocious children do, spoke for the first time since her abduction.

“But I’m really called Camille – Camille Dupuy.”

Colette looked up.

“Oh, my word, Anna. What have you got involved in?” Anna grasped her arm again.

“Don’t believe what you hear in the media. Just give me time to get to the bottom of it.”

Colette registered the urgency and sincerity in Anna’s voice.

“Alright.” she said stoically, then, crossing herself she added, “May the Lord help us.” Fixing Anna with a gaze that gave her a jolt inside, she spoke again, calmly but with a power that Anna had never seen before. “May He protect you, guide you and give you someone amazing to help you, because you surely can’t do this alone.”

Anna was stunned; it was like she’d been injected with some kind of electricity. All she could manage to say was, “Thanks”, but something inside her echoed a word from long ago, *Amen*.

The feeling stayed with her all the way back to where the DGSI vehicle was waiting for her. She parked the borrowed car as closely as she could remember to the spot she had taken it from and jumped into her own vehicle. She had the space of just an hour’s drive to think what she was going to report, what she was going to leave out, and how it was all going to hang together. She took a deep breath and started the engine.

Saturday evening, the present ...

The door was locked, but at least the lights were on at the monastery this time. Anna was about to ring the bell when she heard the sound of the door being unlocked from the inside. The door opened to reveal Sister Colette. She looked at the Count.

"It seems my prayers were answered!" she said to Anna in English with a mischievous smile. In different circumstances Anna would have blushed, but she was focussed on the safety of the child.

"What? Oh, yes." She waved her hand towards the Count to make an introduction. "Colette, this is ... my friend." The Count bowed slightly to Sister Colette.

"A pleasure to meet you, Sister – and thank you for all your help." For all her vows, Colette couldn't help being mildly charmed by the tall handsome stranger, but it wasn't safe to be chatting outside.

"Come in, come in." she said, bustling them through the doorway and closing and locking it behind them. "This way, follow me."

Sister Colette led them from one corridor to another, then stopped outside a door.

"It's nearly bedtime, but she's still up." Knocking on the door gently, Sister Colette opened the door a fraction and called out in a childish voice, "Sister Clarisse? Are you there?"

There was a giggle from inside the room and a young girl's voice called back, "Yes, I'm here, Sister Colette."

Sister Colette opened the door a tiny bit more, teasing Camille, then called out in a sing-song voice, "You have visitors. Anna is here!"

As soon as Anna's name had left Sister Colette's lips there was a scuffling sound and a little face peeped round the door.

"Anna!" she shrieked and threw herself at the surprised,

but delighted, rescuer. They hugged and Anna held her close again, feeling her warmth and fighting back tears of joy to see the change since last time they had embraced.

"Camille, there is someone very special that I would like you to meet." She moved slightly to one side so the girl could see. "This is my friend …" she hesitated.

"Edward." said the Count crouching down and fixing Camille with a warm smile. He held out his hand, palm up, just as he had done for Anna the first time she had met him, thirty-one hours that seemed like three years ago. Camille took his hand like a princess at a ball and giggled as he made a show of kissing it. The Count bowed low.

"At your service, *Madamoiselle*." he said in a mock-serious voice. She giggled again and withdrew her hand with a dainty flourish. Anna looked at the Count, and Sister Colette watched Anna looking at the Count. She leaned over and whispered something in Anna's ear. Anna blushed.

"Stop it, Colette; he's just a *friend!*" she whispered back. Sister Colette shrugged her shoulders.

"If you say so." Then with a roguish grin she added, "But I know what *my* prayers would be if I was in your shoes!" And for a moment they laughed together just like they used to at college. Camille and the Count looked up.

"Sorry," said Anna, "private joke."

The Count whispered something to Camille and she giggled again.

"Now," said Sister Colette, "time for bed."

"Just ten more minutes."

"Time for bed." repeated Sister Colette.

"Just *five* more minutes."

Sister Colette remained unmoved.

"*Two* minutes." persisted Camille. Sister Colette couldn't refrain from smiling any longer.

"Alright, two minutes, then bed."

"Will you tell me a story?"

Sister Colette sighed. "A very short one, then you must

sleep. Now, get into bed, please, *Sister Clarisse*."

Camille giggled again and snuggled down under the duvet. Sister Colette sat down on one side of the bed while Anna sat on the other side. Camille waved to the Count.

"You can sit down too, but you have to listen to the story." The Count nodded obediently, then winked at Anna and sat down beside her. Camille turned to Sister Colette.

"Now, are we all listening ...?"

* * *

True to her word, Sister Colette's story had been a short one – and was, coincidentally about a short man. He'd climbed a tree to see Jesus because he was too small to see over the crowds. Anna started to explain the story to the Count, as the whole conversation had been in French, but the Count held up his hand, smiled, and said simply, "It's okay, I got the gist."

Sister Colette took them to the kitchens to get some food and a drink, and as they ate, she initiated the inevitable conversation.

"So, what happens now?" she asked.

Anna was about to speak, but the Count put his hand on her arm. She turned abruptly towards him as if he was stealing her thunder, but then she realised that had it not been for him, she would have no thunder to steal. This had all been down to him and he clearly had a plan. She held her tongue. The Count spoke.

"From your point of view, Sister Colette, it is simple: in the morning we will take Camille to another safe place."

Anna stared at him.

"But where can we take her?"

"I happen to know somewhere, but it is better for Sister Colette if she doesn't know where we're going. She must be able to speak truthfully in the event that anyone comes asking."

Anna looked over at Colette and then back to the Count, concern etched on her face.

"But no one will come asking." she said, trying to convince herself as much as the others.

"Probably not," replied the Count, "we've been very careful. However ..."

"Hope for the best and plan for the worst." interjected Sister Colette. "It is, unfortunately, very much the same approach in our ministry. We also have many difficult and tragic situations to deal with."

Anna and the Count nodded, appreciating the strange similarity between their very different lines of work.

"And besides," added Sister Colette fingering the cross hanging from her neck, "we do not work alone."

"Indeed we do not." affirmed the Count.

"Now," declared Sister Colette, "We need to find you two somewhere to sleep." Anna almost blushed again, but her friend continued speaking. "Anna, you can have my bed; I will sleep on the mat."

"No!" objected Anna, "I couldn't possibly!"

Colette looked at her friend slyly.

"Don't you know that it is better to give than to receive?"

"That's certainly true of a good beating!" They burst out laughing again, remembering the times when they'd shared this private joke together in their youth.

The Count watched Anna laugh. She was so beautiful, and the joy, the energy – the *life* radiating through it all just drove that beauty to the next level. He felt flashes of the times when the two of them had laughed like this, and it amazed him that they could have become so free with each other, so *close*, in such a short time. Did he believe in love at first sight? And if he did, did Anna?

He refocused as Sister Colette turned to him.

"We have a spare room along the corridor – but you should be aware that the facilities are communal ... and everyone else on the corridor is female."

"Of course – and thank you."

"You always were so down to earth and practical!"

laughed Anna.

Sister Colette shrugged.

"Well, someone's got to say it, so it might as well be me."

Once the mirth had died down, Sister Colette showed each of them where they would be sleeping, then left them in her room to chat while she went to get the extra bedding they would each need.

"You're a real man of mystery, you know." she teased, taking his hand as they sat on the edge of the bed.

"Glad to hear it." replied the Count, gently squeezing her hand in return.

"Careful now, we're in a monastery!"

"Yes, indeed," the Count laughed, but he kept hold of her hand.

"So, you just 'happen to know somewhere', do you?"

"I do."

"Where is this place – and just how do you happen to know about it?"

"Far enough away from here, about six hours' drive. Camille will be safe there." He paused. "As to how I know about it … " The suspense was killing Anna. "… I'll tell you tomorrow!"

"Oooh, you …!" Anna exploded, whacking him with Sister Colette's pillow. The Count put up his hands in mock surrender and they both fell backwards on the bed laughing and shushing each other at the same time.

"Quiet! You're going to wake everyone up!" ordered Sister Colette, who had just returned, arms full of duvets and pillows.

Anna and the Count sat up looking sheepish.

"Sorry, Colette." panted Anna.

"Yes, sorry, Sister." apologised the Count. "We'd forgotten that you all go to bed early and have to be up at dawn for morning prayers. Speaking of which … it's Sunday tomorrow – may we stay for morning mass?"

Simultaneously, Colette looked at Anna and Anna

looked at the Count, each of the women with equal surprise on their faces. They both spoke at the same time.

"When did you …?" – "Shouldn't we get going …?" They both stopped abruptly and the Count stepped in, recognising that he had hit on a sore point for Anna.

"Sorry to cause confusion." Turning first to Sister Colette and then to Anna, he answered each of their questions. "*I* would like to stay for morning mass. And, yes, we need to get going, but we have time – and we will be less conspicuous if we leave with the congregation and travel in the late morning when the roads are busier, giving us more cover."

Anna couldn't fault his logic, although she had no desire to sit through a boring church service. She wondered why it was important to him, and then she remembered the old Bible at the manor. *Does he believe this stuff?* she asked herself.

Sister Colette watched her face as Anna was looking at the Count, and could practically read her friend's mind. She had prayed for Anna for years, but Anna was hard ground; uninterested, even aggressive at times. It had never lessened their friendship, though Anna had found it difficult to take when her friend had told her she was giving up a prosperous career in marketing to take up holy orders.

You're out of your mind! she had told Colette. *It's one thing to have an opinion – everyone's entitled to their opinion, but this is giving up your whole life!*

It had taken a while for Anna to calm down, but they had remained good friends, still seeing each other regularly until Colette had to go away, but even then they had corresponded frequently. She came back to the present as Colette's reply to the Count broke into her thoughts.

"Of course you may stay – if you want to."

"Thank you, Sister." said the Count. "We'll stay if Anna is willing."

Anna mumbled something that sounded like agreement,

but neither of the others could hear it properly; however, neither did they want to press Anna on it, so they took it as read, said their 'goodnights' and the Count slipped away.

CHAPTER 14

A CLOSE CALL

As expected, it was an early start the following morning, but the nuns had already been up for a while. Sister Colette knocked on the Count's door.

"Come in." trilled the Count cheerily, shaved, dressed and ready, overnight bag already packed on the bed.

"I've brought some breakfast for you – it's in *Sister Clarisse's* room. We thought it might be nice for you all to eat together."

"Excellent idea." approved the Count, jumping to his feet and following Sister Colette. On reaching Camille's room he saw trays laid out on the floor and Camille and Anna sat round them. Camille indicated the space they had left for him and the Count sat down on the rug. Sister Colette closed the door behind her and the three of them were left together: a "family" made from different families.

"Sister Colette usually says a blessing." she chirped, "but she's gone for Sunday special prayers or something." She looked at Anna. "Why don't you say the blessing today, Anna?"

Anna felt the colour rising on her neck. "Well, I don't really ..."

"Oh never mind," interrupted Camille, "I'm Sister Clarisse. I'll do it."

What an adorable child! thought Anna, trying hard not to laugh from the mixture of relief and her amazement at this wonderful and hilarious six year-old. *How could anyone want to hurt her?* She had asked Colette how this miraculous transformation from fear to freedom had come about, but she had just smiled and said, "Love and prayer, Anna. Love and prayer." Well, Anna wasn't sure about that, but however it had happened, she was thrilled with it.

Grace duly said by Sister Clarisse, they tucked into their breakfast with gusto, passing each other milk, sugar, butter, jam and so on, interacting, helping, chatting – mostly Camille, now a bundle of fun and energy – and Anna had never felt more part of a family than she did right now. The Count made funny faces and did silly things to make Camille laugh, and although he didn't say much, Anna thought his French was definitely improving.

Towards the end of the meal Anna brought up the subject of moving on. She explained to Camille about taking her to a different safe place, somewhere further away from Paris and the people there. At first Camille was upset to have to leave the monastery, although Anna couldn't imagine why; *Life must be so boring here!*, she thought, but she explained that it wasn't safe for Camille – or for Sister Colette – if Camille stayed there for too long, and Camille seemed to understand. *She's such a smart kid,* Anna thought, *and she's only six years old!*

There was a knock on the door and Sister Colette entered the room.

"How was breakfast?"

"Excellent." said the Count, "Thank you."

"Splendid!" Camille chimed in, making everyone laugh, "And I said the blessing!"

"Well done, my dear." acknowledged Sister Colette, then turning to the Count, "It's almost time for mass, if you would like to come?" The Count looked over at Anna, who nodded.

"You go. I'll stay here with Sister Clarisse." Camille giggled, enjoying the role-play.

"Are you sure?" queried Colette, "There's another mass later. I can go to that, if you want me to stay with this little one?"

"No, it's fine – but thanks anyway."

"Okay – but you know I'll be praying for you, don't you?" Anna smiled.

"I know."

"Can I go to mass?" chimed in Camille, "After all, I'm Sister Clarisse!"

"I think it's better if you keep out of sight, young lady." said Anna firmly but kindly, trying not to raise the child's anxiety again. "Remember, we're playing the hiding game."

"Oh yes. Of course." said Camille quietly. "Yes, we are."

* * *

"How was mass?" asked Anna, when the Count returned.

"Good, thanks."

"So you're Catholic."

"Is that a question or a statement?"

"An assumption, I guess."

"Because I went to mass?" asked the Count.

Anna shrugged.

"Seems logical."

"You don't think a Protestant could – or would – attend a Catholic service? Or a Catholic attend a Protestant service?"

Anna shook her head.

"Interesting." mused the Count. "What makes you think that?"

"I went to a Catholic girls school."

"Ah. And?"

"It didn't take."

The Count raised his eyebrows.

"Do you have something against Catholics?"

Anna thought of Colette.

"I suppose not.

"Neither do I." said the Count with an enigmatic smile

and a tone that implied the topic was now closed.

Anna wasn't sure what that meant. Was he saying that he *was* a Catholic or he *wasn't* a Catholic, or was he simply not giving her a straight answer? That would be typical of him. She had more questions, but she kept them to herself. Anyway, she told herself, she wasn't interested in his religion, she just wanted to know what sort of man she was putting her trust in. And maybe falling for.

He seemed to be studying her closely and she hoped he wasn't reading her thoughts.

"We'd better get going." he said finally. "People are leaving the chapel now, but if we're quick we'll still be leaving as part of the congregation."

What little there was to pack had already been sorted and Sister Colette had made a small picnic in case they needed something en route, so they could avoid stopping in town.

"What about fuel?" asked Anna.

"I went out last night and filled up after we separated. I bought a child seat as well."

"Wow," laughed Anna, tugging at his shirt, "are you like some kind of Superdad?! Is there a costume under there?!" The Count fended her off, grinning as he did so.

"How did you get back in? You didn't wake Sister Rosa up like I did last week, did you?"

"No, I left my window unlocked."

"Sneaky – but good thinking. And smart to get fuel without us. Petrol stations often have CCTV. Even just a glimpse of us when you open your door could leave a trace that someone could follow."

The goodbye hugs and tears were done in Sister Clarisse's room, but Colette accompanied them round to the chapel, so they could leave by the expected door. Anna, wig, hat and sunglasses in place, got in quickly while the Count helped Camille, shielded from potential prying eyes by a small parasol, into her child seat and strapped her in. He closed the door and turned back to the saint who had risked so much to help them.

"Sister Colette, you and the other sisters here have done us – and Camille – a great service. We are very grateful."

Colette put her hand on his shoulder.

"Look after them."

"I will. But you know you can still help us, don't you?"

"I know. And I will be praying for you day and night until I hear you are safe."

The Count got into the car and slipped quietly into the steady stream of traffic. Two weeks later the monastery received an anonymous donation. A very generous donation.

* * *

Madeleine Dupuy was pulling all the political strings she could to find out how the search for her daughter was going, but the fact was, the search wasn't going well. The additional information from the British had been helpful, but there had been no actual sightings of this Anna Parker since. Nothing at borders, railway stations, ports or airports in either England or France. And despite a nationwide campaign, with Camille's picture everywhere in the media, no genuine reports had been made by the public. There had been the usual bogus ones, of course, from attention-seekers, along with well-meaning reports from people who thought they might have seen a girl that looked something like Camille, but they had all been a waste of time.

The stress was affecting her sleep and her work. The President himself had taken the trouble to call her to express his sympathy and had told her to take some time off, but she needed to be close to what was going on.

* * *

Recalled from England, Arturo and his team were experienced border-dodgers. There were so many ways to avoid or fool border controls that he wondered why governments bothered with them at all. It seemed to

Arturo that the only people who were really affected were the people who had nothing to hide. They faced hours and hours of delays, queues, checks and questions, while providing the huge bulk of cover that the real criminals needed to slip through unnoticed.

The Boss hadn't been thrilled with how the operation had gone, but seemed to understand that the shadowy enemy had played an exceptionally good hand, thus relieving Arturo from some of the responsibility. But if he and his team had been captured, the Mécénat code demanded the ultimate sacrifice. Arturo had been happy enough in the past to dispatch a couple of traitors who had refused to follow the code, but he never thought for a moment that he himself might one day be required to follow it.

He brought his thoughts under control. He had never been caught. He was *Le Renard*, the Fox, and he would track down this child and her rescuer, corner them, and kill them, just like a fox in a hen-house.

He put himself in Anna Parker's position. He would have to fill in some of the details himself, making educated guesses as he went, but if he could at least come up with some possibilities, that would give him some potential leads to follow.

He knew where the child had been taken from, and the approximate time. He knew, from what the Boss had overhead Sir Peter saying, that Anna Parker had reported back in to the British in the early hours of the following morning and had been taken under guard back to England. That meant she had only had four or five hours maximum to hide the girl – or pass her on to whomever she was working with – and get back to the Paris base. He got his laptop out and brought up a map of Paris and the surrounding area. He zoomed out until he could see 150km on all sides of Paris. It was a huge area, but all reachable within two to two and a half hours at that time of night. A circle 300km in diameter – it was impossible! No wonder the DGSI and police had got nowhere.

He calmed himself again. *Okay,* he thought, *if she's working with someone, then it could be almost anywhere – and that would be impossible for him, but ... how likely was that? No one outside the Mécénat knew that the girl would be at the weapons cache. No, she had to have been working alone, acting on the spur of the moment.*

Arturo smiled. *Now, little hen, where would you run to?*

Arturo thought hard, his crafty brain imagining all sorts of scenarios, and eventually he settled on one. His reasoning was as follows: Anna Parker had only been brought over from England to work with DGSI in Paris a few days before the raid on the weapons cache, so she would not have had time to make many contacts outside of the British and French secret services. Hospitals, hostels, social services and the like would all have insisted on formal registration of the child, including notifying the authorities. What Anna Parker needed was people who were unquestionably trustworthy, who were sympathetic, caring, and, above all, bound to a higher authority than the government. In short, Anna needed *nuns*.

There were about sixteen monasteries within a couple of hours' drive of the centre of Paris. He picked the most likely ones and allocated two to each member of the team. Arturo himself would check two on the north side of the city: the Carmel de Compiègne at Jonquières and the Clarisses at Senlis. Tired from their overnight ferry crossing, the team were less than enthusiastic about driving around Paris and the surrounding area for hours on a potential wild goose chase, but none of them wanted to cross Arturo. It was already nearly ten o'clock on Sunday morning and he was keen to get on with the chase. Senlis was pretty much on the way to Jonquières, so it made sense for Arturo to go there first. The traffic might not be as light as had been on Monday night, but it was much lighter than on weekdays and he made good time, driving aggressively so as not to lose precious minutes.

He screeched to a stop outside the Monastère des Clarisses, strode arrogantly to the door and tried to barge in, uninvited. The door did not move, but solidly rejected his efforts as if his presence and attitude were unwelcome, and the very building was demanding humility and an acknowledgement of his own personal weakness and limitations. But humility was not within Arturo's character and he pushed the bell button angrily. When the door had not opened within a few seconds, he rang again, twice. There was still no response from within, so Arturo stepped back in order to see if there was anyone at any of the windows. Just then a tall, elderly nun appeared from another part of the grounds and walked crossed the yard. Arturo stepped into her path, blocking the way.

"Can I help you?" she said calmly.

"I'm looking for someone – two people, in fact: a woman and a girl. Have you seen them?"

"There were almost a hundred people here for mass earlier; I didn't see all of them."

"These people would have arrived late on Monday night – maybe early on Tuesday morning."

Sister Rosa tried to remain impassive, but Arturo caught the flicker of recognition.

"So you *have* seen them." Sister Rosa said nothing. "Take me to them – *now!*" he ordered, grabbing her by the arm. She didn't budge and Arturo was surprised at her strength. He let her go and drew out a vicious-looking knife. "Don't tempt me." he growled.

"I am not tempting you." replied Sister Rosa with quiet authority. "You are tempted by your own evil nature."

Arturo's wicked temper flared up. He saw the crucifix she was wearing and held the knife against Sister Rosa's cheek.

"How would you like me to carve a cross on your face?"

Sister Rosa squared up to him, her expression firm as

flint.

"I would wear it with pride!" she thundered in a deep voice that startled Arturo.

"I'll see you in hell!" he bellowed.

"No, you won't." replied Sister Rosa fiercely, staring straight into his eyes. Arturo was speechless for a second, but Sister Rosa continued. "Think about what you're doing! It's not too late. Even you can be saved!"

"What are you talking about? I don't need anyone to save me!"

"Look where you're standing!" roared Sister Rosa.

Arturo looked down. The late morning sun was high over the roofs and the shadow of the chapel spire extended in front of him. *He was standing in the shadow of the cross.* He looked upwards. The light behind the cross was dazzling and he felt dizzy. He was used to people being terrified of him, and here he was being bested by an elderly woman in ridiculous clothing. This was getting weird, and for the first time in a long time he felt afraid. Somehow he had gone from being the Fox to being a cornered rat. For the briefest of instants he felt a hand reach out to him. But like a cornered rat, he chose to bite it.

Grabbing Sister Rosa more firmly this time, he held the knife to her throat and marched her roughly towards the door, but before they reached it, it swung open and Sister Colette yelled, "Let her go!"

"Tell me where the girl is – and the woman."

Sister Colette stepped towards him.

"Let - her - go." she repeated, in a low voice. Arturo pushed Sister Rosa aside, strode up to Colette and held up the knife, but she showed no sign of being intimidated.

"Take that knife away from my face." Arturo lowered it slightly.

"They're not here." Colette stated flatly.

"But they were, weren't they?" hissed Arturo.

"Yes." replied Colette, seeing little disadvantage in admitting it and a potential opportunity to diffuse the situation by doing so.

"When did they leave?"

"About an hour ago."

Arturo's confidence was rising again, feeling now that he had found a weaker woman and gained the upper hand once more. He looked over at Sister Rosa.

"See?" he smirked. "I get what I want."

Sister Rosa fixed him again with her eyes.

"You will get what is coming to you."

Arturo laughed with bravado, though there was something about Sister Rosa that chilled him. He turned back to Colette.

"Where did they go?"

"I don't know."

Arturo grimaced and held the knife to her throat. "Where did they go?!" he growled.

Colette looked him in the eye and simply told the truth.

"They said it would be safer for them – and for us – if we didn't know where they were going."

Arturo could tell that she wasn't lying. He swore. Sister Colette slapped him on the cheek.

"How dare you take God's name in vain!"

Stunned, Arturo raised his knife, but Colette didn't flinch. He took a deep breath.

"Did you see their vehicle?"

"Yes." replied Colette.

"And?"

"It was white."

Arturo was about to swear again, but thought better of it.

"Women!" he spat. "They don't know a tractor from a Toyota, but they always know the colour!"

Sister Colette smiled inwardly, feeling a slight sense of guilt for the sin of pride. *Toyota make tractors, you stupid man. I ran the European marketing campaign for them. I also know it was a Renault Megane RS 230 – but I'll never tell you that.*

"What else?"

"I'll tell you this," said Colette, brushing aside the hand holding the knife and quoting Jesus, "All who draw the sword will die by the sword."

"But this isn't a sword." Arturo sneered.

"Your childish quip changes nothing." said Colette, "Remember that you were warned."

Arturo pushed Colette away, as he had done Sister Rosa, in a move designed to express his dominance, but in reality he was the only one feeling it; the Sisters felt nothing but pity for him.

"Which way did they go?"

"Left," replied Colette, "though I doubt that will help you".

"And why's that?" challenged Arturo.

"It just leads to a junction from which you can go left or right, and from those you can go north, south, east or west."

Arturo muttered a curse under his breath and strode haughtily to his car, but inside he was feeling like a dog with its tail between its legs. He wasn't sure whether the Boss would be pleased with him for tracking down the girl's hiding place, or angry for being too late.

* * *

As it happened, the Boss wasn't sure either. Two failures in succession was poor, but were they really failures? For the first one Arturo had simply been following up information that had been given to him, and the second one was merely a matter of timing. In fact, Arturo's cunning had actually produced a genuine lead that had almost paid off.

On the other hand, getting caught on camera by a drone was careless and potentially dangerous for the organisation. On balance it was even. *One more chance,* thought the Boss, *one more chance.*

CHAPTER 15

HIDE AND SECRET

Gent had done his research on the team that had raided the old manor and had put the intel into the same envelope that Butler had left for him the day before, reciprocating Butler's dual formats: digital information on the USB drive, plus paper files and photos. He put it back in the locker just five minutes before the return deadline. *Close,* he muttered to himself as he shut the locker door. As he did so, he felt a hand on his shoulder.

"What's that?" said Dave, the personal trainer.

"I said, 'Close', these lockers can be a beggar to close sometimes."

"Really?" said Dave. "People usually come to me saying they can't open them. If you ask me, they've just forgotten their combination – idiots."

"And you've got a master key, have you?"

"Yeah," said Dave proudly, "I could get into any one of these lockers any time I wanted."

"You know I'm a police officer, don't you?" remarked Gent casually.

"Er, right, yeah. Well, anyway, just 'cause I *can*, don't mean that I *do*, if yer see what I mean."

"Of course." said Gent with a doubtful stare. Dave shifted from one foot to the other.

"So, what workout are you doing today?"

"Running." Dave looked impressed.

"Great! How far?"

"As far as I can ..." *from here!* He finished the sentence in his head. Dave slapped him on the back.

"Good for you! I'll come and check on you in an hour."

"No need," said Gent, "I'd be at the hospital by then." Dave looked at him, unsure whether he was making a joke or actually had a hospital appointment. "Take it easy, Dave," he said, patting the trainer on his bulky shoulder, "although, you know … you'll never get fit that way!"

Dave stared bewilderedly after him as Gent strode out towards the entrance.

"I thought you were running?" he shouted weakly.

"I have run …" came the reply, "… out of time."

* * *

There was no way that any of them would comfortably have made the six-hour drive without stopping, least of all a six year-old. Whilst it was lovely to drive in the sunshine, the Count would gladly have driven in the rain so that Camille could wear a big coat with its hood pulled over her face whenever they had to step out of the car. As it was, the Count bought a child's baseball cap and some garish pink sunglasses shaped like huge butterflies that covered up half of Camille's face. He also bought everyone a chocolate ice cream and made sure that lots of it was smeared around Camille's mouth and nose, making it even harder to see her true features. Anna had bumped the Count's arm, making him smear his ice cream on his nose and they ended up play-fencing with ice cream cones, with both their faces getting covered. Camille found this hilarious and roared with laughter. Thankfully, she was strapped in and her arms were too short, otherwise she would have joined in and there would have been ice cream all over the inside of the car.

As the Count drove, Anna once again observed the same curious driving style – exhilaratingly quick, but safe, and his invariable practice of only crossing the centre lines as far – and driving only as fast – as his view of the road ahead could safely allow. This time, though, she felt that this was no act, no persona, but was really how he drove, all the time. She wondered what that told her about this strong, daring and yet hugely *considerate* man.

Two rest stops and a roadside picnic later, the latter being hidden behind the car, they were nearly there. Camille had been asking regularly since about half an hour after they had left the monastery, but the grown-ups had been able to distract her with games and songs, things to see out of the window and general chit-chat. She had fallen asleep not long after the second comfort stop, giving Anna and the Count a bit of respite. The Count checked in his rear-view mirror.

"I think she's dropped off – at last!" he sighed.

"Isn't she *wonderful?!*" exclaimed Anna.

"She's hard work." laughed the Count, affectionately.

"Yes, but wonderful." The Count looked round at her. No wonder her psych profile had been inconclusive. She was an unreconciled melting pot of characteristics: she was tough and hard, but she was also soft and caring; a trained liar and assassin, who was also honest and protective. In the animal kingdom she would have made a great mother.

They chatted a little, then Anna herself closed her eyes and nodded off for a few minutes.

"Not far now." whispered the Count in the way that husbands do when they're not sure whether their wife is asleep or not – just quietly enough to show consideration, but loudly enough to wake their loved one if they weren't awake already. Anna stretched.

"Mmm. I think I must have dozed off."

"You did." confirmed the Count.

"How do you know?" challenged Anna.

"Well, you were snoring, for one thing."

"I was not!" protested Anna. The Count pulled an apologetic face.

"Sorry, it must have been a noisy road surface." he

chuckled.

They crested a hill and the view opened up. Anna sat up and leant forward.

"That's amazing!" she gasped.

"Isn't it?" said the Count, delighted that Anna was taken by the sight. And what a sight it was! They could see clearly down the valley for nearly ten miles, most of that taken by a sparkling blue lake. The sun was streaming in from the far right-hand side, shimmering on the water and making the sails of the yachts look like luminescent triangles. The hills rose green and majestic on either side, and behind them were mighty mountains, rocky cliffs and ridges. Millions of pine trees flanked the valley. The natural beauty was breath-taking. Below, between their current position and the water, Anna could see a small city resting on the north side of the lake. It was still a couple of miles away, but as they got closer Anna could distinguish the old part on the north-western corner from the much larger modern areas spreading north from the top end of the lake. She could pick out some of the larger buildings in the old quarter – a medieval château, a basilica, and various other large churches. There was a marina on the right, sweeping round to a huge grassed area and a tree-lined promenade that must have been nearly a mile long, leading to a promontory hosting an elegant luxury hotel, park and gardens, and further round to a beach. The colours were bright and tasteful, without a trace of the tackiness of British resorts. Closer still and Anna could see hundreds of people – couples, families and individuals, walking, cycling, playing, swimming – it seemed like paradise, and for a moment she was lost for words.

"Please tell me we're staying here!" she begged. The Count smiled.

"We are – a little way down the eastern side of the lake."

There was movement in the back of the car and a yawning voice piped up, "Are we there yet?"

"Almost, I think." said Anna turning and smiling at Camille, looking cute in her flamboyant sunglasses.

"Oh, it's *beautiful!*" exclaimed Camille as she gazed out of the window at the lake and boats, bikes, and colourful flowers, flags and sunshades.

"Do you like it?" asked the Count.

"I love it!" squealed Camille.

"Wait 'til you see where we're staying!" said the Count tantalisingly as they drove along the promenade.

"Oooh, is it that big hotel there – the white one by the lake, with the gardens?"

"Oh no," said the Count, "it's even better than that!"

Anna wasn't quite sure that the Count could magic up anything better than the Imperial Hotel, but she didn't want to spoil the moment for Camille. As they neared the lake they went left, rounded the north-east corner of the lake and headed south down the valley. The road climbed, giving a glorious view across to the far side of the lake and the towering pine-clad hills that rose up from the old quarter to a ridge that stretched the length of the lake and beyond. Passing through one small town, the road wound round for a mile or two, until they reached another town of a similar size. Just near the church on the right, the Count turned left up a steep lane that passed a graveyard and some fields. A quarter of a mile or so further on, the Count took a right and followed a tarmacked drive through some woodland, winding its way uphill even further. The Count slowed down and turned to Anna and Camille.

"Ready?" he said, turning the final corner. Anna started to speak, "Ready for wha … ?", but she never finished the sentence. What she saw next left her speechless.

Camille squealed again. "I don't want to be Sister Clarisse any more. I want to be a *princess!*"

* * *

The château was like something out of a fairy tale. Beautifully built with stone quarried from the hill on which it stood, its square towers and rounded turrets looked stunning against the blue sky.

"You weren't joking." she whispered.

They drove through the arched gateway and while Camille was enraptured by the dream-like castle, Anna couldn't help noticing the gleaming Bugatti sports car parked to one side of the courtyard.

The Count pulled the comparatively shabby Renault round and parked parallel to the château wall.

"Hang on a second, I'll be back in a moment."

Anna watched him go up the steps to the grand door and ring the bell. It was one of those old-fashioned ones, where you pull a knob out of the wall and the cord rings a bell inside the house. A few seconds later the door was opened by a medium-sized man in late middle-age and formal servant's clothing. He appeared to recognise the Count, but there seemed to be a misunderstanding. Anna hoped that nothing was wrong, but then she wondered whether the Count's stilted French was the problem. The two men spoke briefly on the doorstep, then the manservant, frowny-faced, closed the door. The Count returned to the car.

"Sorry." he said sheepishly. Anna eyed him suspiciously.

"We've come an awful long way. We *are* staying here, aren't we?"

"Yes – please say yes!" chimed Camille. The Count chuckled.

"Yes, yes, don't worry. We're staying here. I just had to sort something out." He opened the door for Anna. She swung her long legs out and the Count offered his hand. Anna hesitated before taking it, wondering what new scrapes he was getting them into, but his confident smile disarmed her. As soon as Anna was out, the Count opened the rear door, then unstrapped Camille and helped her out. Holding her hand, he led her round the car so she could see the château again.

"Would you like to go in?" he asked, knowing what the response would be.

"Ooh, yes, please!"

"Well, let's go then!"

With the Count holding one hand and Anna holding the other they walked up the steps together like a family on holiday. The Count pushed the unlocked door wide open and they stepped into the château.

* * *

Fifteen minutes after Steve Gent had dropped off the package, Butler entered the complex, sports bag in hand and dressed in gym gear, complete with sweat band and branded hoody pulled up over his head. Dave swooped on him like a seagull onto a bag of chips.

"Hello, mate. You here again?"

"Yes." replied Butler without stopping. Dave was not so easily put off. He attached himself to Butler like a limpet to a rock and followed him down the corridor.

"You were here yesterday, weren't you?"

"That's right." said Butler, turning the corner past Reception and heading towards the changing rooms.

"I mean, it's great that you're back, but it's strange that you don't come for months and then you turn up two days on the trot."

Butler kept moving, but wondered what was coming next.

"You know you'll never get fit like that." continued Dave. "I can never understand this 'binge it – bin it – binge it' mentality. When it comes to fitness, you've got to get on top of it and stay on top of it."

"Right." muttered Butler, entering the men's changing area, Dave still hard on his shoulder.

"I mean, look at me," prattled Dave, pulling up his shirt and showing off a rather small and indistinct abdominal six-pack, "I didn't get these bad boys by coming for two days and then skipping for a month."

Butler nearly laughed out loud. *Bad boys?!* he thought.

More like cheeky toddlers! And it's a wonder you even got those, seeing as you just stand around all day! But he kept moving and repeated, "Right."

"I could give you a personalised training plan for the next six weeks."

Butler reached the locker.

"So, what do you reckon? Do you want my help?" The man was persistent, Butler had to give him that, but then, Butler also had to give him the heave-ho as soon as possible. He bent down and pressed some random numbers on the combination lock. As expected, nothing happened.

"Actually, I *might* need your help. Is there any way to open these lockers if I can't remember the code I set?"

Dave's chest swelled with pride, stretching the seams of his skin-tight lycra top.

"As it happens, I have a master key in the office."

"I think you'd better get it," said Butler, failing a second time. Dave rolled his eyes. Another idiot who's forgotten their code.

"Alright – I'll be back in a minute."

"Great." said Butler, who only needed thirty seconds to get the package out of the locker and swap it with a towel from his bag. True to his word, Dave returned just half a minute after that.

"Here we go, mate – keys to the kingdom!" he crowed, waving the master key like an Olympic medal.

"Great – thanks." said Butler gratefully as he watched Dave open the locker.

"There you are … now, there's two things you mustn't forget." cautioned Dave with a serious face. "One is to set a new code, and the other is … " and at this point his face lit up with glee, "*the new code!*"

Dave roared with laughter at his own joke, even though he used it every time he opened someone's locker for them. Butler laughed politely and bent down to get the towel out of the locker.

"AAARGH!" he screamed, clutching the lower part of his back.

"What's up?" yelled Dave, panicking.

"My back!" groaned Butler. "Help me up, will you?"

Dave stared at him in amazement.

"What about setting the new code?" he said.

Butler almost burst out laughing at Dave's complete lack of perspective, but he turned the urge into a contorted pain-wracked face and let out another, "Aaargh!"

"Okay," conceded Dave, "I'll set one for you – do you think you can manage to remember 1111?"

Butler could've strangled him.

"I think I can manage that."

Dave helped Butler up, set the new combination and carried his bag out to Reception.

"Thanks." said Butler.

"No problem." chirped Dave.

Still holding his back and positively exuding fake pain, Butler picked up the bag and hobbled out of the building.

* * *

Back at 37B, the Count's house in Tooting, Butler quickly reviewed the information provided by Inspector Gent. Contacts within EUROPOL had been able to identify three of the five members of the hit team. One, the female, was Margherita Barbieri, an Italian known to be operating in various European countries, including France. Another was Paul Gardelle, French, ex-military, working as a freelance mercenary. Finally, the leader: Arturo Regnard, nicknamed "the Fox", due as much to his cruel and crafty streak as to the similarity of his surname to 'Renard', the French word for fox. His father had been an abusive drunkard, his mother a petty thief who had died of a drug overdose when Arturo was thirteen, by which time he had already racked up an extensive criminal record. He was a seriously nasty piece of work, favouring hunting knives and a Beretta M9, implicated in several much more serious crimes later on, but with insufficient evidence to convict, and suspected of long-term involvement with international organised crime – specifically, the Mécénat. As for the other two members of the squad, one brought up no matches and the other one, as Butler expected, had not been caught clearly enough on camera.

Three out of five isn't bad, he thought, *and every bit of info helps, but it's a shame Steve couldn't get more. If you don't know who's out there, it's a lot harder to stop them.*

He checked the key pages, kept them along with the photos and the USB drive, in the envelope, and sent everything by secure email ready for the Count to pick up at his earliest opportunity. He was packed and ready to go, having set everything in order at the manor and re-located to 37B the day before. Further instructions had come from the Count early that morning and within a few minutes he was on his way to the airport.

* * *

The inside of the château was every bit as handsome as the outside. A maid in uniform crossed the hall and glanced over at the Count. Anna was sure she was trying to hide a giggle and she swung round to the Count who seemed to be trying to cover a smile with a frown. *Oh, I see,* fumed Anna, *it's like that, is it? One in every town, like the sailor with a girl in every port!* Just then, a smartly-dressed woman in her late twenties came into view and stopped on the mezzanine landing.

"Édouard!" she shrieked. Ravishingly beautiful, she made even the act of descending the stairs two at a time a feast of elegance. Throwing herself at the Count, she hugged him and kissed him repeatedly. *Push her away! Tell her to get off!*, growled Anna inwardly. To Anna's annoyance, the Count did neither. On the contrary he swept the woman off her feet, held her close and kissed her lovingly. Not for a second did he realise that he had burst Anna's bubble. All the excitement and adventure she had felt now lay in her stomach like chewed plastic. Camille, on the other hand, was practically hyperventilating with delight at this romantic reunion. Unlike Anna, she hadn't noticed the wedding ring on the woman's finger, nor would she have known what it meant for Anna.

"Enough, Francine!" laughed the Count, setting her down gently. "Let me introduce my friends." The word *friends* tore at Anna's feelings, and she suddenly realised that she was ... *jealous*. Her darker side abruptly brought to mind all the ways she'd been trained to kill someone. *Stop it!* she thought, fighting to keep at least stable, if not positive. As she calmed herself she realised that she'd been so angry that she hadn't noticed the shift in the Count's linguistic abilities. *He can speak French fluently – all that bumbling about was an act! He's been making a fool of me the whole time!*

"This is Anna ..." he beamed, turning towards her with a huge smile which she did not return. The response – or lack of it – didn't go unnoticed by either the Count or Francine. His smile faded slightly, but then returned with gusto. "And this ...", he said, flourishing his hand like a Musketeer bowing, "... is Princess Camille!" The enraptured Camille giggled uncontrollably and curtsied as best as an over-excited six year-old could. Francine curtsied in response, clearly charmed by the delightful child.

The Count turned to Francine.

"And this is Madame Francine Durand – the lady of the house." Francine took his hand and held it in both of hers.

"Oh, Édouard, don't be so formal!" she scolded.

Oh, Edward, don't be such a cheating low-life! thought Anna, but she smiled falsely, figuring that it might be better not to make a fuss just now; she and Camille needed a safe place to stay tonight.

"So, how did you travel – did you fly or get the train?"

"We drove."

"Not in that old Renault?"

The Count nodded.

"No wonder you look such a mess!" The Count feigned

hurt.

"How dare you!" he laughed, "It's a great car."

"You haven't parked it at the front of the house, have you?"

The Count nodded. "Of course."

"Next to my Bugatti?"

"Why not?"

She slapped him on the arm, pretending to be hugely offended. "You'll upset the neighbours!"

"We don't have any neighbours!" protested the Count, "Not for half a mile, anyway." The use of the word '*we*' was not lost on Anna.

"Well, you're bringing down the whole tone of the area!" teased Francine.

A boy of a similar age to Camille and with a noticeable resemblance to the Count ran into the hall to see what all the noise was about. Anna felt sick.

"Ah, Jean-Luc!" said Francine, "What have you been up to?" The boy shrugged. "Never mind," continued Francine, "how would you like to show one of our guests round the house?"

He shrugged again. "Okay." he said nonchalantly.

"Good. Camille, this is my son, Jean-Luc."

"Hello." said Camille.

Jean-Luc shrugged a third time. "Hello."

"Jean-Luc, this is Camille."

Jean-Luc looked again at Camille. "Why are you wearing those ridiculous sunglasses?"

"Manners, Jean-Luc." said his mother.

"Sorry." said Jean-Luc penitently. He turned to Camille again. "Why are you wearing those lovely sunglasses?"

The Count and Francine seemed to find his response hilarious, but Anna wasn't in the mood.

"I'm Anna." she said, assuming that she was being overlooked.

"She's English." piped up Camille.

"But she speaks excellent French." put in the Count, hoping to melt whatever ice had suddenly formed.

"Not as well as you." *You charlatan!* she added in her mind.

"Now then, Jean-Luc. You and Camille can go and play – why don't you show her round the house and gardens."

Jean-Luc shrugged again.

"Okay."

"Look after her, will you?" added Francine.

"*Of course, Maman.*" replied the boy, as if it had been completely and unnecessary for Francine to mention it.

"Very well. Now, off you go. Be good – and have fun!"

Jean-Luc caught hold of Camille's hand.

"Come on, then!" he called.

Slightly taken aback by the unexpected tug from a strange boy, Camille held back. Jean-Luc stopped and turned round.

"Do you want to see the château or not?"

She hesitated for a second, then started to run, taking Jean-Luc by surprise and passing him.

"Of course I do!" she yelled, "Catch me if you can!"

The two of them disappeared into one of the large staterooms, shouting and laughing as they went. Francine felt Anna staring at her. Their eyes met and Francine could almost feel the daggers.

"Édouard, you must be tired after the long drive. Albert will bring refreshments out onto the terrace shortly. Why don't you go and sit in the sun for a few minutes?"

"Actually, I need to check some things first. I'm expecting an important email. I'll just be in my room for a few minutes and then I'll join you outside. Oh, and Butler will be arriving around 9pm this evening – I've told Albert."

"Very well, "said Francine, "Now, Anna and I will have a little chat and get to know each other a little better."

Anna's stomach turned; she had no desire to get to know the Count's mistress – or worse – *wife*.

The Count turned to Anna and put his hand on her shoulder, but she pulled away immediately. He looked at Francine and raised his eyebrows. Francine raised her eyebrows back at him.

"See you shortly." he mumbled and walked away.

Francine linked Anna's arm. It was the last thing Anna wanted – or perhaps the second last thing; the last thing being the Count taking her arm – but she remembered that she was a guest who needed refuge.

"You must forgive Édouard ..." she purred.

Wow! thought Anna, *even her voice is so smooth it's sickly! And the way she says 'Ay-doo-ar' instead of Edward ...*

Francine continued. "He means well. It amazes me that he is so brilliant and yet, when it comes to women, he can be so *maladroit*."

Where is this conversation going? wondered Anna as they walked through one grand room after another.

They stepped out through a pair of ten-foot high leaded glass doors onto a terrace that overlooked the valley. The view was spectacular. From the terrace the land sloped gently down to a huge lawned area and gardens already alive with a thousand flowers, bushes and trees. There were three ponds – one large circular pond with a massive fountain in the centre and two kidney-shaped ponds, one on either side of it. Beyond that were fields leading down to the graveyard and then the town nearly a mile away. Beyond the town lay the lake in all its glory, with three small towns on the far side and the towering green hills rising up majestically behind them.

Anna was speechless. It was like heaven on earth, if there was such a thing. And yet, if it was heaven on the outside, it was hell for her on the inside.

"Beautiful, isn't it?" whispered Francine.

"Yeah." said Anna in a flat tone.

They sat down on the best quality, most stylish and luxuriously cushioned rattan furniture that Anna had ever seen. The large parasols that had been carefully positioned to provide shade for the seating weren't like the ones you get in England, which are typically black, grey or some other bland colour to match the English weather. These were bright primary colours that complemented the French climate perfectly. Everything seemed so much more alive here – everything except Anna's heart. That had died just a few minutes ago. *Pull yourself together!* she said to herself, *You're supposed to be a tough British agent for goodness sake!* Yes, she could be tough; but she could also be hurt. *Stupid fool, letting yourself get drawn in. They're all the same – and you knew that, but you opened yourself up and now you're getting what you deserve!*

There was a shout from one of the turrets. Anna looked up to see Camille waving from fifty feet up.

"Be careful!" she called, but the face had vanished. *Kids,* she thought. *Oblivious to danger, oblivious to life and its realities.*

Francine leaned towards Anna with a curious expression on her face.

"Can I ask you something?" she said gently. Anna looked at her, but said nothing.

"Am I correct to think that you have feelings for Édouard?"

Anna felt like she had been stripped naked and pushed onto the stage of a crowded theatre. And could it have been more patronising?! It was like she was some kind of demented loser with a crush on the high school hero, being spoken to kindly by his long-standing girlfriend. She had no idea how to respond. At high school, she would have either run away or punched the other girl in the face, depending on the day, but she wasn't at high school now, and there was far too much riding on this. She breathed deeply and evaded the question.

"I've only known him for three days."

Francine smiled. "For me it was love at first sight."

"Really." replied Anna in a deadpan voice.

"Oh yes. We had to work at it, of course. Every meaningful relationship has ups and downs, and lasting marriages are not built without hard work, but I knew straight away."

"Great." said Anna without emotion.

"*He* took a little longer to come round, I admit; men usually do. That's why I was so surprised."

"About what?"

"About *Édouard*, of course."

"I don't follow."

"Oh, Anna," said Francine, putting her hand on Anna's arm, "I can read my brother like a book."

* * *

The Count scanned the information that Butler had forwarded from Gent. Having a range of photos was helpful, especially those out of combat gear. People look very different without helmets, for one thing, as any ski instructor who's tried to meet his or her class in the bar will tell you. Names were good too. Being able to name an opponent seemed to bring them closer, make them more reachable, more vulnerable. And knowing their backgrounds, skills, habits, etc. made it easier to prepare both defence and attack. There was even a fairly recent last known address for Paul Gardelle, who had a family – also useful information.

Then there was Arturo Regnard …

The Count shifted his focus to matters closer to home. He knew that he had upset Anna by trying to surprise her. All he had wanted was that big moment when Anna would be on pins and he would reveal his secret and they would ride the wave of emotion into each other's arms. Now he would have to simply come clean and hope the tide didn't sweep her away from him. He closed the bedroom door and trudged sadly down the grand staircase. A blur of noise and colour flew past him.

"Look out, Uncle Édouard! Coming through!"

He shook his head affectionately at the two children bounding down the stairs ahead of him, still full of energy after climbing every tower and turret, and no doubt heading down to the cellars next, with the gardens and woods to follow. He wished he and Anna were getting on as well the children.

* * *

He paused at the patio doors, confused by the sound of low whispers and conspiratorial laughter. He peered slant-wise through the glass. Anna and Francine were huddled together like a couple of thieves planning a robbery. He moved one of the glass doors deliberately and the two women sat up sharply and looked round, faces gleaming with sly understanding.

"Everything alright?" ventured the Count. Anna straightened her face.

"I was just saying to Francine how your French has really improved these last couple of days."

"Er, yes – thank you." said the Count cautiously.

"Remarkable really." Anna continued with a mischievous glint, "In fact, since we got to the monastery, one might say *miraculous*."

The Count held up his hands in surrender.

"Okay, I'm French – well, half-French, to be precise. Dad was French, Mum was English. I was going to tell you."

Anna tilted her head to one side.

"Were you?" she said doubtfully. "And when were you going to tell me that your name is Philippe?"

"That's my first name. No one close to me calls me that ..."

"Philippe Édouard Thomas de Beaumont – " Anna was striking home. "*Count of Albigny!*"

* * *

Butler's flight had been slightly delayed, but he landed in Geneva around 21:15 local time. He caught the train from the airport terminal to the city centre and then took a taxi to the Count's chalet on the shores of Lac Leman – Lake Geneva, as the Brits call it. From there he had a choice: the Count's Lamborghini, or his four-wheel drive Range Rover Sport. He figured that, as the Count had already taken one practical vehicle to the château, he might as well take the Lamborghini. He would have to watch his speed, as it was all too easy to let the 750 horsepower engine take over, but it would be so much fun, and with handling like this, barring traffic lights, he would hardly need to drop below the speed limit almost the whole way to the château. Forty-five minutes later, wearing a huge grin, he pulled the Lamborghini up next to Francine's Bugatti and let himself in.

* * *

The children had long since gone to bed, the adults had all dined – very well, it must be said, and the Count was sitting beside Anna, talking to Francine and her husband, Max.

Butler knocked politely on the drawing room door.

"Come, in!" called the Count convivially. "Have you eaten?"

Butler shook his head, "Only if you regard economy class airline meals as 'food'." The Count jumped up and greeted him with a firm handshake.

"Thanks for the email – it was very helpful."

"My pleasure, sir – and our drably-dressed friend did most of the work really."

"I sent Albert to bed, as he'll be up before us, but he organised some food for you – put it on a tray and come and join us."

"What vehicle did you drive down in?" enquired Francine naughtily.

"The Lamborghini, Madame."

Francine turned triumphantly to the Count.

"Now *there's* a man with a decent sense of taste and propriety!" she teased.

"But it's *my* car!" protested the Count.

"Exactly!" said Francine. "And you still chose to drive that rust-bucket!"

"The Lamborghini was in Geneva and I was in Boulogne!" the Count persisted, "And we couldn't get three of us in the …!"

Francine cut the Count off by making a signal with her hands, a signal that since their childhood was equivalent to saying "*Gotcha!*" The Count made a face that conveyed affectionate defeat and everyone, including the Count himself, collapsed with laughter.

"Speaking of driving," said Anna addressing the Count, "I've been meaning to ask you about your style of driving ever since you took me to the manor – and it was just the same on the way over here."

The Count looked quizzical.

"What do you mean, *my style of driving?*" he asked.

"Well, you know – fast, but *safe*."

The Count and Francine exchanged glances.

"The truth is … I didn't always drive like that. It just used to be – fast."

"So, what changed that?" queried Anna.

"I used to race with the boys from around the lake. We'd go crazy, trying to beat each other's times for certain sections of road, or for a full circuit of the lake."

"Didn't the police stop you?"

"Eventually." said the Count sadly, "After an accident."

"Oh dear. Were you involved?"

"In a way." He paused.

"What happened?"

"One of the boys was driving his car – on this side of the lake, from the church just down in the village here to the next town – the one just before the top of the lake. He was doing what we all did, going flat out and using the full width of the road to straighten the bends."

"You still do that now – sometimes, but not always, and when you do, you go faster sometimes than others."

"That's right." agreed the Count. "I've learned that it's important to never go faster than your view of the road ahead will allow. You never know what's around the bend. Of course, none of us paid any attention to that stuff back then. You know what it's like. You think your parents know nothing and you don't listen to them. So, this boy – and it could have been any one of us – took a bend as fast as he could go without losing control. He straightened the curve by crossing over to the other side of the road …". His voice trailed off. Anna filled in the gap.

"But something was coming the other way."

The Count nodded.

"It was another car. They hit head-on. No one survived. The police rounded up the boys and we never raced again."

"What did your parents say?"

"Nothing." replied the Count.

"Nothing?" queried Anna.

The Count shook his head and his voice cracked as he continued.

"They were in the other car."

"Oh, Edward!" cried Anna, taking hold of his hand and squeezing it tightly. The Count recovered his composure and carried on.

"And so at the age of eighteen I inherited the title, and became the *Comte d'Albigny*. Francine was only fifteen at the time, so I had to do most of the sorting out. I had lawyers to help me with all the inheritance tax and property, shares in various businesses – and the other businesses that my parents had owned directly, but it was a lot to cope with, especially after the loss of our parents. The government took almost half of the family's assets in inheritance tax, and the rest was shared between Francine and me. We had to use quite a bit of the remaining cash and assets to keep the château, but we desperately wanted it and …", the Count seemed embarrassed to say it, "… in truth, there was an awful lot of money."

"Money which you put to good use, Édouard," soothed Francine, "and doubled within five years."

"Then you met Max and the three of us became a formidable business partnership."

"You make it sound like I married Max for his business acumen!" scolded Francine.

"Didn't you?" said the Count seriously.

"Of course not! How could you say that?"

The Count pulled a face and made their special *Gotcha!* signal. They all laughed, but Anna could see that while he was trying to make out that things were back to normal, he was still hurting.

"Édouard!" laughed Francine, giving him a friendly punch on the arm.

Anna looked on, wondering how an eighteen year-old youth and a fifteen year-old girl had come through such tragedy and emerged from it so strong and happy. They'd probably say something ridiculous like God had helped them through it. *More like a few million euros had helped them through it,* she thought, and then immediately felt terrible for having had such a callous notion.

"You have a couple of sidelines in addition to our joint businesses, don't you Francine?" observed the Count. His sister gave him a conspiratorial look.

"Yes, but they're not half as exciting as your sidelines, Édouard!" she said slyly.

Anna regarded her with astonishment.

"You know about his …?" she started, then stopping herself for fear of giving anything away.

"His covert operations?" ventured Francine. "Of course!" She leaned forward and whispered in Anna's ear, but deliberately loudly enough for the Count to hear, "*I've even been on a couple of them!*"

"What?!" exclaimed Anna.

"Yes! Édouard has taught me lots of things!"

"Hardly." said the Count, rolling his eyes.

"Well, anyway, I've been able to help – a little."

"And Max, you know about all this?" asked Anna.

Max shrugged and Anna could see where Jean-Luc got the gesture from. For all his looking like the Count's side of the family, there was still some of his father in him. The Count and Francine looked at each other. It was the Count who answered on behalf of them both.

"Everyone here at the château knows that the Beaumont family is sometimes called on to assist those in need …."

"Including the government," Francine chipped in, "foreign allies, people in mortal danger – that sort of thing."

The Count glared reprimandingly at her. Francine registered the outstanding perplexity on Anna's face.

"Max knows the basics, but he would worry an awful lot if he knew the details."

"So you're happy for Francine to go off and risk life and limb without knowing the ins and outs of what she's doing?"

Max shrugged again.

"Well, why should he?" said Francine, waving her hand as if they were discussing cakes at the church hall, "I don't ask him about his golf!"

Anna reckoned there was a considerable difference between a 9-iron golf club and a 9-millimetre semi-automatic, but she kept it to herself.

"All the staff here are loyal to the family." added the Count. "They've all been specially vetted and selected – although most of them are local and have been with us through generations. Albert's father served my grandfather, for example."

Anna could understand it. They were a special breed, this family – and she loved feeling part of it.

CHAPTER 16

RECEPTION AND CONNECTION

The following morning, which was Monday, the children were up early and no less full of excitement and energy than on the previous day. Camille had been allocated a room next to Jean-Luc in one of the château's four children's bedrooms that constituted a quarter of its sixteen bedrooms in all, not counting the servant's quarters on the third floor. The Easter holidays meant that Jean-Luc was free, and apart from meal-times, he and Camille could play together all day. The château and its grounds provided a safe and magical place in which they could let their imaginations run wild, which they did to the full.

The grown-ups, apart from Max who had gone to his office in the city, gathered at breakfast, with the usual *Bonjours*, enquiries as to how people had slept, and whether Anna liked her room, but it wasn't long before she interrupted the small talk.

"So, what happens now?" she asked, addressing the Count, whose face lit up with an excited grin.

"I'm glad you asked," he replied, "but it rather depends on my dear sister here."

"Ooh, that sounds interesting!" said Francine, "Why me?"

"Well," said the Count, "the objective of the plan is to kill three birds with one stone, but there are a few ways we could do it."

"O-kay," said Anna, suspiciously, drawing out the word

as if partially hooked, but not entirely convinced, "I'm intrigued. What are the three birds we're going to kill?"

The Count was in his element, playing to the gallery, although without the least trace of pride or show. As far as he was concerned, he was just enjoying explaining a plan that was both satisfying and exciting, and he wanted his audience to feel the same way.

"The first bird is this: We need to let Camille's mother know that her daughter is safe."

Francine interjected straightaway, being a mother herself. "Yes, of course. I can only imagine what it must be like for her right now."

"But how do we do that without alerting the traitor in the camp?" demanded Anna.

"We don't – that is to say, we *do*." replied the Count.

"What?"

"You're talking in riddles, Édouard." chided Francine. However, Butler, being very much on the same wavelength as his friend and employer, came to the Count's defence.

"What he means is that we *don't* avoid alerting them – we deliberately *do* alert them."

"Exactly." smiled the Count, nodding appreciatively. "And that is bird number two."

"It sounds like bird number two to me!" snapped Anna, referring to the alternative meaning of the phrase, "That could put Camille at significant risk!"

"Granted," conceded the Count, "but the second objective is to flush out and identify the viper in the nest. If we don't find out who they are, Camille and her mother will never be safe."

"Alright – for now." said Anna grudgingly, "But the plan will have to be airtight."

"I can't promise that," said the Count, "but I can try to make it at least watertight – and that brings me to bird number three."

"Which is?" prompted Francine.

"To neutralise the threat."

"I'll do that – with pleasure," Anna declared coldly, "after what they've done to Camille."

Francine looked at Anna, shocked at the first sight of her darker side.

"It may take more than one of us to achieve it." said the Count. "We don't know who – or how many – we're dealing with."

"True." admitted Anna.

"But you still haven't said where I come into all this – why does the specific plan we choose depend on me?" asked Francine.

"Because, my dear sister, this is as much your house as mine – and your family lives here."

"Are you suggesting," exclaimed Francine, "that we somehow bring these murderers here – into this château?!"

The Count shrugged. "There are other places we could use, but Madame Dupuy is much more likely to attend, say, a Grand Reception here in recognition of her work and as a show of solidarity and support at this difficult time, than she is to come to our ski lodge for a few runs and a bit of *après-ski*."

"But even if Francine was to agree – and I'm not saying she should, "interrupted Anna, "Camille's mother is at the Ministre de l'Intérieure in Paris; there's no way she'd make a 12-hour round-trip to come here!"

The Count smiled. "I agree, but as it happens, on Thursday she is due to visit a new scheme that has been set up in our fair city to help victims of drug abuse and human-trafficking."

"How do you know?" challenged Anna.

The Count left just the perfect pause to guarantee maximum effect.

"Because I invited her." he said with a smile.

"When?"

"Last night, just after we arrived."

Butler beamed broadly. "Nice one, sir." he grinned.

Francine rolled her eyes, "Oh *Édouard!*"

Anna simply sat there with her mouth open, speechless.

* * *

Madeleine Dupuy had not been especially delighted to receive the invitation to a victims' shelter and rehabilitation centre at this particular point in time; however, it had been one of her personal projects at the Ministry and the Comte d'Albigny had provided a large part of the funding needed. In fact, without his contribution, this victims' centre – the first of a national initiative to be rolled-out across the country – would not have got off the ground at all.

She would have preferred to have stayed near the sharp end of things, but at the moment it was proving to be somewhat blunt. People were in place to search for her daughter, her secretary Emmanuelle had told her, and the President had practically told her to take some time off, but if she wanted to keep working this was a golden opportunity to do that while also getting away from Paris and the constant hounding of the more aggressive media that resided there. The Comte had been extremely sympathetic and supportive, and had assured her – twice – that if there was anything he could do, "*– anything at all, Madame*", she should call on him.

In the end she had agreed to go. It was a long drive, but someone else would be doing that for her.

"And the cars are always *very* comfortable." Emmanuelle had reminded her.

* * *

Francine had still not said yes to the idea of the Grand Reception.

"This week is Holy Week, leading up to Easter Sunday. The reception would be on Maundy Thursday. Would it even be appropriate to host what is effectively a huge party on such a solemn occasion?"

The Count paused, deep in thought.

"The way I look at it, my ass has fallen into a pit." he

said.

Anna stared at him in disbelief, surprised at his apparent coarse reference, while Francine seemed to find it hilarious. The Count caught sight of Anna's expression and chuckled.

"He's referring to when the religious leaders criticised Jesus for healing a man on the Sabbath." laughed Francine.

Anna still looked puzzled, though the shock had gone from her face.

"And Jesus pointed out to them that if their ox or ass fell into a pit on the Sabbath, they'd have no qualms about pulling it out straightaway." explained the Count.

Anna made the connection.

"So the ox or ass falling into the pit is an urgent situation that needs dealing with, whether it's a holy day or not."

"Exactly!" said the Count, relieved at Anna's understanding.

"But you could have said 'ox' instead of 'ass'."

The Count chuckled again.

"I could," he admitted, "but then it wouldn't have been half as much fun!"

Anna felt she was starting – just starting – to understand this complex man who by the nature of his work walked right on the edge of a very thin line between honesty and deception, and by the nature of his own personality managed to combine deadly seriousness and humour with the same integrity. In this latter respect he was like her friend Colette, but while Colette had felt called to a more simple and rigid way of life in the monastery, the Count lived a relatively luxurious and colourful life, and was surprisingly flexible and creative, and yet he was just as serious about his faith. Even so, thought Anna, it was *their* faith, not hers.

The conversation around the Grand Reception continued.

"I will have to clear it with Max." said Francine after a

few moments' thought.

"Not over the phone." warned the Count.

"Of course not!" replied Francine briskly. "I was planning to go up into town this morning. I'll simply call in at his office and have a word in private."

Anna was still overawed by this man who it seemed could bring a government minister to the other side of the country with a snap of his fingers. The Count took her hand and looked at her with curiosity. Butler and Francine excused themselves and left the room.

"What is it?" asked the Count.

"*You.*" she said. "I've never met anyone like you."

"You mean, tall, handsome and brilliant?" he teased.

Anna snorted. "No, I mean short, ugly and ignorant!"

They leant into each other and their foreheads rested against each other as they shook with laughter until the tears rolled down their faces.

* * *

Francine returned at around eleven o'clock with some casual clothes and nightwear for Anna, and to report that Max had agreed – after a little persuasion – and on the condition that he was to take Jean-Luc out on the evening of the reception, so there would be no risk to their son. Had she been entirely forthcoming she would have mentioned that he had also insisted on her coming with them, but Francine had shot that one down.

"Don't be silly, Max!" she had retorted. "I'll be *hosting* the reception – how can I be *out?!*"

Max had wondered why the Count couldn't have hosted the reception, but in his heart of hearts he suspected that Francine actually wanted to be part of the adventure. In the end she had worn him down and he had conceded that aspect of the condition.

"But be *careful!*" he implored.

"Of course I'll be careful!" she trilled, clearly delighted at having achieved her objective. "And anyway, I'll have Édouard, Anna and Butler to protect me – not to mention the staff!"

Max shrugged wearily and let her go.

* * *

Preparations for the Grand Reception began immediately. They had three days to get ready, but as any wedding planner will tell you, there's a lot more to do than you think. Fortunately, Francine was a gifted organiser of social events, and due to their family's situation had hosted numerous soirées, charity balls, and so on. She contacted Madame Dupuy's office and spoke directly to her secretary, a certain Emmanuelle Carnot, who thought it was an excellent idea given that Madame would already be in the area, and booked it into *Madame le Secrétaire's* diary. Francine noted the preference of this particular female minister for the traditional French manner of referring to occupations in the masculine form, rather than moving with more recent trends to accept the feminine form – *Madame* ***la*** *Secrétaire* – for women who were performing the role.

How quaint! she chuckled to herself. *But now that we have the guest of honour we need some more guests, otherwise it will be a very sorry affair indeed!* She opened her long list of contacts and began the process of selecting the most appropriate ones.

While Butler was happily occupied between the garden, the kitchen, and one or two special projects in the garage workshop, Anna was feeling at a loose end. She had nominal charge of the children, but they were quite happy scooting around the place, inventing names and games. Jean-Luc was a natural host and companion. However, Camille lived in Paris which, despite its many tree-lined parks, provided few opportunities for tree-climbing without risking a reprimand or even a fine. Jean-Luc was horrified to hear that she had never climbed a tree and proceeded immediately to take Camille to "the nearest tree suitable for beginners", which made Anna chuckle.

She followed them around for a while, but in the end

decided that they were fine and probably better off without her presence overshadowing them all the time, so she moseyed back to the terrace and sat in the late morning sun. She had not been there very long when she heard a voice from higher up.

"Anna!" She turned her head and looked up. The Count was on his bedroom balcony, which had a stupendous view overlooking the gardens, valley and lake. "I've done what I needed to do this morning. Do you fancy a stroll?"

"Sure." she shouted back, glad of something to do and keen for his company. "Where to?"

"Somewhere special!" yelled the Count and he disappeared into the house. A minute later he came bounding down the stairs and out onto the terrace with a pair of hiking boots in each hand. "Here, you'll be better off with these." he said, thrusting a brand-new pair of ladies boots into Anna's hand.

"Whose are these?"

The Count hesitated. "Well, if you really want to know, I bought them for an old girlfriend – ages ago," he qualified, "but she never wore them. She wasn't really the outdoor type."

"And what type was she?" huffed Anna, feeling a touch of jealousy.

"Well, not *my* type, obviously." said the Count with sly grin. "That's why I gave her the boot!"

Anna laughed at his boyish pun. With that particular piece of ice broken, she took off her plimsolls and put on the boots.

"Mmm, good fit, actually. She must have been my size."

"She was," the Count confirmed, "but she wasn't half as beautiful as you – nor half as much fun to be with!" Anna felt a warm glow. Men had complimented her before – many times, but with Edward, it was the real thing. He meant it, and she felt it.

"Where are the kids?" he asked, feeling momentarily strange at saying the phrase, almost as if it was their kids he was referring to.

"Over there, in that tree." said Anna, pointing to an old oak tree with long, low branches almost touching the ground in places. The Count smiled.

"Oh to be young."

"You think you're too old to climb trees?" Anna said, surprised that he would let a silly thing like adulthood stop him from having fun.

"Not at all!" he countered. He pointed to a smaller tree a few yards from the oak. "I was up that tree last autumn, cutting it back."

He pointed to where the ends of the branches resembled huge fists due to the repeated cycle of growth and pruning. And …" he added with a twinkle in his eye, "I've used the odd tree to get in and out of buildings on some of my … adventures."

"I'll bet you have." laughed Anna, mentally picturing the Count leaping from a high branch like a flying fox. "Anyway, where are we going?"

"Follow me." said the Count, turning and heading back into the château.

"I thought we were going for a walk?"

"Follow me." repeated the Count without looking back.

* * *

The Count led Anna through the hall and down a corridor to one of the two entrances to the cellars underneath the château, then down the old stone steps that turned through ninety-degrees half-way down and led to a sort of underground foyer with stone arches through which corridors went off in three directions. He chose the one on the left. Lights controlled by motion sensors came on as they walked past several closed doors and open-plan storage areas. The end of the tunnel was poorly lit, as the last of the ancient-looking bulbs was a few yards back from it. Some old panelling had been piled up by the end wall. It didn't look particularly interesting to Anna, but the Count seemed to want to show it to her.

"What's so special about this pile of old wood?" she asked.

"It's not the wood that's special," replied the Count, "it's what's underneath it."

He moved the panels to one side, revealing a trapdoor in the floor. Locating the lock, he inserted an ancient-looking key. He turned it, grasped the old iron ring and pulled the trapdoor open. Holding it steady, he waved his free hand towards the opening in the floor.

"After you."

Anna stepped across and started to climb down the metal rungs that had been hammered into the rock more than two centuries earlier.

"Hang on." said the Count, rummaging in his pocket with his free hand. He pulled out a small LED torch and handed it to Anna. She switched it on and pointed it downwards.

"Whoa! That's a fair drop!" she exclaimed.

"About forty feet." confirmed the Count.

Anna started climbing again and the Count followed her, lowering the trap-door back into place as he went. Once he was beside Anna at the bottom, he took the torch and led the way. The tunnel floor was rough in places and although it would've been manageable in ordinary shoes, it was easy and comfortable going with hiking boots on. *He's so thoughtful.* The passage was initially straight, but after about fifty yards it veered gently to the left. Anna became aware of a faint sound that seemed to increase by a tiny amount with every step. As they rounded the long curve Anna could see what looked like a small patch of daylight coming in from the right-hand side.

"What's that?" she asked.

"Something that only a few people have ever seen. Something almost as beautiful as you."

"Charmer." murmured Anna.

As they neared the opening in the tunnel wall, the sound became loud and recognisable – water. Specifically, water falling from a great height. The Count waited by the opening to let Anna go first. She stepped through the gap onto a small ledge. At her feet, about ten feet below, was a round pool of crystal ice-blue water, about twelve feet in diameter. Rising up from the pool was a vast sunlit shaft of a similar width, worn out of the sandy-coloured rock by the cascade of water that surged over the top edge a hundred feet above and falling, falling, falling, like a thick heavy powder, before disappearing into the mist on the far side and crashing into the pool with the force of a jackhammer. After a few seconds transfixed in wonder, she breathed in sharply, realising that she had been so stunned that she had stopped breathing. It was, literally, breath-taking. She felt the Count move in next to her and slide his arm around her waist.

"Do you like it?" he whispered softly in her ear.

"It's magnificent." she whispered back without taking her eyes off the scene. The Count felt the delight well up in him; he had so wanted her to love it. She took it all in again, from top to bottom.

"And you think I'm more beautiful than this?" she probed.

"I think you're the most beautiful thing I've ever seen." he answered.

She turned towards him and their eyes locked. The Count held out his hand, palm up as he had done the first time they had met, when he was posing as the psychologist; but this time he raised her hand to his lips and he kissed it softly. Anna moved closer to him and their lips met.

The Count felt his conscience pricked. He knew Anna did not share his faith, but he had never met anyone like her and, despite having his close family and small circle of friends, he felt incomplete. Even in the Bible, the second thing God said after giving Adam life was, *It is not good for the man to be alone.* But he was – alone. Amidst all the wealth, excitement and adventure of the life that had been given to him, he was desperate to share it with someone. Someone special.

They held hands as they gazed at the waterfall that continued to thunder on and the fine mist that started to dampen their clothes and skin. Anna felt like she was swirling in the pool, while the Count felt like he was among the millions of shining droplets of water falling from the top of the shaft, lost in light and space. They turned towards each other again and the Count whispered softly.

"I …."

Anna kissed him. "Me too."

A wave of relief came over them both as their feelings had finally come out. There were now no 'if's or 'maybe's, no guessing and no doubting. It just felt so good and so right. They looked at each other and laughed, a joyous, happy laugh that came from amazement at what had just taken place and delight that it had done.

Becoming aware of their surroundings once more, they turned again to view the spectacular cascade.

"Where does the water go?" asked Anna, looking down at the pool. "I can't see an outlet."

"That's because it disappears back into the rock directly under the ledge we're standing on."

He knelt down and leaned over the edge. Anna knelt beside him and followed the direction of his finger.

"Lean out a little further."

"I'll tip over if I do."

The Count moved behind her and held her ankles down.

"You'd better not let go!" she warned.

"I won't."

She leaned forward a few more inches, holding herself by tightening her hamstring muscles at the back of her thighs. The Count couldn't help but gaze at her, elegant and beautiful from any angle.

"I can see it!" cried Anna. She pulled herself back up. "It's amazing!"

"It is, isn't it." The Count agreed. He looked at his watch. "We'd better head back."

"Yes – but can we come back here sometime – soon?" pleaded Anna.

"I'd like that very much."

He switched on the torch, took her hand and led her back into the tunnel. They talked as they strolled along, hand in hand.

"I'm amazed that no one has discovered the waterfall from the outside and made it into a tourist attraction." said Anna.

"The whole thing, top to bottom, is on our estate," replied the Count, "so no one comes here. The top of the shaft is pretty hard to get to – you need climbing gear to access it." He interrupted himself. "Would you like to go up there with me sometime?"

"Sure. You know I love climbing, although it's mainly indoor walls and bouldering."

"Yes, I know," said the Count, "it's …"

"IN YOUR FILE! Anna chimed in with him. They pulled towards each other, bumping shoulders and laughing as only lovers do.

"Exactly. And as you saw, there's no way into the shaft from below."

There was a moment's pause as Anna's vulnerable, jealous side took over.

"Did you bring her here?"

"Who?"

"Boot girl." said Anna, pointing to her feet.

"Oh goodness, no!" chuckled the Count. "She wouldn't have got down the ladder in her Dior dress and high heels!"

"So I'm a plain-Jane, am I? Another of your 'drably-dressed friends'!"

The Count looked mortified. "Of course not!"

"You've never seen me in evening dress and heels!"

The Count stopped and pulled her round to face him. "Oh yes, I have!" he said mischievously. "I've pictured you in a cocktail dress and heels, in a ball gown, in a bikini …"

"What?!" shouted Anna, giving him an affectionate slap before collapsing into giggles.

"Anyway," declared the Count triumphantly, "I'll see you in an evening dress on Thursday."

"What do you mean?" challenged Anna, "I can't risk being recognised!"

"Do you think I'm going to miss out on the chance to be seen with the most beautiful girl in France?"

Anna pouted. "Just France?"

"The most beautiful woman in the world." the Count corrected himself. "And, just for the record … about boot girl – we never got anywhere near being that close. I've only ever brought one other girl to see the cascade."

"And who was that?" said Anna with a touch of suspicion.

"My sister, of course!"

They had reached the château end of the tunnel, with its metal rungs. The Count gave Anna the torch and climbed up first. He pushed up the heavy trap-door, hauled himself out and held the trap-door open while Anna came up. He then let it down and locked it, then together they covered it over again with the wooden panels and headed back through the cellars. Anna looked at the doors along the way.

"Are there any more tunnels?"

"Tunnels, passages, hidden rooms … this château has been used for clandestine activity since it was built."

"And when did your family acquire it?"

"Acquire it?" said the Count, surprised. "My family built it."

Of course they did, thought Anna, *this spying stuff is in your blood.* They climbed the stone steps up to the ground floor north corridor.

"So, did you enjoy our little stroll?" asked the Count.

"Which part?" said Anna mischievously.

"All of it." smiled the Count matching her tone.

Anna stopped and kissed him again.

"It was wonderful. *All of it.*"

* * *

By lunchtime Francine had arranged the menu, the orchestra, fifteen special guests ("I'll do the regulars in the afternoon") and the flowers. She really was a whirlwind when it came to matters of society. Even the Count was impressed with her progress when he and Anna returned from their walk.

"Excellent, Francine – you're amazing." lauded the Count.

"And you're wet, Édouard. Where have you been?"

She noticed Anna let go of the Count's hand and observed that she was also wet.

"Oh." she said with a knowing look, and put her head down pretending to review her list. The two love-birds took the hint and slipped off to get changed before lunch.

CHAPTER 17

INSIDE INFORMATION

The interior branch of the French Secret Service, the DGSI, were used to better results than this. They had trawled through the various potential sightings of Camille, or Anna – or both, speaking on the phone and, where the caller was not obviously a time-waster, travelling the length and breadth of the Paris region, also known as the *Île-de-France*. They had even investigated potential sightings as far away as Bordeaux in the south-west of the country and Verdun in the north-east, sometimes using local law enforcement resources as a proxy, but on two specific occasions they had flown agents out to the region on special charters to interview the people in person. All to no avail.

There had been no ransom notes – nothing … except a cryptic message that had been emailed directly to a specific DGSI agent, from an untraceable source. It simply said:

COUNT YOUR BLESSINGS CAMILLE IS SAFE.

The agent quickly deleted it so no one could catch sight of it. It was good news – sort of. The minister's daughter was safe and in good hands, but what was he to do with the information? If the Count had wanted to tell the DGSI – or even Madame Dupuy – officially, he would have done so, he was not a stranger to the French Secret Service, that was how Vincent had come to meet him. The Count had pulled off a daring mission, of which he, Vincent Sadoul, had happened to be a part of and subsequently the Count had seconded him as an occasional covert assistant. No, something was amiss; the Count was putting him on alert.

* * *

A while later Vincent's email client pinged again. He leant forward, shielding the screen.

COUNT YOURSELF INVITED – JOIN THE TEAM
EVEN THOUGH IT'S A CLIQUE.

He scratched his head, wondering what the coded message could mean. As before, he took the precaution to delete the email from his Inbox, but he knew he hadn't grasped the meaning of the message at all.

Keeping the message in the front of his mind he tried to break it down into parts. It was obviously a message from the Count, that bit was straightforward. He thought about the next couple of words – the Count seemed to be asking him to get involved somehow. *Okay,* he thought, *now, JOIN THE TEAM – what team? – the Count's team, maybe?* But that seemed to overlap with the invitation to get involved, and the Count was always super-concise, not wasting words in these emails. He'd come back to that one. Then the last bit … *EVEN THOUGH IT'S A CLIQUE. Something to do with an exclusive club, an elite group, a closed circle of people …?* He was clutching at straws. Suddenly he had an idea. He accessed his Deleted Items folder and viewed the message again. Positioning the mouse pointer over the word CLIQUE … he clicked.

The screen went blank, then in rapid succession two things appeared one above the other. They displayed for five seconds, then the email deleted itself and the screen went back to normal, showing his recently-deleted emails – except for the two from the Count, the other one having self-destructed on a one-minute timer.

The two things that had popped up were: a picture of

Madeleine Dupuy and the name of a victims' shelter followed by the word THURSDAY.

He pulled out his personal phone and quickly did a search on the victims' shelter, then clicked on the ***Latest News*** option. The top story was: **Representative from the Ministre de l'Intérieure to visit the shelter**. He read on to find out when the visit was to take place, although he could've made a pretty good guess. Sure enough – it was on Thursday.

Putting all the pieces together from the two messages Vincent surmised the following:

- Camille Dupuy was safe – probably with the Count.
- Something was going on in the DGSI and he should trust no one.
- Madeleine Dupuy, whose daughter had already been abducted, was in danger.
- The Count wanted him to join the DGSI team escorting the Secrétaire d'État to the shelter.

That last one might be tricky, but he knew it was serious and the Count was depending on him.

He wandered down to the admin hub area, where he knew he would find the people with as much knowledge of what was going on as the Director herself, and spotted Alice, one of the admin team.

"Hi, Alice!" he called cheerfully. "How are you doing?"

"Fine, thanks. And you?"

"Not bad." He pulled a face. "A bit bored at the moment. Too much time behind a desk for me. I could do with a bit of a change, really."

"You should have a word with Aurélie, see if she can find something for you."

"Thanks, I might just do that. So, what's going on this week?" he asked casually.

"The usual: counter-terrorism, a drugs raid in Marseille – the search for the missing girl, obviously."

"Bad business, that." said Vincent shaking his head.

"Who's leading the search?"

"Eric Mazet."

"Doesn't look like he's having much joy with it."

"Bit of a nightmare, if you ask me. It's not Eric's fault, but there's a lot of pressure being put on him."

"By Madame Dupuy?"

"Primarily, yes, but it's got all the ministers spooked; frightened for their own families."

"Can't blame her, though." Vincent sympathised. "I mean, it's her *daughter*."

"Yeah. Must be terrible for her."

"And who's looking after *her* – Madame Dupuy, I mean?"

"Eric's got that as well. They wanted it all to be coordinated from the same place."

"Wow! Poor man!"

"Absolutely." agreed Alice. The conversation lulled.

"Hey, it's been great chatting to you, Alice."

"You too. Hope you get some excitement before too long."

"So do I. See you soon."

"Yeah, bye."

Vincent headed off to find his man. Eric welcomed the offer of an extra pair of hands and a call from his boss to Vincent's supervisor would seal the deal. Ten minutes later he was on the team.

* * *

While Francine was busy with the social side of the Grand Reception, the Count was planning the other side of it: how and when to let Madeleine Dupuy know Camille was safe, whether to try to give them some time together and how that might be done securely, how to identify the bad eggs in the basket, and how to deal with them – all without the other guests having the slightest idea of what was really going on.

Various options were discussed, and every now and then the Count would pop in to where Francine was energetically working away, to consult and confirm – who would be sitting where, what time would the speeches be, and the dancing, what about some fireworks in the grounds … ?

By the end of the day they had a reasonable outline plan and with almost three full days to go, things were looking good. The Count's biggest concern was that they might peak too early and lose focus. Once the children were tucked up in bed and asleep, the group reassembled.

"We need to be absolutely on the ball with this." he insisted. "There's little enough room for error even if things go the way we expect them to, but there are still too many unknowns."

"It would be good if we could decrease the unknowns, sir. Is there anything I can do?" asked Butler.

"Not right now, thanks, but I'm hoping for some inside information from a friend – perhaps tomorrow, Wednesday at the latest. There'll be plenty to do then."

Butler nodded. "Very good, sir."

"I don't mean to be difficult, but we're going to be dealing with people who are armed, potentially heavily. There are a few things in the kitchen I could make good use of, but wouldn't it be a good idea to have some weapons?"

"But we do have weapons!" declared the Count. "All around us!"

Anna glanced round the room and then stared at him as if he had gone mad.

"What on earth are you talking about?"

"The château, the grounds, each other – our wits and imagination!" he cried enthusiastically.

"I was thinking more along the lines of, you know … guns, knives, grenades – *rocket launchers!*" said Anna.

"Have we needed a gun so far?" challenged the Count.

"No, but …"

"But what?"

"They're not gentlemen like you, Edward – they'll have

guns and they won't hesitate to use them!"

"She has a point." agreed Max. Francine glared at him.

"If Édouard says we don't need them, then we don't need them." she said firmly, folding her arms and sitting back in her chair as if to close the matter. There was a moment's awkward silence before the Count resumed.

"It's not that guns are forbidden," he clarified, "in fact, Anna, we have a few. It's just that they are a last resort to be used only in the most extreme circumstances where life is threatened – and the same goes for knives and any other lethal weapons. Our plan will not be founded on the intent to kill."

The quiet authority in his voice couldn't have been more impactful if he had thundered it at top volume. No one, not even Anna, questioned it, or dared in their heart to doubt him.

* * *

It was getting late and folks were saying their goodnights and heading up to bed. The Count and Anna walked up the grand staircase together. At the mezzanine landing two smaller sets of stairs went up, one to the left and one to the right, leading to opposite sides of the gallery that went all the way round in a square. A corridor led off from each side. The Count's bedroom was in the north wing, up the right-hand set of stairs. His was the first bedroom on the west side, which was the left-hand side of the corridor. Butler was in the room opposite as usual. There were three more guest bedrooms on each side of the corridor, making a total of four on each side. The first two on the west side, which overlooked the lake, had been designed for higher ranking members of the family and special guests. They were very grand and had a dressing room, en-suite bathroom, and balcony. The other two each had a sink, but shared a guest bathroom located between them. The rooms on the opposite side of the corridor, where Butler was, were a mirror image, but slightly smaller, with a view up the mountain, and no balcony. The south wing, on the opposite side of the gallery, was very similar in layout, but had the nursery and children's bedrooms instead of four smaller guest rooms. At the end of each wing there were doors on either side of the corridor that gave access to the towers holding the old stone stairways that led from the cellars and dungeons, up past the basement to the first floor bedrooms, the second floor staff quarters, with various storage and other rooms, to the old guard rooms and the turrets.

Anna's room was in the south wing, next to Camille's room, so when she and the Count reached the mezzanine level, they kissed and parted, the Count going up the stairs to the right and Anna to the left. At the top of the stairs Anna turned and looked across the gallery, and was delighted to see the Count had done the same. He blew her a kiss and went to his room. Anna had thought about pretending to catch the kiss, but it seemed a bit too cheesy and girlish. In the end she had just smiled, but it meant the world to the Count.

CHAPTER 18

CROQUET ON THE LAWN

The Count slept well. He dreamed that he was out on the lake with Anna, the sun shining on her tanned body, her long hair worn up but slightly blown by the breeze that sent the yacht shooting over the glistening water. When he woke, he couldn't wait to see her again. He shaved, showered and dressed, then sprinted down to the dining hall.

Anna looked stunning in the chic clothes that Francine had bought for her. She'd given Francine her sizes and had expected a reasonable fit, but the choice of colours and styles were inspired. The Count came and sat beside her at the large dining table where breakfast was being served.

"You look lovely." he said, kissing her on the cheek. Camille giggled and Jean-Luc rolled his eyes. The Count looked over and smiled broadly at them.

"What are you two scoundrels up to today?"

Camille looked at Jean-Luc, who immediately took the lead.

"We're going with Butler to the potting shed."

"What's a potting shed?" asked Camille.

"It's where we plant seeds, and move them to pots – or from small pots to bigger pots, when they grow bigger." he explained, making sure that he didn't mislead the protégé that he had taken under his wing. "Haven't your parents taught you *anything?*"

"Jean-Luc!" chided Francine sternly.

"Sorry, *Maman*."

Anna intervened and spoke gently to the boy.

"Camille has not had the chance to spend much time with her family like you have. Her father died a couple of years ago, and her mother has a very important job that demands a lot of her time."

Jean-Luc turned to Camille with genuine remorse.

"I'm sorry, Camille. I didn't mean to be nasty."

Camille nodded, but remained silent, staring at her plate.

"Now," declared the Count jovially, "I fancy a game of croquet after breakfast. Who wants to challenge me?"

There were no takers. Max put down the morning paper, excused himself and went off to work and Francine announced that she had too much to do for the Grand Reception.

"I haven't even finalised the dances yet, let alone arranged the fireworks!" she declared.

Jean-Luc was still fuelling up for the day, so Camille picked up the paper and pretended to be devouring its contents, despite the fact that it was almost as big as she was. The Count went over to her and folded it up, so she could hold it more easily. She posed with a serious face, like a grown-up who was shocked at the events being reported. The Count chuckled, whipped out his phone and took a picture of her.

"Hilarious!" he cried. Camille giggled, turned the paper round and pulled a frowny face as if reading even worse news. Jean-Luc was laughing while trying to keep his mouth closed, so that the food wouldn't come spilling out. He was unsuccessful.

"You're … sho … funny … Chamille!" he spluttered, spraying bits of toast onto his plate and the tablecloth.

Butler turned to the Count.

"Sorry, sir. I'm afraid you'll have to excuse me from the croquet." He nodded towards the children. "I've got to supervise activities in the potting shed. Now, are you two ready?"

"What about cleaning our teeth?" exclaimed Jean-Luc, swallowing the last bit of toast.

"Good point, Jean-Luc. Camille, you and Jean-Luc go and clean your teeth, then meet me by the side gate."

The three of them exited the room – and by default, the croquet competition. That left Anna. She looked at him sideways, not sure whether to congratulate him or take pity on him.

"Was that just a ruse to deflect the tension, or did you really want to play croquet?"

The Count sensed her likely reluctance to play and looked a little deflated.

"Both."

Anna leaned in and stroked his cheek.

"Go on, then. I'll challenge you!"

The Count's face lit up and he gave her a kiss.

"You're a good egg. Now, what was it you were saying about weapons last night?" But before she could reply he added, "You can have first choice of mallet!"

"Can I let my breakfast settle first?"

"Of course. I've got a few things to sort out anyway."

He squeezed her hand, went back to his room and sent messages to an associate in Paris, his contact in the DGSI and to a friend in England, then spent a few minutes in quiet reflection, thanking God for all that he had been blessed with, and asking for help for the day. After a while he received a reply from his English friend – good, all was well.

He came downstairs and found Albert, who was busily supervising the staff in their preparations for the Grand Reception.

"Sorry to bother you, Albert, in the middle of all this, but would you mind digging out the croquet set and putting the hoops in for me?"

"Of course, *Monsieur le Comte*."

The Count even now couldn't quite get used to Albert

calling him by his title. Albert had been there in the château long before the Count was born, and from the Count's childhood through to the day his father had died, Albert had always called him "*Monsieur Édouard.*" From the moment the news had reached the château he had become "Monsieur le Comte". It was true that such titles generally had no legal status as such, that side had been abolished in 1789; however, hereditary titles had later been restored, albeit merely as symbolic marks of honour.

"Thank you, Albert."

He found Francine beavering away, surrounded by sheets of paper, with her laptop and phone amidst them all.

"How's it going?"

"Just *dreadful*, Édouard. I've still got a horrendous problem with the guest list!"

"I thought you'd already got lots of people confirmed."

"I have."

"Then what's the problem?"

"The problem is, Édouard," said Francine as if explaining to a child, "*there is an odd number of people!*"

"Oh dear," mocked the Count, "that would never do!" He paused. "But I think I may have solved it for you."

"Really?"

"Yes. An old friend from England is coming over and I thought it might be nice for him to visit us."

"Will he …?"

"Fit in?" ventured the Count.

"Well, yes."

"How very snobbish – but quite correct of you in the circumstances!" laughed the Count. "Oh yes, he'll fit in perfectly."

"Wonderful!" beamed Francine. "Who is it?"

To enhance the suspense the Count leaned over for dramatic effect and whispered in her ear. Her face lit up with delight.

"What a lovely surprise! When is he arriving?"

"On Thursday. I'm not sure what time yet, but well

before the Reception is due to start."

"Good. Now, where should I put him?"

"I was thinking we'd just put him in the room next to Butler's."

"Oh Édouard! For a genius you're so dull! I mean, where he should sit at the Reception!"

"I know, little sister," replied the Count with a wicked twinkle in his eye. He looked at the draft seating plan. "I think he should sit here." The Count pointed to the plan.

Francine thought for a few seconds. "Very well. I'll have to move a few people around to accommodate him, but I'm sure you've got your reasons."

"I have." confirmed the Count. He kissed her on the top of her head. "Thanks, Francine. I really appreciate all this."

"You're welcome. And anyway – I owe you for sorting my problem out – you've saved my life!"

"More than once." replied the Count with a wink. His sister laughed.

"Well, now that you've done it again, you can buzz off and let me get on with my planning."

The Count bowed with fake submission. "At your service, Madame."

* * *

"Is it always so sunny here?" asked Anna, shading her eyes as they strolled over to the lawn, where Albert was busy positioning the hoops and peg.

"Is that a genuine question, or are you just airing your excuses up front in case I thrash you?" teased the Count. Anna punched him on the arm.

"A genuine question."

"Not always. In fact we're due a little rain tomorrow, but I can't complain, the weather's pretty good overall – not bone dry like the far south, but then, I wouldn't want it to be. I love the green hills; they're so much better than the rocky scrub of some of the highly-fashionable parts of the Mediterranean coast."

"Although I bet you have a place there." countered Anna.

"Of course!" grinned the Count. "Which member of the French nobility doesn't?!"

"Oh, so you just have it to keep up appearances."

"It's part of my cover, darling."

"But you never go there." she teased.

"Oh well, I have to *drag* myself there a few times a year," the Count batted back, feigning hardship, "otherwise it would look very suspicious!"

Albert stepped politely towards them with a selection of croquet mallets.

"I've set up the court, *Monsieur*, and left the balls there for you, but I thought you might like to choose your mallets."

"Excellent, Albert – thank you." said the Count. "Anna?"

Anna had expected them all to be pretty much the same, but she was surprised. In addition to different shaft lengths, there were different sizes and weights of head. Albert rested the mallets on the ground while Anna deliberated. She tried a couple, swinging at imaginary balls, then settled on one.

"Good choice," nodded the Count, "I think that will suit you nicely."

He took a slightly heavier mallet from Albert's hand without hesitating.

"Thank you, Albert."

The *majordome* bowed slightly and returned to his duties in the house.

Anna looked at the lawn, now converted to a croquet court, and expressed surprise at how far apart the hoops were.

"It's not full regulation dimensions – that would be 35 by 28 yards – but it's a decent size court." the Count observed modestly. He took her through the basic rules and let her try a few practice shots.

"Ready to start?" he asked. "Just for fun, of course."

"Okay – who goes first?"

"Usually we toss a coin or a mallet …"

"A mallet?! Isn't that dangerous?"

The Count laughed. "That depends on how you toss it." He reached into his pocket and drew out a coin. "Let's do a coin toss instead. Heads or tails?"

"Heads." replied Anna decisively.

"Very good." The Count tossed the coin, caught it deftly in his right hand and slapped it down on the back of his left hand. He showed it to Anna. "Heads it is. You go first."

Although Anna had only played croquet a few times – and that had been on holidays as a child and teenager – she was naturally adept and well-coordinated. She had been on the school team for various sports and had captained a couple of them. The Count, on the other hand, seemed quite inconsistent despite obviously having had much more practice over many more years. He would play an exceptional shot, then fluff a couple, then recover, and so on. The match progressed quite evenly between the two and the peg out was going to be close.

The Count's ball was ahead, just a couple of feet short of the final hoop, but slightly to one side, the angle making the shot awkward, as the hoops were only a fraction of an inch wider than the balls. Anna's ball was slightly further back, but nice and straight on to the hoop. She addressed the ball and practised swinging her mallet, then with competitiveness etched on her face, she struck. The ball went cleanly through the hoop and stopped just two yards short of the peg. The Count seemed to have one of his inconsistent moments and, falling foul of the reduced opening due to the angle, got the ball stuck in the middle of the hoop. Anna pegged out and threw her arms up into the air in victory.

"Well done!" the Count congratulated her. She strolled playfully back towards him, a teasing look of superiority on her face.

"So, you were going to thrash me, were you?"

The Count merely chuckled and gave her a kiss.

"I'm thirsty," she announced, turning and walking back towards the terrace, "shall we go for a drink?"

"Certainly." replied the Count, addressing his ball and casually knocking it the full seven yards to the peg, striking it dead centre – as he was perfectly capable of doing, whenever he wanted to.

* * *

Anna was still revelling in her victory over the Count when Francine came in for a short break from the stress and excitement of arranging the Grand Reception.

"It all came down literally to the last shot. It could have gone either way, but I won!" she crowed. Francine looked over doubtfully at the Count.

"It all came down to the last shot, did it?" she commented wryly. "How *exciting!*"

The Count nodded in agreement.

"It couldn't have been closer if I'd planned it."

Francine rolled her eyes and Anna started to suspect that perhaps the Count wasn't really as inconsistent a player as she'd thought. She peered at him with suspicion and then they both burst out laughing.

"You … you … !" she exclaimed, deciding not to say the word that she'd had in mind and throwing a cushion at him instead.

"Careful!" yelled the Count, catching it dexterously, "that came from Versailles!"

He checked something on his phone, then stood up.

"Please excuse me, ladies. I have a little job to do before lunch."

CHAPTER 19

RANSOM

Étienne Dumas, web developer and expert hacker, received the Count's message with excitement, and even more so when he saw that there were two tasks for him. One was more straightforward than the other, but he was confident he could manage them both. Deadline? Twelve noon, today. Not much time, but for the Count he would ditch all other duties and make it happen.

He printed off the photos and information relating to Arturo and his team that the Count had sent him, tucked it all into an envelope, and set about composing a convincing ransom request and online post to go with it. It had helped that the Count had sent him a photo of Camille holding today's paper.

Within an hour, he was ready.

First, he sent a coded message to Vincent Sadoul at the DGSI, then he posted the image of Camille online, bang on twelve noon, using an account that, if anyone was good enough to trace it, led back to an address in a block of flats, somewhere in the Dordogne, that had been demolished two weeks previously. Finally, he took the folder he had packed, put on a grey baseball cap and set off for a café in the next district.

*   *   *

Vincent Sadoul recognised the code immediately. The café it told him to go to was in a different area of the city, but he could get there easily on the Paris Metro. He waited until lunchtime, then made his way to the appointed place, taking precautions to make sure he hadn't been followed. He had timed it well, but still had a couple of minutes to kill, so he stepped into the shop next door to the café and casually browsed a few books. On the dot of 12:45 he was about to enter the café when he was almost struck by the door as it was opened from the inside by a man in a grey baseball cap, who was looking down at his phone as he pushed through.

"Sorry!" he said, stepping aside to the allow the man to pass. There was no acknowledgement, let alone a reciprocal apology. *Parisians!* he thought to himself, *as rude as they come.* He went in and ordered a coffee, then sidled over to the table in the corner, as indicated in the message he had received, and sat down with his back to the wall. He put his bag down and rifled through it, as if looking for a particular item or document, all the while detaching the envelope that had been taped to the underside of the table-top. He pretended to pull it out of his bag and examined the contents. After he had finished his coffee, he put the package into his bag and left. Picking up a sandwich on the way, he took a circuitous route back to base, even more on the lookout than before, if that were possible, because now he knew who he was looking out for.

* * *

The Count rehearsed his short speech, activated a voice distortion app on his phone then made an untraceable call to the office of Madeleine Dupuy at the Ministre de l'Intérieure.

Emmanuelle Carnot answered the phone with her usual efficiency, politeness and sweet tone. The caller, however, was efficient, but far from polite and the voice was clearly being distorted.

"We have Camille. The ransom is five million euros."

"Who is this?"

"Search online for Cam5M..." a short but complex

string of letters and numbers followed.

Emmanuelle searched – and gasped when the page appeared.

"I will be in contact again with further instructions in one hour."

The Count hung up.

Emmanuelle ran to her minister's door and, without bothering to knock, burst in. Madeleine Dupuy looked up, startled and slightly outraged at the intrusion, then saw the look on Emmanuelle's face.

"Madame," panted the secretary, "it's Camille … she's being held for ransom – they want five million!"

Madeleine took a moment to get over the shock, then calmed herself.

"*Who* has Camille?" she demanded.

"I don't know – they didn't say."

"And how do you know it's genuine?"

Emmanuelle pointed through the doorway to the screen on her desk. Even at that distance, Madeleine could recognise her own daughter.

"Call Eric Mazet. Get him here at once!" she ordered.

"Yes, Madame." stuttered Emmanuelle and ran to the phone.

* * *

The DGSI were unable to retrospectively trace the call from the data available to them, but they would be ready for a live trace on the next one. As soon as it came, recording began and the trace was started.

"Listen carefully," said the same distorted voice," I will not repeat myself."

"Wait," stalled Emmanuelle, "I need to get Madame Dupuy."

"Don't stall, Mademoiselle Carnot, I know she is already there."

Eric signalled to her to keep trying.

"I'm sorry … I …"

"Silence!" commanded the voice. "Five million euros,

Madame Dupuy. Tomorrow night. 8pm. Your hotel. No police. No tricks."

"What hotel?" cut in Madeleine, trying to prolong the conversation.

The caller hung up.

Eric looked over in vain at the agent doing the trace. The agent shook her head.

"What happens now?" demanded Madeleine.

"It's an interesting move, Madame. They know, as we do, that the state does not negotiate with kidnappers, so why demand a ransom?"

"Perhaps they think the government will make an exception for a minister's daughter?"

"But that would simply make all ministers' children targets. No, they will not sanction it."

"Then Camille is to be sacrificed to prove the state's resolve?"

Eric leaned back in his chair. "There is another option, Madame."

"Which is …?"

"We pretend that the state *has* sanctioned it."

"They'll never fall for that!"

"Then do you know someone with five million euros to spare?"

"Don't be ridiculous! Who has five million euros to spare?" snorted Madeleine.

It was Emmanuelle Carnot who broke the silence.

"Actually, Madame, there is *someone* …"

* * *

The Count pretended to be surprised to receive the request from Madame Dupuy. He expressed his deepest concern and sympathy, and having no children of his own could only imagine her pain, but he questioned the ethics and wisdom of paying the ransom.

Eric and Emmanuelle looked on as Madeleine pleaded, begged for help. The Count fell silent for a moment, then with a deep sigh agreed to fund the exchange. Everyone in the room with Madeleine shared silent signals of delight and relief, but Madeleine herself looked worn-out.

The Count had lots of questions. Madeleine passed the phone over to Eric.

"So the exchange will be made tomorrow night." he said, repeating the information Eric had given him, as if to get it straight in his head.

"So, when and in what form do you need the money? ... Yes, I see ... and where will we ... ? ... Aha, yes ... mmm ... Very well."

The call was ended with repeated thanks from one end and good wishes and encouragement from the other, and the Count went back downstairs to update Anna and Butler. The latter was particularly excited.

"Things are hotting up now, sir!"

Anna was less casual about it all. She had been surprised when the Count had told them about the five million-euro ransom demand, but understood straightaway that it was a ruse to flush out the enemy before they got to the château. She knew that the Count would not be rash with the life of a young girl at stake. On the contrary, the ploy was designed to remove, or at least reduce, the risk to Camille.

With half the afternoon still remaining, the Count took his leave and headed into town on what he referred to as "a special mission of vital importance". And to the Count it was. He had to buy the most beautiful dress and shoes he could find for the woman he had fallen in love with. When he returned he went straight up to his room to hide his purchases, some of which he would need the next day and some that were to remain hidden until the evening of the Reception.

Butler also went shopping, but with a very different, rather more practical list. And then he went to see a man about a boat.

* * *

The DGSI had already finalised the route for the six-hour drive, with planned rest and meal stops, and booked the two nights overnight accommodation for Madame Dupuy and Eric Mazet's team at the Imperial Hotel. Some of them had originally been feeling like this would be more of a much-needed luxury holiday than a job, but the ransom demand had changed everything. Every effort was now going into planning extra security, potential placement of guards, snipers and "grab" agents to swoop in, recover the girl and arrest the perpetrators. The existing team of five agents was going to be augmented by two more – one male and one female – from the station in Dijon, which was just over half-way to their destination, who would join them en route the following afternoon.

Vincent had passed this information, along with Eric Mazet's mobile number, on to the Count, who was making plans of his own. At times Anna felt a bit left out of the process, but she followed Butler's lead, giving advice and opinions when the Count asked for them, and letting him get on with it otherwise.

Everyone at the Paris end was waiting for the next call: Eric Mazet and his team, Madeleine with her secretary, but after two hours there had been no more details from the kidnappers.

"I suspect that they are deliberately keeping us in suspense," said Eric eventually, "with a view to raising our stress levels in order to undermine our performance, and to give us as little time as possible to plan and prepare."

And he was right.

CHAPTER 20

GRIST TO THE MILL

The next day Butler was very busy, starting early by going up to the north end of the lake in a small, underpowered, bright red boat, and then jogging along the shore path back to the château in time for breakfast. That was only one of the many things that the Count had given him to do that day and he had no time to help the children with potting shed activities or fishing in one of the two small lakes on the estate, so the Count suggested to Jean-Luc and Camille that he and Anna made a movie with them.

"I'll be the director." announced Jean-Luc.

"And I'll be the star!" Camille chimed in.

"Wonderful!" said the Count joyfully. "Do you think there might be a part for Anna – as a supporting actress, of course? If that's okay with the director and the star?"

"Certainly." agreed Jean-Luc.

"Yaay!" squealed Camille.

They spent a happy couple of hours, running round the château, acting out scenes, with "Princess Camille" playing the damsel in distress with just as much drama as any Hollywood starlet, whether pretending to be locked up in one of the turrets or stealthily making her escape. Anna played the part of the wicked Queen who had cast a spell on the King so he wouldn't come to save the princess. Jean-Luc, taking his role as director very seriously, wanted to stay behind the camera, so Camille had to make her own escape, rather than being saved by a charming prince. The

Count helped Jean-Luc with the basic storyline, ideas for shots, etc. and lined up the music for the big finale when Camille, now free again, danced on the terrace in the sunshine.

When shooting was finally finished, the Count went up to his room to put it all together into the four-minute cinematic masterpiece that they would watch together after lunch.

* * *

"Don't rush your meal, Jean-Luc." chided Francine.

"Shorry, *Maman*, he replied, mouth full of food, "Jush want to shee the movie we made."

Both children ate hastily, which meant that Anna and the Count had to eat quickly too, but with every effort to be dignified.

The children were very excited as Anna sat them down in the drawing room in front of the large screen. Somehow the Count had found time to add some dramatic music behind the rather sparse dialogue, which really added to the experience. Jean-Luc nodded in approval here and there, and occasionally commented on things they could have done better.

"Sshh!" said Camille, without taking her eyes off the screen. She was utterly enthralled at seeing herself there, acting out her childish fantasies – *in a real château!!* she thought dreamily.

When it was over, the children wanted to see it again, so the Count graciously obliged with a chuckle, but he said they couldn't keep watching it all afternoon and would have to wait until tomorrow when he would show it to them again. They left with groans of disappointment, but very soon they were having new adventures outside in the fresh air, where Jean-Luc had remembered a den he'd made in the woods that he wanted to show Camille.

When they were alone at last Anna cuddled up to the Count.

"They're a handful, aren't they?" he said affectionately.

"You were very good with them."

"So were you!" Anna reciprocated.

"We're a good team."

"Yes, we are – speaking of which … is there anything else I need to do tonight?"

The Count pondered briefly before replying.

"Don't you think you're doing enough already?"

"Taking the launch out to the rendezvous point and getting away cleanly?"

"Yes. That's pretty key, wouldn't you say?"

"I suppose so."

"We've all got our roles – you, me, Butler."

"He's great, isn't he. Where did you find him?"

"Oh now that's a very interesting story," nodded the Count, "but one that I don't have time to tell you right now. I need to speak to the bank and get a few other bits ready for tonight."

"And tomorrow night?"

"Well, we can only finish preparing for that when we see what comes out of the woodwork tonight."

"You will be careful, won't you, darling?" pressed Anna.

The Count gave her a long, loving kiss.

"I promise." he whispered, then he stood up briskly and bowed theatrically. "Back in an hour or two." And off he went, whistling as if he hadn't got a care in the world.

Anna pursed her lips to temper the smile that she felt rising. He wasn't exactly maddening as such, but at times he certainly played around the edges of it.

* * *

Butler returned mid-afternoon and reported in to the Count.

"Everything's ready, sir. She's a bit weathered, but she'll do the job."

"And you've changed the name and registration code, of course."

"Yes, sir."

"And what name did you decide on?"

Butler smiled. "I've called her the *Mirage*."

"I like it." chuckled the Count. "And the little one?"

"She's ready too."

"Excellent – thanks."

Butler nodded in appreciation and they went to join the others.

The conversation was lively – the children chattering excitedly about the movie they had made that morning and reporting on the adventures they had been having in the den, and Francine giving an update on preparations for the Grand Reception.

"I thought we'd have the speeches *after* dessert, to allow time for digestion before the dancing starts, then have a short interlude for the fireworks – people can come out onto the terrace to watch. Albert's been working with the pyro-technicians to make sure we don't damage any of the plants and trees, or set fire to the château or any of the outbuildings."

"Just how big is this display going to be?" asked the Count.

"Oh, just a small thing – no more than five or six hundred fireworks."

"Six hundred fireworks!" exclaimed Camille, almost jumping out of her seat.

Jean-Luc turned to her and said in a matter of fact manner, "We had a thousand on *Maman's* birthday." There was no trace of pride or boasting; it was typical Jean-Luc, simply stating the facts.

"A *thousand?!*" gasped Camille, eyes wide as saucers. Jean-Luc nodded.

"People were watching from all round the lake – so Albert said afterwards."

"Now, said the Count gravely, looking at the children, "I'm afraid I have to announce that the grown-ups are all busy for the rest of the afternoon."

"Awww!" groaned Camille.

"Hmmm." mused Jean-Luc, assuming responsibility for his companion and trying to think of something new he could introduce Camille to. Francine stepped in.

"Actually, I have a couple of hours to spare, now that most things are nicely in place. How do you fancy a spot of archery?"

"Good idea!" concurred Jean-Luc. "What do you think, Camille?"

"It sounds like fun!"

"Excellent!" said the Count. "Now we've all got exciting things to do."

The two children, supervised by Francine, went off to have an archery competition – or two, as Jean-Luc felt there had been some cheating going on in the first contest.

"Why are you letting Camille stand three yards nearer than me?" he complained.

"Camille hasn't used a bow and arrows before."

"Well, she can have some practice shots, then."

In the end, Jean-Luc won, which would have been fair had it just been the children playing, but as it was, Francine let Jean-Luc have the victory by repeatedly missing the bulls-eye on purpose. Camille didn't mind what her score was, she was just loving yet another new experience – and having a family to share it with.

* * *

Arturo and Margherita Barbieri were en route to Dijon. Following orders from the Boss, they were to neutralise and take the place of the two DGSI agents that were scheduled to join Eric Mazet's team accompanying Madeleine Dupuy. The Boss had provided the location, time, names of the agents and even the make, model and registration of the vehicle the agents would be travelling in.

"Your Boss has good sources." observed Margherita.

"*Le Patron* is well-connected." agreed Arturo. "Keep up your speed, we're only minutes ahead of the DGSI motorcade."

The rendezvous point was the car park of a hotel on the

north side of Beaune, about 30 miles south of Dijon. They had not had time to research and plan, as the Boss had only been able to give them the details at the last minute.

"That's standard DGSI procedure." Arturo reassured Margherita. "Keep the details secret as long as you can – makes it difficult for people like us. Don't worry, I'll improvise, just follow my lead."

They approached the junction. Margherita pulled off the A6 and cruised round the bend, crossing back over the motorway and onto a small roundabout.

"Take the second exit." said Arturo.

"But …"

"Second exit!"

Margherita did as she was told.

"Now, pull over here."

She stopped the car. Arturo got out, walked round the open door and bent down. Margherita could hear the long hiss as Arturo let the air out of the front passenger-side tyre. He replaced the dust cap and got back in.

"Now you can go to the hotel."

Margherita turned the car round and went left at the roundabout, to pick up her original intended direction, then went straight on at another roundabout and took the first left to the rendezvous point. The car park was at the side of the hotel, surrounded by high hedges and trees. It was not particularly busy at that time of day, despite it being the holiday season, and they spotted their target immediately.

"Park next to the DGSI vehicle – on their right, but leave one space in between. I'll speak to them, but you get out with me and keep this needle handy."

He placed a syringe in the cup holder and put another in his pocket. "No time to clean up blood. This will have to do. They'll be out for 12 hours and won't remember a thing."

Margherita parked as instructed and Arturo immediately began his act. Jumping out of the car, he stormed round to the flat tyre and shouted angrily at her.

"I told you it was flat – couldn't you feel it?!"

Margherita followed his lead, responding defensively.

"I'm trying to concentrate on driving – and you shouting at me doesn't help!"

"Useless!" yelled Arturo, going round to the back of the car and opening the boot. He fumbled around.

"Where's the spare wheel?"

Margherita got out and came to help.

"I don't think it has one. What's this thing? It's got a picture of a tyre on it."

Arturo snatched the can from her and peered at it.

"I don't know! The writing's so small, I can't read it - it's ridiculous!"

He walked over to the DGSI vehicle and tapped on the window. The female agent, Marianne Tauzin, had been watching the scene play out. They had seen the car turn into the car park, the alloy wheel practically scraping along the tarmac. She wound down the window. Arturo continued the act and threw in a twist for good measure.

"Hey, do you know how to ...?" he stopped, pretending it was because he'd realised he was talking to a woman. "Oh, sorry." He looked past her to the male agent, Claude Boucher. "Do you know how to use one of these? We've got a flat tyre and there's no spare wheel, just this can thing."

Marianne took the bait.

"What makes you think a woman won't know how to use it?!" she snapped. She opened the door and turned to her partner. "Give me a minute."

Boucher nodded reluctantly.

"But be quick, they'll be here in 10 minutes."

"Okay, relax."

Arturo pretended to look doubtful of Marianne's abilities, but Margherita stepped over.

"Thanks so much. And sorry," she added quietly, "*he can be such an ass!*"

Marianne nodded and the two women smiled. She went round to the far side of the car, Margherita right behind her, knelt down and started to unscrew the cap. Arturo engaged Boucher in conversation to distract him, while Margherita injected Marianne.

A minute or so later, Arturo feigned impatience.

"What's going on with these women?!"

He stormed over to where Margherita was holding Marianne's body in position, as if still working on the tyre. He shouted over to Boucher victoriously.

"I knew it! I knew they couldn't do it!"

Boucher sighed and got out.

"Oh thanks, *mon ami*. That's what we need – a man on the scene!"

Boucher joined them and leaned over Marianne. Before he could register that she was unconscious, Arturo had injected him and he was out cold. Arturo and Margherita quickly stripped the agents of everything they would need, dumped the bodies in the boot of the hire car, and got into the DGSI vehicle.

Five minutes to change the photos in their IDs – a rough job would do; no one was going to be looking closely at them – and they were now DGSI agents.

* * *

The two vehicles carrying the Secrétaire d'État and Eric Mazet's Paris team, arrived at the rendezvous point near Beaune bang on time. Spotting the Dijon agents' vehicle as easily as Arturo had done, they parked opposite.

Margherita flashed their vehicle's headlights three times, as they had been told to do, and Eric's lead car responded with two flashes. Eric got out and came over to the driver's door. Margherita wound down her window as he was approaching and flashed her dark eyes and white smile more than her stolen and doctored ID. It worked. He glanced at it briefly, but only in passing as his eyes went to meet hers.

"Hi. I'm Eric Mazet. I'm leading the team."

“Claude Boucher, Dijon station.” said Arturo, leaning across and extending his hand. Eric shook it firmly, then turned back to Margherita.

“Marianne Tauzin.” They shook hands.

”Good to have you on board.”

“Glad we can help out.” said Margherita with another smile.

“So, you’ll know from the brief that I’m leading the search for Madame Dupuy’s daughter and that we’ve had a verified ransom demand …”

“Five million, wasn’t it?” interjected Arturo, keen to consolidate their good start by demonstrating knowledge that only a genuine DGSI agent would have, then added quickly. “Sorry for interrupting, sir.”

Eric waved it away.

“Not a problem. But, yes, five million. So, in addition to escorting Madame Dupuy to her engagements over the next couple days and then back to Paris, we’re also awaiting further contact from the kidnappers, with a view to getting Camille Dupuy back safely.”

“We’ll do our best to support you, sir.” lied Arturo convincingly.

“Thanks.” Eric checked his watch. “Now, let’s get moving – I’ll brief you more fully when we get to our destination, but for now ….” – he handed each of them a tiny in-ear communications device – ”put these in, take rear car position – you’re Car 3 – and follow my instructions.”

“Will do.”

Eric handed the earpieces to Margherita and returned to his vehicle. Margherita wound up her window, glancing over at the car in which they’d hidden the bodies of the real agents. She checked the comm’s devices were off, then turned to Arturo.

“How long do you think before the hotel people find the agents?”

“Don’t worry, I’ll get someone to come and move the

car tonight – I've hidden the keys under a stone by the hedge. When the agents wake up they'll be sitting in a strange car in a strange place with no idea how they got there."

"No wonder they call you The Fox!" said Margherita.

Arturo smiled, enjoying the attention and admiration.

"That's me. Now, from here on in, no careless chatter. Unless I say otherwise, it's ear-pieces in and switched on – and we're Boucher and Tauzin, DGSI. Got it?"

"Understood."

"Okay – earpieces on."

They activated their comm's devices and slipped them into their ears. The lead vehicle moved off, followed closely by Car 2. Arturo and Margherita slipped in behind them.

* * *

Vincent Sadoul was riding shotgun in Car 2,with Madame Dupuy in the back, next to Simone Pelletier, the female agent on the Paris team. Had he been able to see through the bullet-proof privacy glass of Car 3, he would have identified Arturo and Margherita straightaway, although he would have had a hard time convincing Eric to check the car with the flat tyre for the real agents Boucher and Tauzin without compromising his own position in relation to the Count. As it was, the rest of the journey passed uneventfully and at 16:00 they arrived at the Imperial Hotel on schedule, much to Eric's satisfaction.

Giving orders through the in-ear comm's devices, he assigned each pair an initial position. The agents in Car 1 would clear the way to the minister's room, sweep it for bugs and stand guard outside. Those in Car 2 – Vincent and Simone, plus Eric himself – would bring her up and wait for further details of the ransom exchange. The agents in Car 3 would monitor the hotel lobby. He also thought it would be good – primarily for *Madame le Secrétaire's* benefit, of course – if food and drink was ordered on room service and brought up to the suite.

While they were waiting, Simone stayed with Madeleine Dupuy and remained on comm's while Eric and Vincent familiarised themselves with the layout of the top floor of the hotel and then surveyed the scene from the balcony which overlooked the rose garden and the lake beyond.

"Not a bad view!" whistled Vincent, chronically understating matters.

"And so *inexpensive!*" replied Eric sarcastically.

"I'm glad the DGSI is paying for this and not me!" said Vincent, relieved that no one was listening into their impertinent conversation. "Anyway, what do you reckon, sir?"

Eric scanned the scene, starting from the hotel grounds immediately below them and moving out to the shoreline and lake.

"I can't see the exchange going down inside the hotel. Too many people. Same goes for the front of the hotel, which we saw on the way in – there's the main road, and between that and the hotel people are going to and from the adjacent park and generally milling about. The lake side is the most likely. Doesn't look like there's a wedding on today, so … the rose garden, maybe?"

"What about getting away? What's their exit route?"

Eric pondered the question for a moment.

"Hmmm …" He looked over to each side, following the dirt and gravel path at the far end of the rose garden. "That track leads round the promontory, allowing entry and exit from either side. Too narrow for a car, but it would be easy on motorbikes."

"What about the lake?"

"That's a possibility too."

"So, what are the parameters, sir?"

"Well, recovering the girl is paramount; there's no compromise on that. But once we have her … if we can catch the kidnappers as well, even better."

"So, we have to let them in, keep out of the way until

the exchange has happened, then pounce."

"That's the idea. However, that's all conjecture. If they're any good – and I think they are – they'll keep us guessing until the last minute."

They came in from the balcony and found the phone recording and tracing gear had been set up at one side of the room.

"All ready, Simone?"

"Almost, sir. Just making sure everything's hooked up properly."

Eric looked at his watch.

"Just under three hours to go. Better give our Dijon friends some food. Simone, would you invite them up, please?"

Simone passed on the instruction to come up to the suite.

"Great." muttered Arturo under his breath. "Leftovers – just what I fancied."

Margherita put her finger to her lips and pointed to her earpiece. Arturo sneered and mouthed, "I don't care!"

They headed up, gave their names and flashed their IDs nonchalantly, but briefly, at the two agents guarding the minister's suite. One of them knocked twice and then opened the door and the two imposters walked in. Eric introduced them to the minister.

"Ah, there you are. *Madame le Secrétaire*, these are the agents from Dijon station. This is agent Boucher …"

"Madame." Arturo nodded.

"… and agent Tauzin."

"Madame."

Vincent turned his attention away from the balcony, and it was as much as he could do to keep the shock from registering on his face. There was no mistaking the hooked nose and cunning eyes of Arturo Regnard – *The Fox!* And beside him, Margherita Barbieri.

"Ah, Vincent – and Simone …" Eric tapped Simone on the shoulder. She looked round and removed the headphones she was wearing. "... agents Boucher and Tauzin from Dijon."

"Pleased to meet you." said Simone.

"Hi." said Vincent simply.

"Well, now that we've all met each other ... Vincent, Simone, you take the lobby for half an hour while our colleagues from Dijon have a break."

"Sir." acknowledged Vincent, heading to the door. He knocked twice and waited for it to open. He followed Simone out and to the lift, trying to form a plan, but he needed to contact the Count.

When they reached the hotel lobby Vincent went to check outside. Deactivating his earpiece, he invoked emergency protocol and called the Count's secure phone. After a brief exchange, he hung up. They were both much better informed and the plan now had an extra twist.

* * *

The Count had been working with Butler on final technical preparations while Anna familiarised herself with the layout of the lake, hotel, mooring point, escape route, and the equipment that the Count had given her. She'd piloted a few boats in training and the *Mirage* looked pretty similar, from the photos Butler had given her. It was down at the estate's private stretch of the lake's shoreline, which comprised a low rocky cliff, only a few metres high, on the north side, dropping down to a large boathouse, where Butler and the Count were working, then round to a beautiful curved sandy beach about twenty-five yards long. After that there was a stretch of grass before the tree-covered rocks took over again, giving the whole area a serene air of seclusion.

Viewed from the lake the estate was a huge "L" shape rotated through 180 degrees, with the small town nestling in the vacant corner. The boundary went from the field above the graveyard all the way up to the ridge. From there it ran along the ridge, then down to the lake, back along the water's edge to the town, and up and round the town back to the graveyard. What passed as the "main road" passed through the centre of the town and cut through the estate, effectively separating it into two parcels of land, each of which was secured by attractive stone-walls and gates, rather than defended by ugly and aggressive barbed wire and concrete. A testament to the Beaumont family's sense of style and public obligation.

They had almost finished their labours when the Count received Vincent's call on his secure phone. Vincent only had a minute or so and he was clear, concise and ready to listen. The Count responded in like manner, although he had paused briefly as his quick mind added new aspects to the plan and worked it through end-to-end almost instantaneously to confirm its viability. He thanked Vincent and hung up.

"Trouble, sir?" asked Butler.

"Merely grist to the mill, as the saying goes." replied the Count with a cunning smile, "Grist to the mill."

CHAPTER 21

THE EXCHANGE

The kidnappers' next call came through at 18:00. Simone started recording and activated the trace.

"Yes?" said Eric.

"Do you have the money?" demanded the distorted voice.

"We have a source, but …"

"Good." interrupted the voice. "You will transfer it to the account I will give you when I call again."

"We're at the hotel." stalled Eric.

"I know." said the voice chillingly.

"So, where do you …?"

The line went dead.

Simone shook her head, but Eric had never really held out any hope for a successful trace. It was just standard procedure.

* * *

Tension was rising as the hour approached. Back up in the minister's suite, Vincent had been assisting Eric on multiple scenarios and strategies. A couple of motorbikes had been commandeered, as had a couple of motorboats. These had been hidden in strategic places and two of the DGSI vehicles had been parked at the front of the hotel facing the road, ready to go if needed. The bikes had been hidden in the bushes by the hotel outbuildings where the grounds keepers stored their equipment. The boats had been moored under the huge weeping willow trees that rose up, almost out of the lake itself, on the west side of the promontory on which the hotel had been built. The branches, just now coming into leaf, fell like net curtains right down to water. The team had been allocated provisional roles and positions for each of the three main scenarios: exit by road, exit via the track, exit via the lake. Having spoken to the Count, Vincent now knew which scenario it would be, but kept it to himself as Eric finished the briefing.

"The priority is the safe recovery of Madame Dupuy's daughter, Camille." Eric reminded the team. "Our secondary objective is to apprehend the kidnappers – of whom we suspect rogue British agent, Anna Parker, to be one."

He held up Anna's picture again, in case any of the team had forgotten what Anna looked like.

"All we need now is our benefactor." said Eric, looking at his watch again. He looked round at the agents gathered in the room. "I'm told the Comte is a bit eccentric, but humour him, after all, he is a Comte – and he's bank-rolling the ransom."

Just then there were two knocks and the agent outside opened the door. The Count entered wearing an expensive suit and shoes to match. He was carrying a case containing a laptop that he would use for the money transfer.

"Good evening, good evening," he chattered, "don't mind me, please carry on."

He caught his foot on the rug as he rounded a chair and almost stumbled over, but managed to steady himself by catching hold of Vincent. Arturo rolled his eyes in disbelief at the unfairness of life. *How does such an idiot end up with all that money?* he thought to himself.

The Count put the laptop on the table and fumbled to get it open.

"The room's been swept, *Monsieur*."

"I should hope so." replied the Count, now trying to get the screen to come on, "The rates they charge here!"

Oh my word! thought Arturo.

"I mean, it's been swept for electronic listening devices." clarified Eric.

"Ah, yes, of course!" said the Count sheepishly.

"*Monsieur le Comte*, I believe you already know Madame Dupuy."

The Count looked up with an expression of horror.

"Madame! Madame! Forgive me! I didn't see you there. There are so many people in the room ..."

The minister stood and the agents separated so she could approach the Count.

"Once again, Monsieur, I am indebted to you for your generosity."

The Count took her hand.

"Not at all, Madame, not at all. If we do not help each other in life, what unnecessary suffering will the world have to endure!"

"You are very kind."

"Do not worry, Madame, please believe that all will be well."

Madeleine nodded and returned to her seat.

"May I present the team, Monsieur?" said Eric, slightly overawed by the presence of nobility, however eccentric.

"Yes, yes, of course. The brave fellows – *and ladies*," he stressed, "on whom we daily depend for our safety."

Eric introduced the team. The Count greeted them individually. Arturo held back, hoping that he could avoid having to feign politeness and respect for the privileged clown of whom he was already jealous. However, the Count seemed oblivious to Arturo's body language and held out his hand. Arturo gritted his teeth and shook it.

"Monsieur." he nodded.

The Count paused, then addressed the team in general while looking specifically at Arturo.

"And you're all fully equipped, I assume?"

Arturo opened his jacket, revealing the semi-automatic pistol in a shoulder holster.

“Aha!” beamed the Count with interest. “Is that a Glock 17?”

“Close,” said Arturo, who was actually thinking, *Nowhere near, you buffoon*, “it’s a Beretta M9.”

He suddenly became aware that he had exposed what might be seen as a non-standard service weapon.

“Personal preference.” he explained to Eric. “My boss is okay with it.”

“May I see it?” asked the Count, with the eager look of a child on Christmas morning. Arturo glanced over at Eric, who made a face that said “Be patient” and nodded. Arturo drew the weapon and handed it to the Count, who almost dropped it, but recovered just in time.

“Sorry,” he burbled, admiring the gun, “that’s a beauty!”

“Do you know much about guns, Monsieur?” asked Eric politely, trying to ascertain whether Monsieur le Comte was in danger of accidentally shooting someone.

“I dabble.” replied the Count, “I have a few firearms of my own, but there’s rarely time for practice.”

He released the magazine and slid it out.

“And what bullets are you folks using these days?” he prattled on, sliding the top bullet forward to examine it more closely.

“I wouldn’t do that, Monsieur …”

“Oops!” said the Count, as the bullet flicked out and went under the bureau. Arturo looked furious, but Eric gave him the “Patience!” look again. He started to move towards the bureau, but the Count put his hand out to stop him.

“No, no. Just because I have a title doesn’t mean I expect everyone else to clear up after me.”

He walked over, crouched down beside the bureau and reached under it, his body and the side of his face pressed against the cupboard door. His voice was slightly strained as he stretched and felt around.

“Now, where are you, you little blighter?!” Suddenly,

he craned his neck even further round towards them, clearly at the limits of its flexibility, and with a look of triumph shouted, "Got it!"

He stood up rather awkwardly, brushed off his trousers, slid the bullet back into place and replaced the magazine. He sheepishly walked back over to Arturo like an embarrassed schoolboy and handed back the weapon.

"It's probably better if I leave it to the professionals."

"I think so." agreed Eric, barely managing to conceal his frustration.

At 19:45 the phone rang. Eric nodded to Simone, who began the recording and trace again.

"I'm listening." said Eric.

"Are you in position to make the transfer?"

The Count nodded.

"Yes." said Eric, making no attempt now to stall.

"There is a small red boat on the hotel shore, directly in line with the rose garden fountain."

Eric didn't have time to verify, but had no reason to doubt the instructions being given.

"Understood." he said.

"At precisely 8pm one of your agents will get into the boat. There is a motor launch called the *Mirage* moored three hundred yards straight out from the shore."

"Yes."

"The agent will approach the launch slowly. We will make sure the agent can see the girl."

"Okay."

"At that point I will call you to confirm that the exchange is on and you will transfer the money."

"Agreed." said Eric.

"Just one agent." stressed the voice. "*And no tricks!*"

The call ended abruptly.

Eric looked at Madeleine and the team.

"Well, at least we know which scenario we're working with. However, we're going to have to put someone in the exchange boat."

“I’ll go.” volunteered Margherita, in the guise of Marianne Tauzin.

“Okay, you’ll be Boat 1. Vincent, you go with Boucher in Boat 2.”

“Yes, sir.”

Arturo looked over at him and smiled, but Vincent didn’t get a warm feeling from it.

* * *

There was a buzz as the agents gathered their gear and left to get into position. The Count remained with Eric, Madeleine and Simone, who had now ditched her telephone equipment for night vision binoculars like Eric’s. In addition to the glass doors opening onto the balcony, the suite had a long window to the side of the balcony, giving a clear view without having to conduct the operation in public. The Count remained by his laptop on the table, while the other three took up positions by the window.

Eric and Madeleine both checked their watches repeatedly as the seconds ticked by. Simone focussed her tension through constant checks on each agent within her field of view. She could see the motor launch out on the lake, seeming to hover over the dark waters.

At precisely 8pm Margherita got into the little red boat that had been moored in the shallow water at the edge of the hotel grounds, started the engine and moved out slowly. As Margherita’s boat reached two-thirds of the distance a light came on in the launch, momentarily blinding Eric and Simone, the brightness ironically making it impossible for them to see the launch through the night vision binoculars.

“You stay with night vision, I’ll switch to daylight for a minute.” said Eric, putting down one pair and fishing around for his other pair.

From the small motor boat Margherita could see the name *Mirage* painted on the side of the launch as she drew nearer. Then she saw movement on the boat.

"I have a visual on the girl. Repeat. I can see the girl."

"Is there anyone else on board?" asked Eric.

"Stand by … yes. Anna Parker is with her."

Eric's phone rang.

"Have you confirmed that we have the girl?" said the distorted voice.

"Affirmative – yes." replied Eric.

"Pay attention. This is where you are to transfer the money to." The voice recited the bank details. "Make the transfer."

The Count looked at Eric, who nodded.

"We're making it now."

The Count had already started typing on his laptop, then he spoke on the phone in a low voice over in the corner of the room, apparently giving security details and confirmation to someone at the bank, then more tapping and, finally, he looked up triumph.

"There we are!" he declared.

Five million euros, thought Eric, *just like that!*

"Confirmed." said the voice and hung up.

Margherita was just a few yards away from the launch now.

"Anna Parker is on the move! She's going to the back of the launch – I can't see her now."

Above the noise of her own boat, Margherita heard another engine kick into life. She steered to the side and saw a small, fast motor boat accelerating away from the launch, down the lake and into the darkness.

"There's another boat. Looks like she's left the girl."

"Go after her, Boat 1, before we lose her! Boat 2 – support Boat 1. Boat 3 – get the girl. GO!"

Margherita gave it full revs and began the chase while simultaneously Boats 2 and 3 roared out of their cover and round the promontory towards the launch. To the surprise of the DGSI team, a fourth boat appeared out of the reeds on the far side of the hotel promontory and sped towards the launch in a frantic race for the girl.

"Mécénat!" exclaimed Eric. "Boat 2 – forget Parker – engage!"

A hail of bullets flew across from the Mécénat boat. Arturo ducked and Vincent slumped backwards.

Eric's binoculars were trained on the mystery boat, while Simone had been following Arturo's boat. She saw the spray where the Mécénat bullets were hitting the water, well to the side of the boat, and a movement on the boat that made her think her eyes had deceived her. What she had witnessed was Arturo, in a single move, pretend to duck and turn, bringing his gun arm around the front of his head as if for protection – and shoot the agent sitting behind him.

"What happened there?!" she exclaimed, pointing.

"Where?" responded Eric immediately, sweeping his night vision binoculars to the right.

There, on Boat 2 – it looked like … Boucher just shot Vincent!"

"Nonsense!" snapped Madeleine.

The Count stared in sudden clarity. In a flash everything fell into place. Camille's fear of returning, how easy it had been to carry out her kidnapping, the threatening letters putting the DGSI onto the trail of the Albanians, how the Mécénat had always managed to stay one step of the French Secret Service, how Arturo had known the route, stops, and which agents he and his associate would need to eliminate and impersonate, how they had known about the ransom exchange ... even the use of the name Le Patron. He recalled what Francine had said about Madeleine's choice to be referred to as *Madame **le** Secrétaire*, rather than the feminine form *Madame **la** Secrétaire*. *Le Patron*, rather than *La Patronne*. It all made sense. And in that moment he realised that he was looking directly at the indignant face of Madeleine Dupuy – the Boss.

The Count showed no flicker of emotion, no sign of recognition. On the contrary, he seemed to back the minister's stance.

"That's a rather extreme accusation – the darkness can play all sorts of tricks on the eye."

"Exactly!" agreed Madeleine.

"That's true." conceded Simone, turning her attention back to the lake. "Sorry. What's happening now?"

Eric zoomed in on the launch with the daylight binoculars. The three boats were homing in on it. Arturo's boat, with Vincent's inert body sprawled at the stern, was just slightly nearer to it than the others. The second agent in Boat 3 was returning hostile fire as his partner piloted the craft. The Mécénat boat was swinging round wildly, the helmsman having been hit. Arturo realised that unless he blatantly blew his cover, his team was now outnumbered and lost. He knew what capture would mean for the other surviving team member, and his cruel and cunning mind saw a way to strengthen his position in the DGSI and save his comrade the trouble of suicide. He steadied his boat, took aim and shot the other Mécénat operative. To his amazement, the man didn't go down. He just stood there and looked at Arturo in confusion. Arturo fired again and this time Paul Gardelle fell backwards. Arturo sighed with relief. Behind him, the agent in the back of Boat 3 was lowering his weapon.

Eric was wondering how things had got so crazy. And just when he thought things couldn't get any worse, his phone pinged and vibrated. He glanced down at the message.

I SAID NO TRICKS!

"Oh no …" breathed Eric. He looked up.

The launch exploded in a ball of fire.

* * *

The two boats nearest to it were thrown up into the air by the blast. Arturo managed to hang on, but Vincent's body was tipped into the dark water. Crashing back down onto the surface and ploughing into the smoke, Arturo crouched low as burning debris fell on and around him.

Eric stared, mouth open. Madeleine Dupuy gasped in shock, but the Count observed that there was no immediate expression of grief.

"Boats 2 and 3, report in!" shouted Eric frantically.

"Boat 3 – we're OK. Enemy threat eliminated."

"Boat 2?!" yelled Eric.

"Boat 2 – agent down. I'm OK and I got one of them, but Vincent Sadoul's been shot … " there was a pause and through his daylight binoculars Eric could see Arturo, illuminated by the burning remains of the *Mirage*, look round to check, "… he's not in the boat, sir. He must have fallen out when the boat tipped up."

"Boats 2 and 3, can you see the girl or any other survivors?"

"Boat 3 – negative. No one on the launch could have survived. It's been blown to pieces."

"Boat 2 – negative. It looks like Vincent's gear has weighted him down. I… I think he's gone, sir." Arturo was proud of his performance; he actually sounded as if he cared.

Madeleine collapsed onto a chair with heart-wrenching sobs. The Count regarded her coldly, wondering whether any of this show of emotion was real, then resumed seamlessly back into character.

"Madame! Oh Madame!" he flustered. He turned to Eric. "Some brandy – quickly!"

"Hang on." barked Eric. "Boat 1 – Status."

"She's gone, sir. They only gave us a low-powered engine; there's no way I could keep up with her."

Eric hung his head and exhaled slowly in despair.

CHAPTER 22

THE BOSS

Just nine days previously, notable French politician, Madeleine Dupuy, Secrétaire d'État and well-known campaigner against organised crime, was enjoying the success of both sides of her morally bigamous life. She was successfully advancing her public career by outspokenly decrying human trafficking and the smuggling of weapons and drugs, while simultaneously benefitting from those very activities on an international scale.

She had not always been the Boss. Her late father had begun building the Mécénat nearly forty years ago, growing it from a small-time gang in one area of Paris to a regional network across the whole of the Île-de-France. But his vision had always been too small for Madeleine. Having been born into it when it was already established and growing, she had never appreciated how much work was involved in building an organisation from scratch. In her view she had made the Mécénat an international force, not by standing on the shoulders of a giant, but by treading a stunted man into the ground.

Her father's attitude of loyalty and care for those who had come under his patronage and sponsorship was too soft for Madeleine. Even before his death she had been the harshest of his lieutenants, and when they had argued violently about an opportunity for expansion, she had retired him – permanently.

She had realised soon afterwards that while expanding

the Mécénat operation had raised the organisation up to the next level, it had consequently brought significantly more attention from both rival gangs and the law enforcement agencies. It was of paramount importance that her identity as Mécénat Boss was kept secret. It had struck her that one way to ensure that no one suspected her of being involved in organised crime was to publicly stand against it. And the best way to do that was in the brightest of spotlights – politics. When the opportunity for a position of trust and influence within the Ministre de l'Intérieure, which governed not only the Police Nationale, but the DGSI as well, it was a match made in heaven – or in hell, depending on whether you were Madeleine Dupuy or one of the tens of thousands of people whose lives had been ruined through kidnap, extortion, drugs or illegal weapons.

She had also seen an opportunity to use her position in the French government to disrupt the activities of rival gangs, putting more business to the Mécénat, while using her privileged access to information to keep one step ahead of the law enforcement agencies and intelligence services.

In the early stages of her career she had had an affair that resulted in her becoming pregnant in the run up to a crucial election to higher office. She had never been the maternal type, and her decision to keep or abort the child was simply a cold political calculation as to whether she would win more votes as a single mother or as a pro-abortion feminist. She had chosen the former and kept the child – a girl, but for all the public displays of love and attention, she was an uncaring and sometimes cruel mother behind the scenes.

Not long after the child's second birthday, she had married a respectable businessman. It had given her additional propriety and, as he was often away on corporate affairs, not too much of a problem with her double-life. When she had found out a couple of years later that some of his affairs were more than corporate, she had given the order for his assassination. The clever part, of which she was particularly proud, had been how it had been made to look like the Mécénat were attacking her family because of her campaign against organised crime. She had gained publicity, sympathy and votes, while making it virtually impossible for anyone to even imagine that she was involved with – let alone the head of – the Mécénat.

It made life easier for her too. She had gained the respectability, but now had one less person to keep her dirty secrets from. However, another problem was growing – literally. Camille was an intelligent girl who was developing fast. For the first few years it had been easy to keep secrets from the child, but as the girl grew more inquisitive, aware and demanding, it became increasingly tiresome for Madeleine. Nevertheless, she worked round it until one day, when the child was six years old, the inevitable happened.

The wretched child had overheard her giving orders to clear out a trafficking post and leave no traces – including killing the Mécénat lieutenant who had compromised the site. She had tried lying to the girl, saying that she must have misheard or misunderstood, but the brat had heard very clearly and wasn't fooled by the lies.

On reflection, Madeleine was not surprised. Camille was her own offspring, so she was bound to be clever and perceptive. Madeleine looked at her. She was pretty, yet vulnerable; the sort of vulnerability that had not yet developed a defence mechanism. It was soft and exploitable. The child would have to be dealt with, of course, but in that moment Madeleine wondered if she might not have to actually kill it. In fact, if she played her cards right she could get rid of the girl and make both money and political capital out of it.

The plan would have to be put into effect swiftly, as the child could not be trusted to keep silent for long, but as it happened, she thought, the very incident that had sparked this chain of events could be used as the vehicle to resolve the problem. The child would be trafficked to the Far East tonight along with the weapons shipment from the compromised smuggling post, and once that was on the way, Madeleine could announce that her child had been kidnapped by one of the Mécénat's rival trafficking gangs, "evidenced" not only by the mysterious disappearance of the girl, but also by a series of notes that Madeleine would manufacture and claim to have received over the past few weeks, threatening that her daughter would be next to go if Madeleine didn't stop her campaign – no, *crusade* – against the organised crime gangs. By naming the gang she believed to be responsible, she could in a single stroke squeeze a rival group and divert law enforcement resources and attention away from the Mécénat operation. It was, she thought modestly, quite brilliant.

All that remained was to make the child so afraid that it wouldn't blab at the first opportunity.

CHAPTER 23

THE SECRET OF THE MIRAGE

The evening's activities had meant a much lighter and earlier dinner than usual for the Count and his extended family, including Anna, Butler and Camille. No four-course meal with the adults' conversation drifting on until nine or even ten o'clock tonight. They had said their goodnights to the children early and left them in the care of Francine and Max, the latter having only just returned from the office.

The Count went to change into a suit, ready for his performance at the Imperial Hotel, while Butler had driven with Anna down to the town, turning left to head south along the main road to where the houses stopped and were replaced by fields and woodland belonging to the Count's family estate, through the gate on the right-hand side and down through the pine trees to the boathouse. She got her first real-life glimpse of the *Mirage* and thought it looked much nicer than in the pictures Butler had shown her earlier, in which the deck and cabin had been covered in tools, cabling and various pieces of equipment.

"I don't see why I couldn't come down and have a look this afternoon." she complained to him.

"Sorry. I didn't have time to come and get you and the Count didn't want to take the risk of you being seen in the daylight – not even for a minute while you opened and closed the gate. It might be a small road, but it's surprisingly busy because of the tourists – and because it's the only road round this side of the lake."

Anna remembered the Count's promise to Francine that the plan would be, if not airtight, then at least watertight. She also suspected that Butler felt he had enough to do without her disturbing or distracting him, but he was too kind to say so.

"I guess." she conceded.

At around eleven and a half metres in length, the *Mirage* was a single cabin motor launch with a 270 horsepower twin engine. Butler had attached a small tender, which he had converted from manual to remote control.

"No drones this time?" laughed Anna.

"No, but just as much fun, though!" grinned Butler.

He had spent the morning taking a few pictures of the inside of the cabin, sending those on to the Count, and installing a screen and projector to which he could stream from a distance. After that, he'd rigged the explosives. On the deck was the scuba gear that Anna would need. She changed into her drysuit and went through the standard scuba equipment checks – all good, naturally, as Butler had readied it. Seeing once again the efficiency with which the Count and Butler gathered together from existing supplies, devised and made, or bought in whatever they needed for a given operation, Anna surged with confidence and with pride at being part of the team.

Butler did final checks on all his equipment, then gave Anna the nod. She moved through the cabin to the cockpit and started the engines. Butler opened the boathouse doors that gave onto the lake and cast off for her. Anna guided the *Mirage* out into open water and steered the launch to starboard, towards the north end of the lake, two and a half miles distant.

Butler drove a little over two miles up the road that curved in and out, sometimes towards and sometimes away from the lake, round sheer cliffs fifty metres high, and through the last small town on the eastern side of the lake.

Turning off the main road, he parked in a secluded spot, close to the shore, from which point he could see the whole north end of the lake, the Imperial Hotel, majestically lit up on its promontory, and the *Mirage* making its way unobtrusively towards a set of mooring buoys.

He watched Anna attach the launch to the mooring, slip on her scuba gear and slide gently into the water at the stern of the boat, out of sight from the hotel and nearby shoreline. A few minutes later she appeared a few yards away from him, having surfaced behind some rocks. She removed her gear and carried it over to where Butler was already getting a towel and some dry clothes ready for her.

Her part now complete, she sat down beside Butler. It was all down to him and the Count now – and timing was everything.

* * *

The Count had enjoyed editing the video clips he'd taken that morning with Anna and the children. He chuckled repeatedly, recalling their antics and at Camille's passionate performance. He smiled softly at the way Anna sometimes looked at him when he was recording her on video. They were clips to keep and treasure, he thought. Having finished putting the movie together, doing final editing, and adding the additional music to heighten the mood of each scene, he redirected his efforts to making a second movie, one that the children would never see. For this he used only a couple of specially-selected scenes that he had guided Jean-Luc, as director, to include. He had also ensured that they had been filmed against a plain background, to make it easier to replace with the best of the pictures that Butler had sent him of the inside of the *Mirage*'s cabin.

When he was finally happy with the second movie, he sent it back to Butler.

After their early dinner, he had changed, picked up all the things he would need for this evening's activities which he had been gathering together during the day, as and when time allowed, and set off for his appointment at the Imperial Hotel.

He was very much aware of the risks and of what was at stake; however, he loved the thrill of the game and he particularly enjoyed playing the part of the bumbling Comte, which had the double advantage of putting people off seeing him as any kind of threat, and also of creating situations in which he could execute sleight of hand manoeuvres and such like.

This evening's most flamboyant example had been to manufacture the situation in which he could replace Arturo's pistol magazine with one full of blanks, as a precaution against him shooting Vincent or any of the other DGSI agents. This he did by talking Arturo into giving him the magazine and "accidentally" flicking one of the bullets under the bureau, so he could turn his back on the room and switch the magazine and bullet for blank equivalents from one of the hidden pockets in his jacket. He was also glad he'd brought blanks for both the standard Glock and Arturo's preferred Beretta just in case Arturo was arrogant or clumsy enough to bring his own weapon.

This had been preceded by his supposed tripping over the rug, enabling him to grab onto Vincent and slip a small underwater breathing device of Butler's own design into his pocket. When Vincent had told him that he would be in Boat 2 with Arturo, the Count had figured it might present a tempting opportunity for Arturo to improve his odds by taking Vincent out. It would be especially easy a few hundred yards out on the water, in the dark. If it happened, Vincent would have to make it look convincing and then disappear without a trace. The breathing device was an ad-hoc measure that the Count had suggested, just in case. So-called micro re-breathers with a longer range were available, but outside of science-fiction and Hollywood blockbusters, they were anything but micro. There was no way the Count could slip such a kit to Vincent, or that Vincent would be able to conceal it.

Butler's device was small enough to hide, and would give Vincent just a few breaths which he would have to make the most of to get far enough away from the action to safely surface in the dark.

Butler had done well, and not only with the breathing device and the boats. He'd also delivered the last two ransom calls bang on script and with a decent approximation of the Count's own timing and delivery, which they had practised together for a few minutes after lunch. The voice distorter had done the rest. The Count wouldn't have been able to make those particular calls as he was in the room with Eric and Madeleine, but it had been the Count who had sent the text and triggered the explosion. He knew there were lives at stake if the timing was even a fraction off, and he knew that he would have the better understanding of who was where and what was happening from his position in the DGSI control room. He also recognised that the plan was his, and he did not want to offload the responsibility that came with it.

The video had projected realistically enough to convince Margherita Barbieri, acting as the agent in Boat 1, that Camille and Anna were on board the launch, and of Anna's leaving Camille there alone. In the original movie this had been where Camille had got the chance to escape from the wicked queen. And it had been Butler's timing that made it all hang together, watching the video at his end as he streamed it to the launch, and just waiting the exact number of seconds required before remotely starting up the tender's engine, to match the time Anna would have needed to go round to the back of the launch, get into the tender and start it up. He was just as good with a remote control tender on the water in the dark as he was with a drone in the daylight, and thanks to his skill the higher-powered tender was able to lose the low-powered boat that he'd left by the hotel's shoreline that morning, ready for the DGSI agent to use for the exchange. And Anna hadn't needed to be put at risk by being anywhere near the exchange when it actually took place. He'd steered the tender off south west, towards the opposite side of the lake and a mile further down, to throw the DGSI and anyone else off their trail, then slowly brought it round back to the boathouse.

The Count was very glad that he'd prayed for help and had felt prompted to switch Arturo's bullets for blanks. Had he not done so, Vincent would be dead.

All in all, the *Mirage* – and the projected mirage – had worked a treat.

* * *

Vincent Sadoul held his breath as he retrieved the breathing device that the Count had slipped into his pocket during his contrived stumble over the rug. He knew it would only give him a few breaths and he would have to hold each of these as long as possible, while using up oxygen with the effort of swimming fully-clothed underwater. He could feel the weight of his gear pulling him downwards ever so slightly, so he released a few small items one at a time until he achieved neutral buoyancy just below the surface. If the biggest risk of surfacing was being spotted, the biggest risk of staying just under the surface was that of being caught by the propeller blades of one of the DGSI boats, so he put some distance between himself and the boats before checking the compass in his watch and turning towards the eastern shore, where Butler and Anna were waiting for him. With slow, deep breaths and a relaxed efficient stroke, he swam, submerged, until he felt safely out of the area likely to be scanned by the team. Gasping for breath, he surfaced and quietly swam towards the shore. He could see the faint green light that marked the rendezvous point and adjusted his course accordingly.

* * *

By 10pm they were all gathered together at the château, each with a glass or a cup of whatever they chose to celebrate and warm up with. Butler was having a port and brandy, as the excitement and stress of the evening had given him heartburn. Anna joined the Count in a hot chocolate with brandy in it – courtesy of Albert, who made it almost as well as Butler had back at the Manor. Francine was drinking a sweet white wine from the Loire region, while Max had his twenty year-old Scotch whisky. Vincent, somewhat overwhelmed by the setting and the company, was wearing some of the Count's old clothes that had been put to one side for one of the local charity shops up in town. He was drinking straight brandy to warm up after his 500-metre swim without the benefit of a drysuit.

"Relax, Vincent." the Count encouraged him.

"I had no idea you really were a *Comte*."

"Join the club." laughed Anna.

"Very few people have been trusted with knowing me as *Le Comte* – or the Count – in both the public and covert sides of my life. The fact that you are here with us, means that you are …"

He paused, thinking of how different his relationship was with the people he employed and supported, from that of the Boss with those supposedly under her *mécénat*, or patronage. He himself would die for his people, whereas in the Mécénat, people were expected to die for the Boss. No, his relationship with those closest to him was not one of patronage, it was something much deeper. He brought himself round and completed the sentence.

"… family."

"But don't get any ideas about inheriting part of the estate!" joked Max. "I married into the family and even I have to make my own way!"

"Quite right too!" exclaimed Francine mischievously. "We can't have people sponging off us, can we, Édouard?"

"Heaven forbid!" laughed the Count.

"Well," said Francine, bringing things down to earth, "the house party is growing – where shall we put you, Vincent?"

Vincent opened his mouth, but then realised that Madame Durand was really talking to herself.

The Count waited for the excited chatter to die down, Everyone had their own story to tell from the events of the evening, but it was the Count's perspective that would bring the biggest and most shocking revelation. Knowing that, he deliberately waited until the end, wanting the others to be able to express their experiences without feeling they had been already been overshadowed.

The reaction to the news that Madeleine Dupuy, Secrétaire d'État and champion of human rights, was in reality *Le Patron* – the Boss, the head of the Mécénat – was no less than the Count had anticipated. There were gasps, shouts of "No!", and a dozen questions, but the Count calmly dealt with it all.

"Above all," said the Count, wrapping up the debrief, "we must treat Madame Dupuy as before. Not even the slightest hint of this knowledge must cross our lips or show in our expression, manner or tone. This will possibly be our greatest challenge, but everything ..." he paused and looked at everyone, "... *everything* depends on it."

* * *

Meanwhile Eric Mazet was debriefing his own team. They had recovered the Mécénat boat and bodies, conducted a failed attempt to find any survivors – which was not surprising. Given the size of the explosion and the weight of Vincent's equipment, he had not expected there would be any trace of either Camille or Vincent.

Thankfully, the flustering Count had gone. He had very nobly, but utterly impractically, offered for the Madame Dupuy to stay at his château overnight, but both she and Eric had insisted that she would be better off at the hotel, with the DGSI team around her.

"And what of tomorrow's Grand Reception, Madame?" he had effused. "Should we cancel?"

"Not at all." Madeleine had replied firmly. "We must show that we are strong and that we will not be intimidated by these evil cowards."

The Count suspected that, now assuming she was rid of the problem child, the Boss would play the strong, determined mother and politician for all it was worth. While that sickened him, he welcomed it. It would be to his advantage. If all went to plan, she would fall into her own net.

Eric was thinking about the five million euros that the Count had generously paid to ransom Camille – and now he had neither the money nor the girl. Had he known that the money was merely being transferred from one of the Count's personal accounts to one of his offshore accounts, he would have been less impressed with the sacrifice, but as it was, Eric just wondered whether the Count was hugely generous or just massively rich. The truth was, he was both.

CHAPTER 24

THE GRAND RECEPTION

Over breakfast the next morning, the Count was asking Vincent about his experiences on and subsequently off Boat 2.

"Quick thinking." said the Count, referring to Vincent's tactic of ditching items of gear to achieve neutral buoyancy just under the surface. "What exactly did you let go?"

Vincent thought for a moment.

"My gun, a spare magazine, … and two grenades."

The Count nodded and made a mental note to have a diving excursion to retrieve them at an early date. It was necessary, given the hazardous nature of the items. And, besides, it was a good excuse to go diving.

"Is there anything else you need for the reception, Francine?" asked Anna.

Francine thought for a moment, then shook her head.

"No, I think everything is prepared."

"Not quite." disagreed the Count. "We have a little reception of our own to prepare."

"Yes, on that note," said Max, "I'll be coming back early from the office to pick up Jean-Luc."

"Where are we going, *Papa*?"

"Well, first we're going to your favourite place to eat, then we're going to a concert at the Bonlieu."

"Hmph," sighed Jean-Luc, "It doesn't sound as exciting as the Grand Reception that *Maman* is organising."

Max looked over at Francine for help.

"Well, it might *sound* exciting," she admitted, "but before the fireworks and the dancing, there'll be a number of *speeches …*"

"Okay." said Jean-Luc, cutting in at the thought of having to sit through boring adults talking about things that didn't interest him in the least.

"Can I come as well?" chimed Camille.

Now it was Francine's turn to look at the Count. Without missing a beat, he made a shocked expression.

"But you are the *invitée d'honneur*, *Mademoiselle Camille!* The guest of honour can't miss the Grand Reception!"

Camille looked puzzled.

"I thought someone else was the guest of honour?"

"On paper, *ma chérie*, on paper. You are the *surprise* guest!"

"Can I jump out of a cake?!" she squealed.

"If you like," said the Count hesitantly, "but you'd be covered in crumbs and cream!"

The thought of that didn't appeal to Camille.

"Alright." she conceded. "We'll have to think of something else for my surprise entrance."

"Indeed." smiled the Count, "In fact, I have a bit of an idea already."

* * *

The children amused themselves playing *cache-cache*, as the French call the game of hide and seek, in the towers, the cellars and the garden – there was no end to the château's possibilities for anyone with a half-decent imagination. While they did so, the Count set out the plan and assigned tasks to the adults. As always, Butler was delighted to be part of the plan, whether his part was large or small, although it was very often the lion's share of the work.

"Very good, sir." he nodded and left the room, whistling as he went, totally in his element.

Anna and the Count had their roles and Vincent's job

would be to protect the Englishman who was due at the château later that day.

* * *

Madeleine Dupuy had slept well for the first time in over a week. The child was gone, and the risk of exposure had gone with it. She had a Grand Reception to look forward to tonight with the associated adulation, and even the visit to the victims' shelter this morning, though tiresome, would be good publicity. Over the next day or two she would, no doubt, receive great amounts of sympathy from voters, colleagues and, most likely, from *Monsieur le Président de la République* himself.

Anna Parker had escaped, but she would get a team onto that. Whether it would be led by Arturo or not was proving a difficult question yet again. For a second time the operation had not gone smoothly; but on the other hand, it had worked out quite well in the end. The fact was, Arturo was here now and she would make use of him and what was left of his team until this particular circus was over.

* * *

The visit to the victims' shelter went well. The Count was a super, if slightly clumsy, host. He knew the names of every staff member and a fair few of the clients who were staying there. He seemed to listen to and genuinely care for them all.

Quel idiot! thought Madeleine, for whom the words of the people whose hands she was shaking and faces she was nearly, but not quite, kissing went in one ear and out of the other. Still, the lunch was excellent and the media were there.

She returned to the hotel with Arturo and Margherita, who had been her escorts all morning. In the afternoon she met with Eric who wanted to confirm security arrangements with her for the Grand Reception that evening.

"Now that …" she hesitated for effect, "… it's over, I

don't feel the need for a huge team of bodyguards – and how will it make the other guests feel? It would throw a wet blanket over the whole affair."

"Well, I can see where you're coming from …"

"Good." said the minister sharply, "Then in that case, I think Boucher and Tauzin will be sufficient escorts this evening – they were excellent on the visit to the victims' shelter this morning."

"They could probably use a rest …"

"Yes, yes, give them a rest this afternoon – excellent idea."

Eric wasn't sure how he had ended up caving in, but Madame le Secrétaire was quite forceful. No wonder she got things done.

* * *

Anthony Bright, OBE arrived mid-afternoon at the château. He was welcomed warmly by Albert, who showed him into where the Count was having a final run through his plans for the evening, surrounded by his loyal team, Anna nestled up at his side. Everyone heard the knock, but Anna and Vincent were surprised that Albert had not waited for an invitation to enter.

"Uncle Tony!" cried the Count, jumping to his feet and racing to embrace the elderly Englishman.

"Edward, my boy! How are you? I was delighted to receive your invitation."

Francine rose to her feet and walked gracefully over. Bright bowed.

"Madame." he said with sober deference in his rich baritone voice.

"Oh, stop it, Uncle Tony!" she laughed, giving him just as warm an embrace as her brother had done.

"Beautiful as ever." said Bright. Francine blushed. "And I see another beauty here." he continued, indicating Anna. "Someone special, I think?"

"Very." the Count confirmed without the slightest embarrassment or formality.

Bright strode over to where Anna was still sitting, took her hand and kissed it.

"Miss Parker." he said, with a slight nod of the head.

Anna was completely taken aback. First the sudden entry of a visitor who was welcomed so warmly, and then the shock of the stranger knowing who she was.

"Have we met before?" she enquired tentatively.

"No, my dear, but it is my pleasure that we have met now."

You old charmer! thought Anna, enjoying it nevertheless.

"Thank you, but …"

The Count intervened.

"Darling, may I introduce Anthony Bright, OBE. A colleague of my father's, a dear friend of the family, and my current employer."

If Anna had been standing up, she could have been knocked back down with a feather. She looked at the Count in confusion.

"I thought Sir Peter was – or had been, your employer?"

"Do you remember us talking about Pyramus and Thisbe?"

"The play within a play. You said that Sir Peter's play was the farce within the bigger production." The penny had not yet fully dropped, but it was edging it's way over.

"Edward and I have been working together for a few months now on stemming the Mécénat's attempts to spread into the United Kingdom." said Bright.

"You were already working for the British Secret Service when Sir Peter contacted you?!" gasped Anna.

The Count nodded. Sensing a modicum of tension, Bright stepped in again.

"At a much higher level than Sir Peter, you understand. He had no idea of it."

She still looked confused.

"Don't be fooled by Sir Peter Shackleton's more

exalted honour. He received his knighthood for reasons that have nothing to so with the Service."

"So you're his superior?"

"That depends on whether you mean his immediate superior, or just his superior in general."

Now it was the Count's turn to step in.

"Uncle Tony is somewhat further up the chain of command than Sir Peter."

"How far?" asked Anna warily, realising too late how insubordinate that sounded.

Bright laughed.

"Your young man told me you were spirited! He was right about that too."

Your young man? The phrase did not pass Anna by. *And what did he mean by 'that too' – what else had Edward told Bright?*

"Uncle Tony and I were trying to identify the top level of the Mécénat organisation – specifically, the Boss." continued the Count hurriedly. "When you rescued Camille you inadvertently triggered a sequence of events that led us to our goal."

"And now that we know the identity of the Boss, we have one more hurdle to get over." added Bright.

Anna looked at the late middle-aged man who had suddenly burst onto the scene with more impact than any twenty year-old she could imagine. She turned to the Count, unsure whether or to what extent she had been used as a piece in the game. She thought of the young girl whose life she had saved and whose outlook had been transformed by the love she had received at the monastery. And now perhaps they were both going to be used again.

"You need evidence." she said flatly.

* * *

Vincent felt out of his depth. It was one thing to be given specific tasks to do, even challenging and risky ones, without needing to understand how they fitted into the bigger picture. It was another thing altogether to be with people who saw the whole thing from the top down. In the Count's case it was even more stupefying, because, not only did he grasp and operate at the top level, he designed it right through to the finest detail – and he was out there, in the field, face to face and hand to hand with the enemy.

He looked over at Butler and Anna, and wondered whether they felt the same. Butler seemed completely at ease and Anna was nestled up against the Count. If he could have read her mind, though, he would have observed that she was not quite so much at ease as it appeared.

What, wondered Anna, *was really true in this world of espionage?* The Count didn't lie, she had come to be sure of that, but he did play parts and people believed what they wanted to believe. What did she believe? She knew what she *wanted* to believe, but was that just part of the game?

* * *

The Count gathered the remainder of the adults, staff included, and ran through the plan for the evening one more time. Francine gave him a wary look.

"Now, you're not going to break anything, are you, Édouard?"

The Count laughed.

"I'm hoping to break a couple of things tonight – the Mécénat, for one."

Anna hoped that the other wasn't going to be her heart. She also wondered how her young ward would take the news that the Grand Reception – at least on paper – was in honour of the mother that she was so rightly terrified of, and the scheme involved the two of them meeting up.

"So," the Count said as he rounded off, "is everyone happy with the plan and their role?"

There were general nods and even a few smiles from those, like Butler, who were looking forward to the action.

* * *

Camille, however, was not so easy to persuade when the moment came to tell her.

"I'll be with you the whole time." Anna reassured her.

"And I won't be far away." added the Count.

"She'll kill me." sobbed Camille.

"No, she won't." said Anna firmly, fighting back tears of compassion and anger. "I won't let her."

Camille looked at her, then across to the Count and back to Anna.

"Do you promise?"

Anna stared at this sensitive, intelligent, wonderful human being and reminded herself that Camille, for all her grown-up speech and behaviour, was just a child. A small, vulnerable child who had had the fear of – not God, but a monster – put into her.

"I promise." vowed Anna softly.

* * *

The orchestra was playing at half-volume in the background as the guests arrived, received their welcome drinks and mingled.

The hush that fell on the people in the ballroom as Madeleine Dupuy entered the room with her escorts turned to applause that grew louder and louder until it drowned out the orchestra and the minister had to wave her hands to quell the ovation. The decision had been taken that afternoon to issue a press release on the murder of Camille Dupuy in a private, non-governmental ransom exchange that had gone tragically wrong. The level of sympathy and admiration had gone through even the château's elevated roof.

Arturo had been enviously admiring the château from the moment they had turned into the courtyard and seen the towers and turrets, not to mention the gorgeous Bugatti supercar with the equally gorgeous woman getting into it.

Madeleine did the rounds, working the room. *You never know when one of these country yokels might come in handy*, she told herself.

Francine, who had just come back in after having to move her car due to the large number of guest vehicles combining with a severe lack of good parking sense, came over to greet her.

"Madame Dupuy – welcome! Thank you so much for coming – especially in the dreadful circumstances."

Madeleine nodded sadly in an attempt to project both humility and strength.

"We cannot let them win." she said huskily. Then, clearing her throat, she spoke again, this time with renewed vigour. "We will not let them win."

The Count bustled his way through the crowd, spilling some of his drink on Arturo's shoes as he reached the minister.

"Madame! Madame!" he fussed. "We are so glad you have come!"

Arturo looked down with annoyance at his feet and felt the irritation move gradually towards anger, but the Count continued his carefree banter.

"And you too, Boucher!" he said, raising his glass and spilling a little more of his drink, this time on Arturo's arm. Arturo was practically glowing with rage and the Count could sense it. *Excellent*, he thought, *nothing makes a man more rash and careless than anger – except, perhaps, a woman.* He turned his attention to Margherita.

"And Madame – or is it Mademoiselle? – Tauzin! Did you enjoy your visit to the shelter this morning?"

Margherita attempted to reply, but the Count carried on as if no reply was necessary.

"Isn't it shocking? The things these people have had to endure! Those responsible – those against whom you have so doggedly campaigned against, *Madame le Secrétaire*," he emphasised the title, "must be brought to justice! Don't you agree, Madam … er … mois … er … *agent* Tauzin?"

Margherita tried once again to speak, but the Count was giving no quarter.

"Of course you do!" he cried triumphantly. "*Everyone* here does, don't they?!"

Margherita didn't bother to answer. The question,

indeed the whole monologue, had been rhetorical. Madame le Secrétaire excused herself and moved on. Francine took the Count gently by the arm.

"You're laying it on a bit thick tonight, aren't you? Don't overdo it, Édouard." she giggled. He chuckled and patted her hand.

"Me? Overdo it?!" he responded in mock-horror. "How could you say such a thing!"

* * *

The meal was a triumph. Numerous compliments were passed back to Maurice, the chef, and Suzanne, the sous-chef he was training up for a chef's position in the city. Madame Dupuy – paper guest of honour – was seated in the middle of the top table, between Francine and the Count, facing the other tables, which had been set out in pairs along the ballroom floor. To Francine's right sat Bright.

Butler, dressed as one of the staff, was accompanying Frédéric, the youngest of the château employees. His boyish looks gave him a non-threatening appearance, but like every member of the château staff, he was a black-belt in at least one martial art.

Anna sat with Camille in the secret mezzanine room that lay behind the great mirror hanging on the end wall, just above the orchestra. The bullet-proof one-way glass gave them a good view of the ballroom, while also delivering a sense of separation, and Anna felt it helped Camille to be at the opposite end of the ballroom to where her mother sat eating. If it had been an adventure with Jean-Luc, Camille would have been squealing with delight and excitement, but as it was, the experience was a very different one in the current circumstances.

Anna spotted Arturo and Margherita with Madeleine straightaway, and was not surprised at Camille's reaction. The young girl tensed with fear when she saw the three of them enter the ballroom through the grand doors half-way down one wall.

"Don't be afraid, Camille," soothed Anna, "I won't let her hurt you."

"It's not just her ..." replied Camille, shaking, "... it's *him!*"

Anna stared at her.

"Do you know that man?"

Camille nodded.

"He killed my *papa*, and he's come to kill me!"

"How do you know he killed your father?" asked Anna.

"Maman told me. When I heard her on the phone, saying those terrible things, she got angry and said that if I told anyone, a man with a hooked nose would come to kill me, just like he killed my papa."

Anna's hatred of Madeleine Dupuy rose to new heights. *So Madeleine had ordered Arturo to kill her own husband!*

She put her arm around Camille's shoulders and held her tight.

"I won't let *him* hurt you either." she said through gritted teeth.

* * *

After the meal came the speeches. Francine was right, Jean-Luc would have been bored. First up was Francine herself, as the organiser and hostess of the reception, then Madeleine Dupuy, thanking everyone for their tireless work and support over the years and for their sympathy at the present time, then looking forward to the future, etc., etc., and finally the Count, who managed to mention every type of crime, misdemeanour and scam the Mécénat had ever been involved in – and how incredible it was that *Madame le Secrétaire* had stood against it all this time. There were moments when Madeleine wondered whether there was a touch of sarcasm in his voice, but the Count's delivery was perfectly nuanced.

And then ... the fireworks.

* * *

The one remaining member of Arturo's team who wasn't in the ballroom was hanging around in the trees –

literally. He had been told by Arturo to stay on hand, just in case, so he'd parked down near the graveyard and walked up the lane to the château. Not being either invited or properly dressed for the occasion, he went round the huge stone walls and into the gardens. Seeing the pyro-technicians doing last-minute checks for the fireworks display, he had slipped into the adjacent wooded area to avoid being spotted and had found Jean-Luc's rope swing, which he used to climb up into one of the trees and get a better view of what was happening and who was where. It was Béatrice, the maid, who had seen him enter the courtyard on the CCTV and had reported it directly to Albert. Albert, in turn, had sent Frédéric to investigate. Butler had asked to see the footage and, on recognising the intruder from his own drone video at the old manor house in England, he had gone to the Count and whispered in his ear.

"Apologies, apologies!" declared the Count. "It is almost time for the fireworks and it appears I am needed outside."

Francine looked at him with an expression of curiosity, but he simply smiled and said, "Two minutes, dear sister, two minutes – start without me if you need to!" He bowed politely towards the minister and took his leave.

* * *

The pyro-technicians had not seen the unwelcome visitor, so Frédéric guessed rightly that he had gone into the trees. It was the obvious place to hide. However, finding the general area was not the same thing as finding his quarry. Even with his torch, Frédéric could not see the man anywhere. On the other hand, the man could see Frédéric. Crouched on a branch six feet above Frédéric's head, the Mécénat intruder saw his opportunity to strike before he was discovered. He readied himself to leap …

* * *

The Count saw Frédéric's flashlight among the trees and could tell that he had not yet spotted the intruder. A test flash from the pyro-technicians was all the Count needed to spot the man just above Frédéric. Sprinting across the lawn, he leapt onto one of the low-hanging branches of Jean-Luc's "beginners tree" and ran up it like a squirrel in full flow, barely breaking his stride as he jumped to the next branch. Flinging himself into the void he soared across the gap, turning in mid-air to lead with his shoulder.

As the intruder prepared to pounce, he was hit from the side by what felt like an express train, knocking the breath out of his body. Almost all of the Count's momentum transferred to the intruder, sending him crashing into an adjacent branch and tumbling down to the ground.

"All yours, Frédéric!" called the Count as he grabbed the branch and swung down. Frédéric was already in motion. Having heard the commotion above him he deftly side-stepped the falling man and rendered him unconscious.

"Well done, Fred!" said the Count, grinning at the lad who was panting more with excitement than effort. "Now, what shall we do with our careless friend?"

"Well, they used to put people like him in the dungeon."

"Excellent idea!" replied the Count. "Can you manage him?"

Had it been anyone else than the Count – or his mother – Frédéric would have given them the sort of look that young people give when they say, "What do *you* think?", but Frédéric knew better than to give cheek to the Count.

"Of course, Monsieur." he said, hauling the inert figure over his shoulder.

CHAPTER 25

REUNION

The fireworks were just starting as the Count brushed himself off and slipped silently round to the terrace where the guests were gathered excitedly. Moving noiselessly round the back of the crowd, he spied Francine with Madeleine. Arturo and Margherita were lurking in the shadows a few yards away. He made his way towards them, stopped just behind the minister and whispered into her ear.

"I have something much more interesting to show you, Madame."

Madeleine turned sharply. The voice was not the one she had been used to. It oozed confidence and challenge.

"And what is that?" she replied in like manner.

"Your daughter."

Madeleine froze. Without hesitating, the Count grabbed her arm firmly and steered her off the terrace and into the house via the patio doors, rather than back round the corner and into the ballroom. Her bodyguards, who had positioned themselves near the corner, reacted, but were on the wrong side of the crowd, giving the Count time to disappear. As Arturo and Margherita reached the patio doors, they found the way blocked by Butler and Albert who appeared to have chosen just that moment to reposition one of the couches. After a moment of to-ing and fro-ing, the confusion was rectified with humble apologies from the staff, and the two fake DGSI agents stumbled into the house. The Count and Madeleine had disappeared.

"Where did they go?", growled Arturo, turning back to the hired hands.

"I couldn't say," replied Albert, "although I recall someone mentioning the dungeon." This was entirely true, as the Count had referred to getting the rogue agents into the dungeon in his briefing earlier that day.

"Check it out." Arturo ordered Margherita. "You – old man," he said, pointing to Albert, "show her the way."

"As you wish, sir." replied Albert with a slight bow.

"Now, you." he pointed to Butler, "where else might they go?"

Butler raised his eyebrows, then spoke slowly as the city-dweller's stereotype of a simple country peasant might.

"The château is very large, … there are many rooms …"

"Oh, for goodness sake!" roared Arturo and stormed off.

* * *

Albert led Margherita through the majestic hallway onto the corridor that ran the length of the château between the two towers on that side of the building. Taking the right-hand direction, he ambled past a couple of doors to the top of some stone steps that, like their companions that the Count had used to take Anna to the waterfall, led down to the cellars – and on this side, on to the dungeon.

"Hurry up, old man!" ordered Margherita, drawing her gun and pushing him with the other hand. Albert, being only in his mid-sixties, did not appreciate being called "old man" any more than he appreciated being pushed. But he was a consummate professional, and maintained both his cool and his dignity.

"This way, *Madamoiselle*." he said politely.

The dungeon was on a level below the main cellars and had two ways of being accessed. One was a metal grill gate and more steps, the other was via a hole in cellar floor that dropped fifteen feet into the largest of the cells. The hole was covered by a thick, heavy wooden hatch, that had been replaced a hundred years previously after the original one had finally rotted and one of the staff had nearly gone through it. As they approached the metal grill, they could see it was slightly ajar and there was light behind it. Margherita took it as confirmation that the Count had brought Madeleine down.

"After you, *Mademoiselle*." said Albert politely, opening the grill wider and holding it for her to pass. Margherita sneered.

"You must think I was born yesterday!" She pushed him again. "You first!"

"As you wish." he replied.

As Albert took the lead, Margherita pulled in close behind him and put her gun to his head.

"Careful, now." she whispered.

"Of course, agent Tauzin." said Albert a little louder than usual.

"You're well-briefed." snorted Margherita.

"The Count takes security very seriously. Intruders are not welcome here." He placed a slight emphasis on the word *intruders*.

They reached the foot of the steps and turned the corner into the dungeon area. Margherita could see where the guards would have sat, monitoring their prisoners in days gone by. She could see the six cells with their iron bars, and in one of the cells she could see her fellow Mécénat team member. What she did *not* see was Frédéric stepping out of the shadows behind her.

* * *

While the guests were on the terrace watching the fireworks, the tables and chairs had been moved to the side of the ballroom, the floor had been swept and spilled drinks cleaned up, ready for the dancing. The start of the fireworks had been the signal for Anna and Camille.

"Ready?" Anna asked, holding Camille's hand for reassurance.

Camille nodded, but said nothing.

"Brave girl."

She led Camille out of the chamber, up the narrow steps built inside the thick château walls, and out through a secret door in the storage room at the nursery end of the first floor. They entered one of the two spare nursery rooms in which Butler had been busy earlier in the day, and waited.

A minute later the door opened.

* * *

The Count frog-marched Madeleine up the stairs and onto the first floor gallery.

"Where are you taking me?" she demanded, but the Count said nothing. He tightened his grip and pushed her along the corridor.

"You're hurting me!"

"What a shame." said the Count scornfully. "How does it feel?"

He dragged her to the last bedroom on the right.

"In there." he commanded.

* * *

It was hard to tell whose face registered more horror, Madeleine's or her daughter's, but at least Camille had had some time to prepare for it.

"No!" cried Madeleine.

The Count pushed her forward and closed the door behind him.

"A rather strange reaction to finding out that your daughter is alive after all, wouldn't you say, Madame?" observed the Count.

"And you!" exclaimed Madeleine, staring at Anna.

"*Enchantée* – not!" came the reply.

The cogs whirled in the Boss's brain. No wonder she had been unable to track down the shadowy man whose forename or surname began with a "C"; wasn't his name at all. It was his title.

She wheeled round to face the Count.

"*Count!*" she spat. That's what Sir Peter was going to call you."

"At your service, Madame – at least …" he said, reaching for her clutch-style handbag before letting go of her arm, "I'm going to carry your bag for you. Just in case you have any unwanted surprises in there."

Madeleine cursed inwardly. He was right again. Her Smith & Wesson Bodyguard micro-compact pistol was tucked neatly at the bottom. Anna stood with her arm round Camille.

"Have you anything to say to your daughter?"

Madeleine sneered and lent forward.

"Do you remember what I said would happen if you told anyone?"

Camille's eyes widened and her lip started to tremble, but Anna crouched down beside her.

"And do you remember what *I* said about your mother and her bullies?"

Camille nodded slowly and clasped Anna's hand. Madeleine leant closer.

"And who do you believe?"

Camille hesitated, then looked her mother directly in the eyes.

"Anna."

The two women glared at each other, Madeleine in defiance and Anna in triumph. The atmosphere virtually crackled with electricity. And then the door burst open.

* * *

Arturo's search of the ground floor had proven fruitless. There were a couple of locked doors, but no light or sound came from behind them. He turned his attention to the first floor. Moving cat-like up the stairs, he reached the mezzanine and listened. Faint noises seemed to be coming from the left, so he mounted the stairs on that side and crept down the corridor, gun in hand. He could hear voices coming from the last room on the right. Putting his ear to the door, he could identify three voices – one was Madeleine, another sounded a bit like the Count, but much stronger and without the fussing. The third was a woman's voice, but not one that he knew. Then a fourth voice, a child's voice, said one word. A name – *Anna.*

He put it all together and made a mental picture of the scenario. Then he went in.

* * *

The Count, still holding Madeleine's clutch bag, narrowly managed to avoid being hit by the door as it flew open. Madeleine spun round.

"Arturo! The girl!" she screamed.

Arturo pointed his weapon and pulled the trigger. Anna threw herself in front of Camille, shielding the child with her own body. The Count ditched Madeleine's bag and hurled himself at Arturo, catching him around the arms and chest, and hammering him against the wall. Seizing her opportunity, Madeleine grabbed her bag and ran down the corridor to the grand stairway. Realising that she had not been hurt and without thinking why she was unscathed, Anna leapt to the Count's aid. The two men were closely entwined, wrestling each other like judo players. Anna recognised the move that the Count was trying to force through and grabbed one of Arturo's legs. She pulled hard and between them they lifted Arturo up bodily and smashed him down on the floor.

"Get Camille safe! I'll take the Boss." said the Count, delivering a blow to the side of Arturo's head that would have knocked most men out, but Arturo was a quick and seasoned fighter, and the blow only stunned him momentarily.

"Camille! Quickly"

Anna grabbed Camille's hand and was about to turn towards the main stairway, but Camille pulled her the other way.

"The tower!" she cried, dragging Anna round to the right as the Count burst past them, racing after Madeleine.

Arturo's head was clearing. He stood to his feet and started towards the corridor, trying to make sense of what had happened. He couldn't have missed Anna Parker from that range! He recalled how the Mécénat operative on the boat hadn't gone down when he had shot him. *Blanks!* he suddenly realised. Someone had switched his magazine. But he still had his knife. What had he heard? *The tower!* It must be the door just there, at the end of the corridor – it was ajar! But up or down? He stopped and listened. The sound of footsteps was definitely from below. They had a head start on him, but one of them was a child. He would soon catch them.

Outside the fireworks were exploding in a spectacular display of sound and light and colour, but the interior of the château, with its thick stone walls, was as oblivious to them as the cooing crowd was to the events inside.

Arturo raced down the stairway, past the ground floor and down to the cellars, following the sounds that were getting louder and nearer. He chased Anna and Camille down the ancient stone steps into the underground labyrinth that was the cellars of the château.

"This way!" yelled Camille, pulling at Anna's arm. "Jean-Luc showed me."

Jean-Luc's knowledge of hiding places in the château was almost as good as his mother's and his uncle's. They had played hide and seek many times there.

"Okay, go!"

Anna could hear Arturo on the steps behind them.

"This way!" whispered Camille, panting.

She led Anna into a side room half-filled with boxes, crates and old pieces of furniture. Camille ran over to where an old piano stood in one corner. Anna wondered how they'd managed to get such a heavy thing down all those steps, but there was no time to dwell on it.

"In here!" breathed Camille, wriggling in behind it and

sliding half the back panel across. Anna could hear Arturo's shoes rapping on the stone floor of the cellar corridor. He was almost there.

"You get in and close it up." said Anna. "I love you."

Drawing the gun that the Count had given her as a last resort measure, she moved swiftly into the central space. Arturo rounded on her as he heard her steps.

"Anna Parker." he sneered.

"Arturo Regnard", she replied," – the Rat."

"The Fox, Miss Parker, if you please." breathed Arturo, eyeing her weapon slyly as she edged towards him.

"No, I think the Rat suits you better."

As she neared him he held his hands up a little, as if surrendering, locking his eyes with hers to draw her focus. *First field mission, Anna – rookie error: the safety is still on.* Suddenly he snatched at the gun, twisting it out of Anna's grasp. In the scuffle it fell to the floor and Arturo kicked it away, under a broken wine vat by the wall. He pushed her back with an evil grin, confident now.

Hand to hand, then, thought Anna. Arturo drew out an eight-inch hunting knife, sharp as a razor on one edge and serrated on the other, equally capable of killing and gutting prey.

"*The Fox.*" he smirked, "And now I have you, little hen."

He took a step towards her, but Anna had a knife of her own. In a flash she pulled it out and threw it with deadly speed and accuracy. It struck Arturo in the throat, just above his protective vest. He staggered back, gargling blood, unable to breathe through his severed windpipe. He slumped against the wooden vat and as the room started to dwindle from view he remembered Sister Colette's words, *Those who draw the sword will die by the sword.* He remembered the dazzling light behind the cross, and the mysterious hand that had reached out to him. But it was too late; the light was fading and he felt himself being dragged down into darkness.

CHAPTER 26

RACE TO THE FINISH

Francine was a good hostess, but her brother had not returned. There were still at least five more minutes of fireworks, during which she would not be missed, so she re-entered the house in search of the Count. Hearing someone coming down the stairs, she headed for the hallway. Someone was at the foot of the stairs and running towards her. But it wasn't the Count.

Madeleine Dupuy pointed her Smith & Wesson pistol at Francine.

"Car key." she demanded.

"What?" stammered Francine.

"Give me the key to your car!"

"But you have transport of your own." stuttered Francine, stalling for time. The Boss slapped her.

"Don't be smart with me, Madame! Give me the key now!" Francine fumbled in her bag and the Boss snatched it out of her hand the moment it appeared from the bag.

"In there!" ordered the Boss, waving the gun towards the library door. Francine moved round, keeping Madeleine in her sight all the time. As Francine approached the doorway, Madeleine shoved her into the room.

"Come out and I'll shoot you." she said, and shut the door. Movement at the top of the stairs caught her eye. It was the Count. Madeleine ran out of the château door, thanking her stars that she had seen how Francine had opened the driver's door as she had moved the Bugatti to make space as they arrived. She felt under the door, found the hidden latch and jumped into the driver's seat. It took her another couple of valuable seconds to get the key into the ignition, but once it was in and turned the EB110, with all its 600 horsepower, came to life. She fumbled around for the headlight switch, expecting some weird and wonderful feature in such an expensive vehicle, but was surprised to find it was on the indicator stalk, just the same as any other car. That had cost her a few more seconds and the Count was already at the château door. She released the brake, hit the accelerator and the car leapt forward, almost crashing into the wall as she wrestled with the steering wheel. She made it through the archway – just, tyres screeching as the Bugatti roared away from the château and onto the lane.

Having grabbed the car keys from his jacket hanging in the cloakroom, the Count gave chase. On a race track the Renault would have been no match for the Bugatti, but the Count had been driving these roads since he was teenager. He knew every bend, every bump, every camber. The RS 230 had been a great leveller – after all, he could hardly have joined in with the local boys if he'd turned up in a million-euro supercar. They'd raced on these roads time and time again, until the tragic night of the accident that had cost his parents their lives. He had vowed from that day on to never drive like that again. He knew all too painfully now that it was not just about throwing a car round the bends, any fool can do that – and many fools do. It was about realising that *you don't know* what's round the corner and that *real* driving is being able to control the car whatever happens. Youth is so short-sighted. When you're young, everything revolves around *you*. With experience you realise that there are other people in this world too, and what you do impacts on them – sometimes massively – for good or for bad. Tonight, however, the Count was going to have to exceed the speed limit – and by a long way, but even now he would not allow himself to take chances where the limit of his vision could not match the speed he wanted to go at. He turned the key, engaged first gear and thundered out into the night. Neither of them had spent precious time on fastening their seat belts.

Passing the graveyard, Madeleine slammed on the brakes, changed down into second gear and threw the car to the right, onto what the locals called 'the main road', but was really only a country lane, barely wide enough for two cars to pass in some places. The Bugatti screeched and slithered as Madeleine struggled to control the phenomenal power and acceleration.

The Count saw her turn right and power-slid the Megane round after her. There was no way he could catch her on the straights, the Bugatti was far too quick, and it simply wasn't safe to overtake on the bends. He racked his brain for a plan. At the very least he wouldn't lose her. He glanced down at the gauge and realised that the long journey from Senlis had left only a little fuel. When that ran out, she was away. As the trees flew by, out of the corner of his eye the Count could see a strip of moonlight reflecting on the lake. It seemed to cruise alongside him, effortlessly matching the frantic pace of the cars, with a still calmness that starkly contrasted with the wild frenzy of the chase. They rounded a bend and an idea entered his head. He remembered the roundabout with its high kerb surrounding a bed of flowers set around a small stone block with the name of the town carved into it. Madeleine would have to slow right down to go round it. He could picture the approach, the raised pedestrian crossing right before the circle, the ramp up, the flat crossing and the ramp down, then the turn onto the roundabout. What if he didn't turn? What if he hit the ramp going as fast as he could? How high and how far would he go? The road dipped down and he could see the roundabout over the low roof of the sleek Bugatti. The road was clear on the other side and the roadworks were still blocking the only other exit. He allowed the Bugatti to get well ahead of him, so there would be space for it to brake and the Megane to accelerate without hitting it. Then, as the Bugatti's brake lights flared up, he floored the RS 230.

The rear end of the Bugatti seemed to race towards him as it decelerated rapidly and the Megane's 230 horsepower accelerated him towards it. He prayed that his timing was right. The Renault hit the ramp of the pedestrian crossing and, with an impact that pressed the Count into his seat, the front end of the Megane flew up. He never saw exactly how close he had come to hitting the Bugatti, which would probably have been the end of him, but he saw it below and to his right as he soared over the stone block and flowerbed before landing heavily a few yards the other side of it. He was now ahead of the Bugatti. His head ached and he felt dizzy from the thump it had received as a result of not having his seat belt on, but he quietly thanked God for the clean jump.

Madeleine Dupuy almost crashed in surprise as the white Renault flew over the roundabout and onto the road in front of her, initially putting distance between the two cars due to the difference in the speed at which they had each crossed the roundabout. The Count only had the Renault's sidelights on – he had no need of the headlights; he knew the roads well enough to drive by moonlight, and he had no desire to assist the Boss by lighting up the road ahead for her. There was no traffic coming the other way, so the Count's plan was to prevent the Bugatti from overtaking, get to the section where the road narrowed to a single lane, and then force her to stop. That was almost a mile further on, but if he could keep in front and hog the middle of the road, it was possible.

The next stretch, to the two ninety-degree bends in quick succession, was pretty straight and the Megane's 230bhp engine was no match for the Bugatti, which was coming up on him fast and getting faster still. He was lifted out of his seat as the impact jolted the Renault forward, lifting its back end slightly as the sleek nose of the Bugatti sports car caught the lower part of its rear bumper. He suddenly realised that the Boss would never back down and capitulate, she would rather die trying to run him off the road. It was now less than two hundred yards to the first of the two sharp bends where a huge cliff bulged out of the hillside. He could see the Bugatti accelerating towards him again and although in the dark he couldn't yet see the bend, he knew exactly where it was and visualised it in his mind's eye. For a second time he prayed, more of a flash of thought and feeling than words, then just before impact he hit the brakes hard.

The nose of his car dipped, the back end came up and the Bugatti went right underneath it, powering through with such force that the Megane slid up the bonnet, over the roof and came crashing down behind it, tyres screeching as they hit the road at fifty miles an hour with the brakes full on. Still accelerating, the Boss glanced in her mirror and saw the lights of the Megane receding rapidly. She smiled smugly, then looked forward, only to see the ninety-degree bend and the sheer rock face a few yards ahead. The front of the Bugatti crumpled as it hit the cliff and the huge engine that sat behind the twin seats came rushing forward.

Breathing heavily, the Count sent up a quick prayer of thanks and steadied the Megane to a halt short of the crumpled Bugatti. The sight was not a pretty one, but he had neither time nor desire to dwell on it. His thoughts turned back to the château.

"Anna!" he said out loud, selecting reverse gear. He screeched the car through 180 degrees, and floored the pedal once more.

* * *

The Count arrived back at the château to find that, much to his great relief, all was well. He silently offered a prayer of thanks and there were hugs and tears all round.

Recovering his composure, the Count asked Anna and

Camille to wait a moment in the drawing room. He returned a minute later with four boxes, beautifully packaged and each wrapped with a silk bow. He put them down on the table, then took two of them, gave them to Anna and kissed her softly on the lips. He then gave the other two to Camille.

"Don't I get a kiss?"

"But, of course, *Mademoiselle!*" laughed the Count and gave her a gentle peck on the cheek. Camille blushed and giggled.

"Now," said the Count, "both of you go up to Anna's room, open the boxes and then meet me in the ballroom in five minutes."

Camille squealed with excitement.

"Come on, Anna! We only have *five minutes!*"

* * *

The orchestra was nearly half-way through its programme and the dancing was in full swing. No one seemed to have noticed that Madeleine Dupuy was no longer there, and those that had noted her absence simply thought either that, as a Secrétaire d'État, she would probably have many things to attend to and an early start in the morning, or that she had left the reception to go and grieve over the loss of her daughter. They would be shocked to read in the following day's afternoon papers, or hear in the media, that the minister had met with a tragic accident.

The Count stood with Butler just inside the door. Bright and Francine were waltzing together, having already wowed the room with their foxtrot. Butler, who was facing more towards the doorway than the Count, was momentarily immobilised.

"Sir." he said simply, looking past his employer.

The Count turned. Standing in the doorway on the threshold of the ballroom was the most beautiful sight he had ever witnessed.

"Oh, Anna," he whispered in delight and awe, "you

look … I can't find the words."

"Try 'ravishing'!" called Bright, as he led Francine into a spin turn right next to them, and away.

"Well, it's a start." said the Count smiling deep into her eyes.

"And what about me?" chimed in Camille.

"Exquisite." replied Butler, stepping towards her with his hand outstretched. "May I have the pleasure of this dance, *Mademoiselle*?"

"Oh alright, then." said Camille, with a note of disappointment. "Although I was hoping to dance with Édouard!"

While Butler whisked Camille round the ballroom floor, sometimes picking her up and twirling her round in huge circles until she was dizzy, the Count stepped towards Anna and took her hands in his.

"I told you I wanted to be seen with the most beautiful girl in France."

"In the *world*, wasn't it?"

"Yes, darling, in the world."

* * *

When it was all over and the guests had all gone, Max had been given the all-clear and returned with Jean-Luc, and the children had gone to bed, everyone gathered in the drawing room.

"So …" said Francine in a leading tone, "tell all!"

The Count spoke first about the intruder, then recounted the encounter in the nursery, once more thanking God that he had been prompted to swap Arturo's bullets for blanks. Anna followed on with her tangle with Arturo in the cellars.

"And Madeleine – the Boss – what happened to her?" pressed Francine.

"Dead." stated the Count flatly. "I attempted to stop her, but she tried to run me off the road."

Anna was amazed. He seemed genuinely sorry about the death of a monster.

"Edward, she deserved whatever death she got!"

"Don't we all, really? It's just that some of us have had our slates wiped clean."

"What are you talking about? She was evil!"

Francine stepped in to lighten the mood.

"So, let me get this straight. She went off in my Bugatti and you caught her up in that old banger of yours?"

"That's right. In fact, I overtook her at the Velliers roundabout."

"Your Renault overtook my Bugatti?!" hooted Francine. "I don't believe it!"

"The thing is, she went round it, and I went … over it."

"Over it? How could you go over it? There's a great big stone sign in the middle of it!"

"Well, I was four feet up in the air at that point."

There was a stunned silence and then everybody collapsed with laughter, knowing that every word was true – and it was just the sort of crazy, brilliant thing that he would do.

"Nice one, sir." said Butler, using his classic response.

"Oh, *Édouard*, you're so irresponsible!" declared Francine, "I'm surprised you didn't wreck the thing – mind you it was a wreck to begin with!"

The Count feigned hurt.

"It's a great car. It's a little battered, but I'll get it fixed up."

"And what about my car?" demanded Francine. " I hope *that* isn't battered."

The Count sighed.

"Sorry, Francine. 'Battered' doesn't even get close."

CHAPTER 27

GOOD FRIDAY

The next day was Good Friday and the family were preparing to go to the service at the small church on the main road, just opposite the turning up to the graveyard and the château. Anna didn't want to go, even though Camille (or Sister Clarisse, as she wanted to be called today) was going, and the Count didn't try to force her. She stayed at the château, gazing out from the terrace across the beautiful valley with its lake and trees, and reflected on all that had been said and done over the last eleven days, and on where it might all lead, or not lead.

When the family returned, her mood lightened and lunch was a more pleasant experience. Later on, however, plans were starting to be made. Despite it being Good Friday, it was not a public holiday in most areas of France and the appropriate authorities needed to be involved in determining Camille's future care.

* * *

The three of them sat on the couch, Camille in the middle. The Count stroked Camille's hair.

"I'm afraid you can't tell anyone about our adventures."

Camille looked at him and he could see a trace of fear there, rising from the memories of what her own mother had done to her because of what she had seen and heard.

"Because people will hurt me?"

"No," said the Count, "but they may come to hurt us."

Camille nodded solemnly. "In that case I won't breathe

a word – ever."

"Thank you." he smiled, stroking her cheek and cupping her chin in his hand.

"But if someone asks me if I've ever been here – should I lie?"

The Count thought for a moment.

"No." he said squarely. "Just say you and your mother visited here when you were younger. That will be true."

Camille's face lit up. "Can I tell them I climbed trees and I potted plants and …"

"Yes, yes," chuckled the Count, "all those lovely things. Just don't tell them about the bad things."

Her face clouded over a little.

"But what if I need to talk about the bad things? What if I remember and get scared, or have nightmares?"

The Count took her hand in his.

"There is someone you can always talk to – about anything, even our adventures."

Camille frowned, a confused, hopeful frown. The Count continued.

"Someone who loves you and will always be there."

"But no one can *always* be there." countered Camille.

"This person can."

"Who is it?! Who can always be there with me?"

With his free hand, the Count put his finger on her lips, then reached over and picked up a book. He placed it in Camille's hands.

"Everything you need to know is in here."

Camille opened the cover. Inside the Count had written a little message for her.

TO MY DEAR CAMILLE.
MAY THIS BOOK BE A LAMP TO YOUR FEET AND
A LIGHT TO YOUR PATH.
WITH LOVE.
ÉDOUARD

Anna looked over Camille's shoulder. She thought back to the worn-out Bible at the manor and wondered whether it really had lit up the way for the Count, like his mother had hoped. It certainly seemed to have been a huge influence on him. *The manor*, she thought – *seven days and a lifetime ago*.

Camille flicked through the Bible.

"It's very long!"

"Well, it's a book of books. A collection of books, if you like."

"It'll take me a year to read it!"

"Probably even longer than that. But that's okay, just read it a little bit at a time." The Count took hold of the ribbon sticking out of the bottom edge of the pages and lifted it to open the book at the chosen place.

"You can start here. This is Mark's Gospel."

"Gospel?" said Camille, scrunching up her face.

"It means "Good News." laughed the Count. "It's a short book about the life of Jesus."

"Okay," said Camille, "I'll remember to read that first."

"Remember me too." added the Count, a tear welling up in his eye.

"I will!" cried Camille. She threw her arms round him and gave him a big hug.

"Now," said the Count, "Anna has something for you as well."

"I do." said Anna excitedly.

"Ooh, what is it?" squealed Camille.

Anna took off her necklace and put it around Camille's neck.

"You can think of me whenever you look at it."

Camille fingered the little gold dolphin that hung from the cord.

"It's beautiful! Thanks, Anna!"

She flung her arms around Anna's neck and they shared a long and emotional embrace. Anna didn't want Camille to go. She didn't want any of it to go.

* * *

Bright, however, had to go. He had seen all he needed to see, having watched the recordings that Butler's equipment had made of the meeting between Madeleine and Camille in the nursery bedroom. They would do very nicely.

"Miss Parker, you've certainly proved yourself as an exceptional – and loyal – agent."

Anna's eyes shone with the faintest trace of tears of relief and pride, as Bright continued.

"And you've worked exceptionally well with Edward – how would you like to work with him again in the future?"

Anna looked at the Count and almost blushed.

"I'd like that very much, sir."

"Very good. Well, we'll have to wait and see what further crises arise in the future that require me to call once again on the young Count, won't we?"

Édouard smiled at being called "the young Count", in deference to his father who, to Bright, was the original Count. He refrained from pointing out that his father had also at one time been "the young Count" continuing the work of his own father – and so on, back over generations.

* * *

A search of the minister's home and office brought to light a number of things that were helpful in dismantling the Mécénat, including key names within the organisation and outside it, customers, accounts, and so on.

The British Secret Service was officially grateful to Anna Parker and secretly to the Count. On the French side, Eric Mazet, was congratulated, while Vincent Sadoul was promoted, thanks to communication between the top levels of the respective Services, namely between Anthony Bright and the Director of the DGSI, and relations between the two agencies had rarely been sweeter.

Sir Peter Shackleton, on the other hand, was discharged on the grounds of conduct unbecoming, which, in the circumstances, was fairly generous of Anthony Bright, given Sir Peter's failures and misdemeanours. Bright also made sure that the Count received full payment, not only for his over-arching work with Bright himself on tracing the Boss and stopping the spread of the Mécénat, but also for the work commissioned by Sir Peter in retrieving both Anna Parker and *the item* – namely, Camille Dupuy.

Speaking of whom, the other thing that Bright had done while speaking to the Director of the DGSI and briefing her on the events of the last few days, was to defer the involvement of the French social services and arrange for Camille to have a few more days with Anna and the Count, along with the rest of the family. The arrangement was that it would be publicly announced that a joint operation between the Services had managed to recover Camille Dupuy safe and sound. Her whereabouts were to be kept secret, but the Director had agreed to advise the French social services that after her trauma she was being gently debriefed and looked after for the next few days under the general protection of the DGSI. This was true, as the Director had agreed to Bright's proposal that she should "commission" the Count to provide this service on the DGSI's behalf.

As for Camille herself, more time at the château with Jean-Luc and the family was wonderful. Now that she could be seen in public there were even more things they could do, more places they could go to and more adventures and games they could create and enjoy. She seemed to be developing almost as many personas and aliases as the Count himself: complementing her existing characters of Sister Clarisse and Princess Camille with the new additions of Camille the Pirate, Nurse Camille, and Mademoiselle de Beaumont, lady of the château, helper of the poor and general righter of wrongs. That said, Jean-Luc matched her for imagination and energy, being as he was, Prince Jean-Luc, swordsman extraordinaire, Jean-Luc the pilot – or spaceman, depending on whether he was flying inside or outside the earth's atmosphere, Professor

Jean-Luc Durand, scientist and inventor, plus – and here he changed his name, for obvious reasons – Jean-Pierre de Luc, adventurer and spy. The two of them became great friends and were an inseparable pair, much to everyone's delight, although all the grown-ups knew that it in just a few days life would be very different for them all.

* * *

The Count's love for Anna had blossomed, as had her love for him, and their longing to be together had grown with it. Those next few days were a whirlwind of hiking, diving, skiing, laughter and love. But whirlwinds rarely pass without stirring up dust and leaves, uprooting trees and, sometimes, demolishing what has been built.

EPILOGUE

The Count found Francine in the château library. She could tell that something was troubling him.

"Francine, have I done the wrong thing?"

"About what?" she asked, although she already knew the answer.

"Anna."

He hung his head, then looked up at her. She had never seen him like this; he looked lost.

"I don't know – maybe."

"I've never met anyone like her. She's all that I could ever hope for. She's the one I've been waiting for all these years."

"Someone you can share both sides of your life with – the secret stuff as well – and she's beautiful and exciting, strong, clever, caring – you name it." acknowledged Francine.

"She's *everything* - apart from …"

"Don't be afraid to say it, Édouard, it's who we are."

"She's not a Christian." He breathed in and sighed deeply. "I should never have let it go this far. It just happened so naturally – like it was meant to be. I guess I hoped that somehow …"

"You would win her over?"

"Yes."

"It's just been a few days. People rarely change that quickly; not on things like this."

"Maybe. I just hoped so much that she would … see something in me that would change her mind." He wiped his eyes. "But she's adamant."

Francine went over to him and held him close.

"Oh Édouard. I'm so sorry."

"What for?"

"I think I encouraged her at the start."

"When?"

"The day you brought her here. She was clearly besotted with you – and, I have to say, I could tell you felt the same about her. You've been so alone, Édouard. I know you've got Butler and so on, but it's not the same. I just wanted you to be happy, and I felt that perhaps God had brought someone to you at last."

"It really felt like He had, but now we've run out of road and there's nowhere left to go."

He was pacing now, back and forth, desperately trying to find a way to make it work, but he knew that this wasn't like a mission that he could plan for and engineer success. This was someone's heart and mind, a decision that had to be made freely, otherwise it was meaningless.

"I could have spoken up earlier," confessed Francine, "but you were getting on so well together, both as friends and on the mission. I didn't want to risk things turning sour between you at such a crucial time, there was so much at stake."

The Count nodded.

"But what do I do now? I feel that to carry on would be hypocritical. Can I really keep going forward in a relationship that's inevitably heading for conflict, just in the hope that somehow it will all turn out right?"

"I wish I could give you the answer, Édouard, but I can't. It's between you and God."

* * *

Anna was on the terrace revelling in the morning sunshine when the Count stepped up quietly behind her. He put his hands on her arms and gently turned her round. Her smile faded when she saw his face.

"What's the matter?" she asked.

The Count dropped his head, then raised it again and

looked deep into her eyes.

"Anna – darling. You know that I love you."

"Yes …" she replied, wondering what was coming.

"We can't be together anymore – not like this."

"What do you mean, Edward?" her voice trembled and she was shaking slightly as she waited for his answer.

"I want to be with you, desperately, but our lives are built on different foundations. Our values and priorities – although we share many in common – they're not aligned. Our direction and our deepest yearnings are different."

"You mean, " said Anna coldly, "that I don't share your faith."

The Count sighed and closed his eyes for a moment, then looked at her, with all her beauty, all her wonderful personality that he had come to love and admire, all the character and abilities that he respected, the close friendship and trust that had developed so rapidly and held firm through all manner of adventures, dangers and decisions, the laughter, intimacy and togetherness, and the burning physical attraction that raised his passions even now. All these things that had made him feel like he finally understood what it meant when God had said it was not good for the man to be alone, and so He created woman for them to be together – one flesh. Could he really sacrifice all that, to be true to what he believed God wanted? Was that what God wanted – demanded? He knew deep in his heart that it was. He could never truly be one with someone who did not share His love for God, with whom he could not share his deepest thoughts, hopes and joys with any expectation of them understanding or reciprocating; who could not comprehend or accept the mystery of the Divine, or willingly participate in the responsibilities and sacrifices involved in being a disciple of Christ; someone with whom he was not truly one in spirit.

He hung his head again and tears welled up in his eyes.

"Oh, Anna! My darling, darling Anna ... Yes."

Anna felt cold, devoid of emotion. She had feared this conversation – this moment, for some time and had wondered whether she would react with rage or tears, but somehow she felt neither. What she felt, above all, was resentment. Resentment towards a God who could tear lovers apart. Resentment for Him destroying her life, for dangling perfection in front of her and then cruelly snatching it away. And for what? To make Edward prove his loyalty? And she resented the Count for breaking her heart. For putting this so-called 'faith' first, for choosing *it* over *her*.

"Anna, darling, say something!" he begged.

She stood up straight, almost but not quite matching him for height, looked him squarely in the eyes and said simply, "Goodbye, Edward."

And with that she turned on her heels and disappeared. Camille ran up from the garden, Jean-Luc on her tail. "Where's Anna?"

The Count hurriedly wiped his eyes and put on the best smile he could muster.

"She's going home, *ma chérie*. Back to England."

"No!" cried Camille, "I love Anna!"

"Me too." whispered the Count.

* * *

Three months later the Count was at the château, in the library. He had been away twice on "special business" since then, once to Italy and once to England, but he had had no contact with Anna. His ordinary business interests, charity work and his covert operations had kept him occupied, but the ache was still there. In one sense he had peace about his decision; he knew it had been right and necessary, and that to indulge himself any longer would only have made it more difficult for them both when the inevitable finally came, but in another sense he was restless, as if part of him had been lost.

He talked to God about it often, both in his regular times of prayer and just as he was going through the day –

and often, the night – but no answers came. Family and friends were a great support and comfort to him, but he still felt the pain. He prayed that somehow Anna would come to faith, not just so they could be together, but because he loved her and firmly believed to the root of his being that the life God had in store for her was the best life she could imagine – both on earth and forever.

Butler was out in the gardens, "earning my keep" as he insisted on saying, not that the Count felt or expressed any need for him to do anything but relax at the moment – he had earned his keep many times over in the Count's reckoning. In fairness, Butler loved gardening almost as much as he loved cooking – although he loved adventures with the Count most of all. But he was happy with the flowers and trees, and chatting and bantering with the real – that is to say, the regular employed, gardeners.

The Count looked out of one of the library windows, up the hill to the rocky outcrops, each one nearly a hundred feet tall, towering out of the top of the ridge a mile away, like teeth protruding from the gums of a child. *I must climb them again*, he thought. *Soon*. He glanced to the right, towards the Col from which the colourful chutes of the paragliders launched. They could be up there for ages, riding the air currents coming up from the valley. He watched them as they swayed and reeled, some making horizontal and then vertical circles in the azure sky. *That too*. He wandered to the other side of the château and out on to the terrace, taking in the incredible view and watching the brightly rigged yachts cut through the sparkling blue waters that melted into turquoise shallows before lapping against sandy beaches. *And that*, he said to himself.

He looked over to the green hills beyond the far shore, that mirrored those on his side, and further to the snow-capped mountain where a small family-run ski resort complemented the numerous larger ski resorts within just an hour's drive of the château and provided a wonderful day out for families. He looked up at the sky, love and adoration swelling in his heart and quoted Psalm 16 verses 5 and 6:

Lord, You are my portion and my cup of blessing;
You hold my future.
The boundary lines have fallen for me in pleasant places;
indeed, I have a beautiful inheritance.

Thank you, Father, he whispered softly, eyes misty with tears of gratitude.

His reverie was broken by the sound of his secure phone. He answered it immediately, not bothering to wipe his eyes.

"Yes?"

"Edward?"

"Anna?"

"Edward, I have something to tell you …"

THE END

WHAT'S NEXT FOR THE COUNT?

The Count Volume II:
PROFANA FAMILIA

Following the surprise phone call that ends Volume I and the Count's daring recovery of a stolen painting, the action moves through England and France to Spain, where the Count takes on a powerful family whose criminal activity and personal vendetta against the Roman Catholic Church culminates in a plan to destroy one of the world's most famous landmarks in a single shocking strike – even if that means taking thousands of lives with it.

.

Due 2026

AFTERWORD

Some readers may find it difficult to accept a character who is supposed to be a man of integrity, but who hides his real identity from all but a handful of trusted people, who almost always masks his true appearance and who goes by a variety of names. A man who often says one thing while actually meaning another in order to veil the truth; who sometimes avoids giving a straight answer – and, in some cases, avoids giving any answer at all. A man with secret hideouts and clandestine meetings.

I am, of course, talking about Jesus Christ.

I mention the above in order to set the scene for the discussion questions that follow, so that anyone approaching the discussion with a prejudiced mind to simply pooh-pooh it as trite nonsense might appreciate two things. First, that the idea of a Christian undercover operative is not as far-fetched as one might initially think. Second, to understand that to send a Christian out to operate in the world of espionage and crime – a world of cold, cruel deceit, of manipulation, torture and violence, where even the supposed "good guys" are often heartless and amoral – is like tying someone's hands behind their back and pushing them into a Mixed Martial Arts cage fight. Like sending a sheep out among wolves. And yet that is exactly what Jesus said He was doing to His followers. The Christian would have to be far more capable than their opponents in order to succeed, would need to call on resources above and beyond the natural, and would have to be prepared to give their all rather than be unfaithful. Far from being weak ineffective characters, despite their appearance they would be the bravest and strongest of people, the cleverest, most inspired and most dedicated agent. Not a raving fanatic, nor the cold-blooded killer so much glamorised and glorified in today's novels and movies – but loving humans who cared even for those whose atrocities they had to bring to an end.

Such a man was Jesus Christ. How hard it was for Him to fulfil His mission while subjected to these constraints! And yet He succeeded. Braver, stronger and cleverer than any other secret agent before or since – fictional or otherwise. And, unlike James Bond and Ethan Hunt, perhaps He actually *did* save the world?

DISCUSSION QUESTIONS

1. Do you think a Christian could be a spy today – either within the intelligence services or alongside them, like the Count?

2. What values might be at risk of being compromised?

3. Do you think the Count tells lies? Why do you think that? Give an example and explain.

4. Is the Count perfect? If not, do you think that he ought to be and would that be realistic?

5. How do you feel about the Count's changes of appearance and persona?

6. Comparing the Count to a con artist, for example, are motives and methods important in this?

7. Are circumstances important in this? *(A con artist causes a bad situation, whereas the Count intervenes to prevent or end a bad situation)*

8. Do you think the Count employs a "the end justifies the means" philosophy, or does he draw reasonable boundaries? Where would you draw the lines?

9. Does it make a difference that the Count has been commissioned from the top to operate in this way?

10. What do you think about the Counts decision on whether or not to end his romantic relationship with Anna?

11. Were you surprised by the Afterword that precedes these questions – what do *you* think about Jesus Christ?

12. Are you looking forward to the next book? Why / Why not?

Printed in Dunstable, United Kingdom

75164156R00167